Laurel Lake Remembers

KAREN GIBSON

PENBROOK PRESS

Also by Karen Gibson

Pieces of Grace
In a Heartbeat
Standing Still

Copyright @ 2023 by Karen Gibson

Cover design by Paper & Sage

All rights reserved. This book or any portion thereof may not be reproduced or used in any manner whatsoever without the express written permission of the publisher except for the use of brief quotations in a book review.

The characters and events portrayed in this book are fictitious or are used fictitiously. Any similarity to real persons, living or dead, is purely coincidental and not intended by the author.

Printed in the United States of America
First printing 2023

www.karengibsonauthor.com
Facebook.com/KarenGibsonAuthor
karengibsonauthor@gmail.com

*For my beautiful, curious, intelligent granddaughters
Willa, Leighton, Brooklyn, Penelope
I love the memories we create*

Chapter One

THE SUNLIGHT DANCED ON THE WATER'S RIPPLING surface, diamonds shining so brilliantly Madison had to close her eyes momentarily, bright explosions of light still visible behind her lids. When she opened her eyes, the scene was already changing as a single, gray-rimmed cloud moved slowly toward the sun, determined to cut short the brilliant show—as if jealously seeking to dim, even for a moment, the always-revered warm orb. The ripples rapidly changed to a chop on the lake's surface as the cool breeze turned to a cold gust of wind.

Pulling the camera away from her face, Madison Keller gazed out at the vastness of Laurel Lake, caught up in imagining what it would have been like in the mid 1800's when brothers Liam and Johan first arrived at this spot and decided to make it their home.

"Your ancestors must have fallen in love with this area the moment they saw it."

"They probably picked it for convenience." The woman next to Madison coughed, sniffled, and then turned her back on the lake. Pausing, she faced Madison again. "I know my family gets all the recognition for establishing Fairview, but in no time at all other people started to settle here. Somewhere along the line, our name was attached to this property, and since the town expanded outward from this spot, we were given all the credit for settling the town. All I'm saying is that the credit doesn't belong solely with my family." This time, Liz Erikson started walking toward the office building, her voice as matter of fact as everything else about her. "I really have to get back to work now."

A direct descendent of Liam, Elizabeth Erikson, now in her early seventies, was as no-nonsense as what Madison imagined her ancestors to have been all those years ago when they arrived as early Scandinavian immigrants to the lakeshore. Wisconsin winters would have been harsh, but the rest of the seasons on the idyllic lake would have made it worthwhile, or so she assumed, wanting to slip back into the daydreams of a few moments ago.

Liz clearly didn't share Madison's almost fairytale view of her family's early existence. And worse, she didn't like to talk about herself—which happened to be the bane of existence for a newspaper feature writer.

"I'm sorry I took so much of your time," Madison shouted to the receding back. "Thank you!"

The woman, clad in a man's button-down chambray shirt and ankle high brown boots, simply waved an arm in the air without turning back to look, pushed her hands through her close-cropped silvery white hair, and then covered it with a stocking cap she pulled from her jacket pocket. She walked with an almost imperceptible limp, listing slightly to the side with each step.

Madison closed her eyes for a moment, turning her face toward the lake to feel the cool air blowing into shore. She could imagine the voices of the past swirling around her, sharing their stories of early life on the lakeshore. The breeze grew colder and she opened her eyes, sighing loudly. She should have heeded the warnings of the colleague who told her before the interview how unlikely it was Liz would be a bubbling font of ancestral stories. He had been correct.

And he had also been correct that a storm front was moving in. A single raindrop plopped onto the top of her camera and the wind picked up even more, sending a shiver through her as she scurried to put her camera back in the case before the downpour started.

Once in the warm protection of her Jeep, the large raindrops leaving splotches on her windshield, she continued to scan the horizon. This part of Fairview hadn't changed in decades, which was one reason she felt especially comfortable here. While every thing else was a whirlwind of shifting, altering, and modernizing, this part of her lakeshore community could be counted on to remain intact.

That hold on tradition was what made her especially excited about researching and writing this story, because the town was changing rapidly everywhere else. Looking down at her notepad, she was disappointed to see little of value from the time spent with Liz. The woman took over managing the cottages back in 1980, shortly after the death of her mother, and five years after her dad died.

Before meeting with her, Madison had carefully researched the basic facts, realizing Liz would have been 28 when she started overseeing the properties—Madison's current age—so she somehow believed she could connect with her interviewee on that level, but nothing had made Liz feel talkative.

There was much she couldn't put in the story, although it would certainly spice it up. Rumors in the small town once swirled around this last member of the family still in Fairview, one even going so far as to intimate that Liz ran away with friends to attend Woodstock and then traveled to California to get lost in the drug and free love culture, estranged from her parents, returning only because her dad died. It was long before Madison's time, and it wasn't exactly something she could ask her about in an interview for this feature—and probably not any, to be perfectly fair.

Sighing, Madison looked out over the lake, wondering how she would capture the heart and soul of the lakeshore community she loved so much if she couldn't get a direct descendant of its founding fathers to give her more than simple, non-informative answers to her questions.

Since this story was to be the first in a series to feature the 150th anniversary of Fairview, it had to be riveting, focusing on the trials and tribulations of the two brothers as they tamed the wild lakeshore. Pinning down Liz for an interview had been no easy task, but even after spending the last twenty-five minutes interviewing her, it was clear the woman wasn't interested in her family taking credit for the town's establishment.

She wondered if the original settling family members kept to themselves as much as Liz seemed to do as they cleared the land for houses and brought their brides over to establish themselves in a new country.

Her phone dinged, alerting her to a new text and she was oddly startled by the sound—an anachronism of sorts as her brain was stuck someplace in the 1800's with Johan and Liam. She snapped back to the present, smiling as she saw Natalie's name on the screen. She'd been waiting for this message all day, hoping her friend was able to solidify plans for a visit.

It's settled. I'll stay with you while Byron is at his conference. Talk soon!

A whoop escaped her, and she did a modified happy dance in the front seat, arms jiving to imaginary celebratory music. Natalie was coming home. Even as she thought it, she could hear her friend's voice in her ear, scolding, reminding, keeping her in check. "I'm *visiting*, Madison. Fairview hasn't been my home for a decade." Excitement coursed through her despite the imagined warning, and she knew she was worse than a kid waiting for Christmas morning. But that's exactly how Madison felt.

It was impossible to go back in time from their 28-year-old existence to the younger teenage version of themselves, but for those upcoming few days, she would give it a try. If it were up to her, they would go even farther back in time to their elementary school days, when she had her small group of close friends and nothing bad ever happened to them.

Before she slipped too far into a walk down memory lane, Madison typed a brief reply. **Lots to do before then. I can't wait!**

And there was a lot to do. She turned the wipers on, clearing enough of the windshield to give her one last view of the vast lake. A lone fisherman braved the elements, appearing and disappearing with each rhythmic swish of the blades, his small craft bouncing like a child's toy as the wind gusted and then died down. Late May in Wisconsin meant cold weather was not simply a possibility but a probability. Tomorrow's forecast was much warmer.

A shiver ran through her, and she thought about how wonderful that hot cup of coffee would taste right now. She sent Patrick a text to let him know she was on her way, having been tasked with picking up the coffee order for her mom's class that evening.

Despite her busy schedule, Madison remained in place another moment, remembering how life used to be in her beloved lakeshore community, seemingly sheltered from the evils of the world. Mostly, anyway. Illness and death were going to creep in, no matter how perfect life in Fairview seemed to her. She quickly shifted into gear, the motion serving to push the negative thoughts out of her head. As she drove toward Water Street, the downpour was already slowing to a light rain.

She had her choice of parking places at this time of day, so she chose a spot halfway between the diner and the flower shop. The diner was still operating on off-season hours, so it was technically closed this late in the afternoon, but Madison, dodging stray raindrops, dashed through the unlocked front door, the jingling of the bell overhead heralding her arrival. The place was empty, except for Patrick in the back, singing loudly and off-key to the Bon Jovi song playing through hidden speakers.

"Hey rockstar, I'm here," she shouted to her brother.

The old-fashioned façade and interior gave the place the charm of a 1950's diner even if it had the efficiency of a modern restaurant. When he took over, Patrick renovated the small galley kitchen, disposing of the old appliances, installing a huge grill, and expanding the deep fryer space. Patrons seated at the counter were given a first-hand view through a cut-out into what was the original kitchen where someone—usually Patrick—would be flipping fluffy pancakes or pulling up baskets of golden-brown French fries, depending on the time of day. But hidden away in the fully remodeled back area beyond the grill, were very modern, very shiny, very high efficiency appliances needed to run the restaurant.

She was pouring herself a cup of coffee as Patrick pushed through the swinging saloon style doors separating the dining room from the grill, his forehead damp with sweat. Madison was glad he'd decided to leave the old doors in place when so many other updates were made to the restaurant. Memories of childhood games with her brother, swinging the doors back and forth until their grandmother shooed them outside, flooded her brain. Nostalgia seemed to be the flavor of the day for her.

"Hey, sis." He wiped his hands on his apron and glanced around the cluttered countertop for something. Madison smiled, pointing to the top of his head where, as usual, he had put his glasses and promptly forgotten. Pulling them over his eyes, he looked at the flat piece of what appeared to be cardboard before him, trying to decipher the instructions written there. "Let's see. It says to pull it apart at the corners until they snap in place, fill the cavern, and then lock the top section together to use as handles." He popped the cardboard sides out and folded down the top as instructed, then held the contraption out for her to admire. "My new coffee to-go containers. People are going to love these."

Madison watched him pour the contents of an entire coffee pot into the box and slide the tabs together to form a handle. "Impressive," she said, taking it from him to mockingly admire, amused by the whole concept. "Do you get a lot of calls for boxes of coffee?"

He ignored her sarcasm as he reached for a nearby bag. "I put cream and sugar in here so mom should be all set."

"Perfect. Are you heading home soon?"

"Nope. I'm dealing with deliveries all day tomorrow, so I'll have my hands full this afternoon making room for everything. Just when I think I'm ready for the busy summer season, something else crops up. As of Friday, I'll be back to full operating hours." He offered a grimace and exaggerated shudder at the thought, but Madison knew he loved everything about owning and operating the diner that had been in the Keller family for decades.

"And that means only three days until the ice cream window opens." Madison smiled, fully aware of her brother's love/hate relationship with the summer tradition. "I *love* when the ice cream window opens." She drained her cup and handed it to her brother.

"I hope you are still saying that after you've worked a few weekend shifts at said window scooping ice cream until your arms are ready to fall off." He'd talked often of ordering a frozen custard machine to ease the burden, but the rest of the family vetoed that idea each time. Nothing beat a waffle cone stuffed with hard pack ice cream on a hot summer day at the beach. She could picture the little kids, a sticky mess trickling from their chins and hands as mothers ran behind with moist towelettes to clean them up, and then giving up, shooing them into the lake to rid them of their stickiness.

As she turned to leave, pushing the entry door open with her hip, Madison wrinkled her nose at her older brother. "Don't spoil my fun."

"I'm putting you down for a shift every weekend then. It'll be *fun!*"

She didn't respond to his good-natured ribbing as she walked out the door, the bell again jangling as she turned east, away from the lake, and took the short walk four storefronts down to her mother's shop on the corner of Water Street and Golf View Drive.

A few sprinkles were all that remained of the earlier rainstorm, but dark clouds still loomed on the horizon.

The yellow and blue awning flapped in the wind as she approached the shop, the windows decorated with multi-colored tulips sprouting from puffy white clouds. Sprigs was the only flower shop in what Fairview residents considered "old town," which meant any holiday heavy on flower-giving was an especially busy time for Nina. With the whole family pitching in during that hectic weekend, they'd survived Mother's Day earlier in the month and now her mom was back to teaching her weekly flower arranging class. She started one each spring, a ritual to chase away the winter blahs and welcome in a new growing season.

"I come bearing caffeine," Madison announced as her mother held the door for her with her hip, her hands filled with baby's breath. The small white flowers bobbed their heads in the breeze sweeping in with Madison. Her mom set the flowers down as Madison shook the raindrops from her ponytail.

"Thank goodness." Nina smiled appreciatively at her daughter as they walked through the store with its cash and carry flower arrangements and variety of small gift items to the workroom in the back. Tendrils of dark blonde hair with slivers of gray had come loose from the bun on top of Nina's head and curled around her face. She set the flowers on a workbench, wiped her hands on the front of her apron and then pushed the stray hairs behind her ears. "Luckily, I found a whole sleeve of Styrofoam cups in the back." She smiled at her daughter. "Thanks for doing this. Patrick was so sweet to offer the coffee. He said I was the first one to use his new to-go containers, so he wants a full review." She checked her watch as Madison found a spot on the counter to set her armload. "You're a lifesaver, Mads."

Nina handed her daughter a green apron, adorned with the name Sprigs in looping vines forming cursive letters across the front. Her own apron was already in need of a good washing, but Madison could tell she was too focused on prepping for her class to worry about changing into a clean one just yet. Nina poured half of a cup for herself, took a sip, and turned to Madison, ready to give her instructions. Nina's shop assistant would have normally done the coffee run and the prep work, but Julie's son was rushed to the hospital for an emergency appendectomy, leaving Nina stranded. That wasn't entirely true, Madison knew. None of them ever felt stranded because someone in the Keller clan would willingly step in and help.

"Roses first. Snip off the bottoms and put them in that pail." She indicated the five-gallon bucket on the floor near the cooler. "Once you've finished those, I'll probably have you start on the carnations and then..." She did a slow turn, taking in the entire workroom and shrugged, "We'll just play it by ear from there."

Madison smiled at her mother's back as she dashed away to continue setting up. Pulling on a pair of gardening gloves, she settled onto the stool to start trimming the stems of the red, white, and pink roses piled before her. Their fragrance tickled her nose, and she fought the urge to sneeze. She was more than happy to help her mom, just like she never hesitated to pick up the slack at the diner when Patrick was short-handed. Heck, she'd offer to take a dental hygienist course and fill in at her dad's office if he asked. She would do anything for any one of them. Her vision blurred as her eyes started to water, and she quickly shook off the feelings. When it came to her family, she couldn't help being sentimental. They meant the world to her. She blinked away the tears and continued cutting the flowers, removing the extra leaves. She was always especially emotional this time of year, so she took a couple deep breaths to fend off the memories, forcing herself to think about *anything* else.

Across the room, vases in various shapes and sizes had been removed from tissue paper and bubble wrap and were ready for Nina's students to fill as they learned the art of flower arranging.

Jenny Whitebird, her long gray hair pulled into a single thick braid down her back, was the first to arrive. Lean, slender and readily identifiable by the scar that ran the length of her face, from her hairline to her jaw, Jenny carried an attitude that said, yes, I have a scar, and yes, you can look at this scar, but I highly recommend you don't ask me about this scar. Her yoga studio was housed inside the boutique hotel two blocks from the flower shop. Armando, the hotel manager, trotted in moments later, his light brown skin shiny with raindrops.

"I was sure I was late. I'm already running around like a chicken with its head cut off and we haven't even started the busy season." He blotted his forehead with the back of his hand as Jenny clucked her tongue in sympathy. (Sincere or not, Madison couldn't quite tell).

The two shared nothing in common but the roof that covered both of their businesses, yet their friendship was obvious. Before seating herself on a stool, Jenny stretched, lifting her leg behind, and extending her hands to the front. Armando mimicked Jenny's movements, almost toppling over as he tried to stand on one leg as she was. He jumped out of the way just in time as Jenny playfully swatted at his arm, surprisingly quick for someone in her seventies.

"Can I get either of you a cup of coffee? You should have some while it's still hot. I'll pour." Madison slid from her stool, started to stretch out her back and then stopped herself as she saw the look on Armando's face, indicating he'd be happy to mimic her actions, too. "On second thought, mister, get your own coffee."

"What? I wasn't going to do anything." His feigned innocence made both women shake their heads.

From the other room, Nina's voice reached them. "Help yourselves to some coffee. I'll be there in a sec."

"If this is Patrick's coffee, don't mind if I do." Armando wiggled his eyebrows at them and then helped himself to a cup, pouring in three packets of sugar, stirring, and then adding one more.

"That stuff is going to kill you, man." Jenny wrinkled her nose as he pretended to reach for yet another packet. Jenny pulled a bottle of green juice from her bag, while he made gagging sounds.

His antics were interrupted by two elderly women struggling to lower their umbrellas as they entered the shop. They were dressed alike in white blouses and flower print skirts with matching ribbons in their hair. The Lambert twins were well-known around Fairview as spinster sisters who looked, dressed, and sounded alike but couldn't seem to agree on anything. They smiled and said hello, then immediately argued about where they should sit. Madison hid a smile, wishing she had her camera with her.

When her mother returned, her hair was pinned back up and she was wearing a fresh apron, looking much younger than a 58-year-old should, Madison couldn't help thinking.

"We're waiting for just a few more people so make yourselves comfortable and we'll get started as soon as they arrive." She placed a frog-shaped planter in the center of the worktable.

The others inspected the planter, painted light green with purple polka dots. Its eyes were red and bulging and its tongue, a deep pink, lolled to the side. Pansies, yellow and orange, sprouted from its back.

Armando rubbed his chin, examining the unusual color scheme. "I sure hope that's not what we're learning to create tonight." He furrowed his brow. "Could we at least change the flowers for...maybe some nice herbs? Cilantro, perhaps?"

Nina held up her hands, laughing. "That poor little guy has been sitting on the shelf for over a year now. I felt so sorry for him I decided to fill him with a little bit of color. He can be our centerpiece tonight even if he isn't inspiring you, Armando."

Madison carried the flowers she'd trimmed over to the table, scattering them around so they would be in arm's reach of every participant. She grinned, perpetually amused by the people of Fairview with all of their quirks—and nosiness, she decided as Armando sidled over, reaching for a pile of roses to pull closer to his work area. "What are you writing about these days, Madison?"

"The paper is running a whole series on the sesquicentennial. Each week, until the celebration in July, we'll be featuring the development of the lakeshore and businesses. I was given the Erikson Cottages as my first assignment."

"That's interesting." He waved a hand, making it clear he had no interest in that topic. "Now, give me some gossip. You work for the paper, so you must be in the know."

Madison laughed. "I'd hardly say that." Nobody was a bigger gossip than Armando, so even if she knew something, he would probably be one of the last with whom she'd share it, and chances were, he would have already known about it. She picked up the clippers and started snipping the bottoms from the carnations before spreading them out on the table as well. She figured she was safe talking about her current project. "I interviewed Liz Erikson this afternoon, but she didn't have much to say. She is one tough nut to crack so it might not be much of a story."

Realizing she didn't have anything exciting to share, he resorted to offering an uninspiring, unenthusiastic string of platitudes. "Be persistent. Keep your head in the game. Be a team player. U rah rah." His dark eyes lit up as Jenny moved closer to the worktable and he grinned mischievously. "You know, you could have been describing Jenny. She's a tough nut to crack, too."

"I heard that, Armando." Jenny stretched her arms over her head and took a cleansing breath before responding further. "As a general rule, he has the attention span of a gnat. That is, of course, unless he's plying someone for gossip. Are you doing that right now, my friend?"

He waved his hand in the air, dismissing her insult and then turned his attention back to Madison, staring pointedly at her head, the expression on his face a clear indication of his distaste. "You know that hair isn't doing you any favors. How do you expect to snare a lover looking like that?" He reached out to flick the end of her ponytail, oblivious to the color rising in her cheeks. "Girl, you need to do something with that. Summer is almost here." He fluttered his eyelashes at her and made kissing noises. "All the boys will descend on Laurel Lake soon."

Madison groaned and pushed away from the counter, ready to get another bucket of flowers from the cooler. "There's more to life than *boys*, Armando. I'm focusing on my career right now. Who knows, maybe there's a Pulitzer Prize winning story in my future." There was a time when she cared about "all the boys" descending on them, but that was so long ago it was nothing but a very distant memory.

"Leave her alone. She doesn't need a man to prove her worth, you know. She might be

perfectly content to live alone. Marriage isn't for everyone."

Madison winced, then quickly recovered by smirking at Armando, conveying a sense of camaraderie with Jenny that belied her real feelings about relationships. She wanted one. She wanted the happily-ever-after of a perfect marriage. She was also the first to admit she didn't go out of her way to make any of that happen. Thoughts of Carl tried to plant themselves in her mind, but she refused to let them in. This had nothing to do with Carl. Even as she thought it, she knew it wasn't true.

Desperate to focus on something else, she replayed the earlier interview with Liz Erikson in her head. Liz was eccentric, that was for sure, living alone, self-sufficient, but she never seemed...happy. Maybe she had loved someone who betrayed her. Maybe she didn't even prefer men. Turning back to Jenny, she decided to ask the question that had been on her mind all afternoon. "Speaking of which, Jenny, do you have any idea why Liz Erikson never married?"

Jenny studied Madison's face for a moment, and although her own was expressionless, the message carried a pointed tone. "I don't know, and I don't think that's my business to know. We all have our histories."

"I agree. I was just curious, that's all. The family has all that property and now she's the last Erikson so..."

"She had her reasons, I'm sure. I know you ask questions as a reporter, but that's probably not a question a lot of women would be comfortable answering, is my guess."

Madison was saved from responding as the door opened again and three young women stepped in, chattering away about babysitters and play dates. A loud clap of thunder seemed to herald their arrival and the start of class.

"On that note," Nina said, "let's get started."

Madison bit her lip as she turned her attention to the flowers before her, thankful she had never asked Jenny about the scar. Someone knew the answer. Someone in Fairview always knew... but they were probably better at keeping secrets than she was.

Maybe she did focus more on her career than on finding a man. At 28, she was in relationship limbo, and no matter how she tried to spin it, she expected to be stuck there for a long time.

Armando leaned closer. "You'll never guess who made a reservation at the hotel for the big 150th celebration *and* will be staying for the entire weekend."

"I have no idea," she whispered back, amused as usual by his joy at being in the know and having an audience with whom to share his knowledge. She could play along.

The lightness of the moment disappeared, however, when he responded, "Our resident shining star." His fingers tapped a drumroll on the tabletop. "Ladies and gentlemen, the one and only...Becca Ristow."

Chapter Two

THE MINIATURE SLEDGEHAMMER PERSISTENTLY tapping away inside Madison's head was becoming more than a minor distraction, and especially problematic since she still had an article to write. But finding the focus she needed for writing was out of the question when all she could think about was Armando's news about Becca. It had been an innocent announcement, but it shook her to the core. She hadn't seen her good-friend-turned-enemy in ten years.

How she got through the previous evening was still a mystery. Armando didn't know the history she had with Becca. He was simply doing what he did best—sharing information. He couldn't know that the town's homegrown "celebrity" was the last person Madison wanted to hear about. Sighing loudly, she thought fleetingly of Jenny and her scar. That she had a history that left her scarred was, literally, written on her face. Perhaps it would be easier to wear your scars so obviously, because the ones that people couldn't see sometimes caused the most angst. Nobody knew the depths of your pain, sorrow, or loss when nothing showed on the outside.

Her childhood could be defined by a finite set of important factors. She could always count on her family and her small group of best friends to be her support system, and the Laurel Lake community was the best place on earth to grow up. Every single memory she held dear was set in Fairview with her special people.

Then things in Fairview took a turn, redefining her.

She wondered if she had any ibuprofen in her purse. Rubbing her temples, she contemplated the unsettled feeling building within her. In the course of one day, she learned that two people she hadn't seen in ten years would be returning to Fairview. One she was excited to see; the other, well, she would be quite happy never to see again.

Natalie had been surprised, too, when she called the night before. They had lost touch with Becca Ristow years prior and neither followed her on social media, so in some respects, they felt as though they were being visited by a ghost.

"Why would she be interested in coming back here? What could she possibly want?" Madison had asked.

"Maybe she's just like me. You know, coming back for a visit." She'd grown serious then, adding wryly, "Hopefully she's a changed woman. Maybe even a bit more, oh, I don't know, human?"

"Maybe."

"You'll have to stand up for yourself, Mads. You can't let her get to you like she did before."

"I know." Madison cut her off, not wanting to think about the last exchange she'd had with Becca, and fully aware Natalie didn't know the half of it—and she had every intention of keeping it that way. Becca probably hadn't changed at all, and quite possibly she was even worse, given her rise to what could be called "fame," Madison guessed.

Many townspeople were familiar with the name Becca Ristow. Beautiful, talented, and destined for a life in the spotlight, according to her mother anyway, the quintessential stage mom. She became the town's darling as she starred in every local stage production, was featured in local print ads, and then moved to New York where she landed an agent and a part as a regular on a popular soap opera. Mrs. Ristow made sure the paper ran stories on the great successes of her daughter until, thankfully, she too moved away from Fairview, putting an end to the public updates. The townspeople knew her as their rising star, but Madison and Natalie remembered her as something very different.

Madison had to do something about the nagging headache. With a quiet but victorious "yes," her fingers closed around a travel-sized container of Tylenol deserted long ago in the bottom of her camera bag. She shook out two, hoping they weren't expired beyond usefulness, and washed them down with a long drink of water. Relief from the nagging thud couldn't come soon enough.

She turned her attention to the article, closing her eyes and channeling herself back to the early days on the shores of the lake, envisioning Liam and Johan building a house together. They started families here, sons and daughters carrying on the traditions of their parents, generation after generation. It was strange to think that only one single family member remained here after all that time.

Her fingers, poised over the keyboard, refused to move.

Madison opened her eyes, struck by the thought that she was the only one of her friends still living in their hometown. Taken aback momentarily, she dropped her hands in her lap, considering how that had happened.

She could tolerate Becca as long as Natalie was around. But when Natalie's dad deserted his family, everything changed. For reasons no one would ever know, he woke up on a Tuesday morning and decided he'd had enough. Natalie's mom, Nancy, found him, his head lolled to the side, arms dangling, his body suspended from the rope attached to the rafters in the old, detached storage shed in their backyard. (Madison hadn't seen him, but vividly imagined the scene in her waking hours and in her nightmares). Natalie and her mother were left alone and confused, unable to comprehend what happened to their once happy family. And the Lutheran church was left to grieve without the pastor who usually helped them through such tragedies. Everyone felt betrayed.

The house went on the market, and when it sold a couple months later, Nancy moved back to her hometown of Minnetonka, Minnesota, leaving her nursing job and life in Fairview behind. Natalie had enough credits to earn her high school diploma, so she graduated early instead of waiting around to cross the stage with her classmates.

Apparently, Nancy couldn't find the solace she sought there, because once Natalie married Byron, she sold the Minnesota house, joining an international medical unit providing care to children in Africa.

Neither of them ever returned to Fairview.

Madison never stopped missing her best friend. They remained in touch with calls, texts, and emails. Even though Madison traveled to Minnesota to spend time with her, and continued to visit her as she wound her way through homes in Arizona, Maine and Iowa, she was never able to convince Natalie to come for a visit. Until now. She was happy to know something had finally changed for her friend and she could return to where they'd once been so happy. Unfortunately, news of Becca's return was a dark cloud over the happiness of that visit.

And now, after a night of restless sleep interspersed with troubling dreams, Madison didn't have any clarity regarding Becca or a lead for her story.

Liam and Johan Eriksson, brave Scandinavian brothers, left behind the political strife and social upheaval of home to travel across the ocean to what we now call Fairview, on the shores of beautiful Laurel Lake. Elizabeth Erikson, the last living descendent of the original Norwegian immigrants, dropped the extra s in the family name, remodeled the original twenty-four log homes, and created a vacation haven and enviable business model. In her seventies, this feisty, no-nonsense businesswoman continues to manage a hospitality empire she has overseen for over forty years. But even the well-established business known as Lakeside Cottages cannot escape change.

Madison re-read the start of her feature, sighed, and deleted all of it. Ben couldn't have picked a worse writer for this first story in the series if he wanted her to highlight the changes as progress. Her fervent wish was for everything to stay the same. But an assignment was an assignment, so she turned her attention back to her notes, ready to try again.

Instead of a story idea, however, an image of Becca appeared again. Becca would be back in Fairview. She pushed the thought away more firmly this time. It shouldn't matter. Becca didn't matter.

She opened a file on her laptop, skimming the notes there, desperate for inspiration for the story. The mayor was hosting Fairview's 150th anniversary celebration in July to honor Fairview's establishment as a town. The lakeshore's new pavilion and amphitheater would be the epicenter of all the events. The articles would serve as a lead-up to the big day, so she wanted readers excited about the town's fascinating history. What she had so far wasn't exactly fascinating.

She tried again.

The Lakeside Cottages, a name given to the twenty-four log cabins that were part of the original settlement Liam established with the assistance of his brother Johan, were updated and given fresh new facades, first in 1980 and then again in 2001, making them a popular choice for families vacationing on the lakeshore. According to owner Liz Erikson, she is at near-capacity for summer bookings. Fall is filling up quickly and winter reservations are already trickling in.

Although summer is the most popular season for tourists, the hardy vacationers enjoy Fairview's winter season for its snowmobiling, cross country skiing, and even ice fishing. The winter visitors are usually content to finish their cold weather activities and then huddle in the cabins, woodfires burning, and unfazed that the attractions popular in the other three seasons are closed, according to Erikson.

She held the backspace key down, once again erasing the start of her article. Madison stared at her laptop, the cursor blinking on a now blank screen. Frustration built. Maybe she could convince Ben to start with a different story...perhaps the new boat landing or the Dockside Bar and Grill.

That wouldn't work. The Eriksson brothers settled the area, so it was only right to start the series with the lone descendent still in Fairview.

She hadn't seen Becca since... No! She put headphones over her ears, turning up the volume as if music might help shut out everything except the assignment before her.

Madison tapped the keyboard, pulling notes up on the screen. If this didn't work, she would take a short walk to get some blood flowing to her tired brain and limbs.

Her own Great-Grandfather Keller moved to Fairview during the Great Depression, married a local girl, and raised his family, and it was the only home both of her grandparents had ever known. Madison had heard stories about Liam Eriksson and his brother and the hardships they endured when they settled in this northeast corner of Wisconsin, but most of her information came from the extensive research she'd done in preparation for the feature. The brothers built a single room log-style home when they arrived, totally unprepared for harsh conditions, and surviving the first winter by burning every log they'd cut down for the second house they planned to build. While some found that fact amusing, Madison always felt sorry for them. She couldn't fathom how difficult it would have been, leaving their homeland and starting over in a strange new land.

Spring eventually arrived, though. Even before they started the second house, they sent for their brides, twin sisters who could only be told apart from one another by the scar one had just above her eye—the result of an altercation with local police before leaving Norway. For some reason, nobody knew what the dispute had been about—or even if there was any truth to it. Madison loved the mystery behind the story, even if it might be simple local lore.

Although the Eriksson brides were scheduled to arrive in late summer, the brothers hadn't yet built the second house that next year, supposedly because of an exceptionally wet, miserable spring, so all four of them lived together in the original house, even after the births of their first babies.

A one-room cabin. No plumbing. No nearby grocery store. Madison couldn't begin to fathom what that would be like for the four adults and two babies.

When the brothers finally got around to completing the second house, it was larger than the first. Liam's wife, Sarah, decided *they* should have the larger home since Liam was the older of the two men, causing a rift between the families. So, Johan and Leah chose to build yet another house, but they decided not to build it next to Liam and Sarah, wanting ample space between them. Madison shook her head at the thought that even twin sisters could be jealous of one another.

Eventually, their families grew and filled in the entire area between the nearly estranged brothers with their own houses, and that was the start of the current lakeshore development known as Lakeside Cottages, and the spot from which the rest of the town of Fairview expanded. The Spanish flu wiped out a significant number of family members in 1918, and eventually, the cottages were rented out to other Scandinavian immigrants unrelated to the Eriksson clan. Ownership of the property and the buildings on it remained with the family, however, as one future-thinking ancestor after another realized the significant value of the property, thus buying up as much as possible when opportunity arose.

Although the cottages ranged in size, each had a similar Scandinavian style, and as the Eriksson family used the cottages for income in later years, they maintained as much of the style as possible in the furnishings and décor. The property was on some of the most prime real estate in the county, rivaled only by the golf course on the adjacent acreage.

Madison paged forward in her notes, skipping decades until she came to 1980. That was the year Liz Erikson, at 28, became the sole proprietor, having buried her mother that spring. A few years later, Liz converted what had originally been the only remaining barn on the property into the registration center for the rental business, and added a recreation space with a pool table, foosball, and tv lounge.

Not only did the vacationers renting the cottages start using the space, but some local teenagers enjoyed the hangout as well. Patrick was there one night when the Kim family checked in for a weeklong stay. He was mesmerized by the dark-eyed, dark-haired Mya. By the end of that stay, Patrick had stolen a kiss from the beautiful Californian, and she had stolen his heart.

But now she was getting into a different history, she realized, and this article wasn't about her. Her family had strong ties to the community, even if they weren't as historically prominent as the Eriksson family. The diner, her mom's flower shop, and her dad's dental practice were all important squares in the quilt that made up Fairview. She couldn't write about her own family, though, so she turned back to her notes.

If she *could* write about her family, she would extend it to include Natalie and Becca, because they were squares in her personal quilt. Oh, the fun they'd had.

A groan escaped as she yanked the headphones from her ears, and pushed the top of the laptop down, the satisfying snap of it a signal that her workday was done. (The part that included sitting at her desk, anyway). She had allowed thoughts of the past—not those of her perfectly wonderful childhood but the other, not-so-perfect part—to take over, leaving little space for the necessary creativity to finish her assignment. Armando's news had shaken her to the core, sucking the breath right out of her, and she wasn't sure how to deal with it.

Pinching the bridge of her nose, she closed her eyes, and took a couple deep cleansing breaths. She needed to regroup. There were photo assignments in her inbox, for although she had been recently promoted to the features desk, she was still the staff photographer for the paper. If she focused on something else, taking pictures instead of writing the story, it might be better. Maybe she needed to step away completely for the day and tackle it tomorrow. Sometimes it only took a good night's sleep to gain a better perspective. Perhaps a new approach would come to her in the meantime.

If not...she couldn't think about it. The assignments had been given out and she had to produce. Unfortunately, she hadn't found the inspiration she needed when interviewing the elusive Liz Erikson. Liz, as she quickly learned, kept everything close to the vest, so putting all her eggs into one basket hadn't been smart and now, one by one, those eggs were cracking before her eyes.

She knew very well what the problem was. Her own personal history was too intertwined with the town and the people who lived here. *And even those who return for a visit*, she thought.

"Heading out for the day, Keller?"

Of course, Ben would choose this specific moment to stop by her desk. She had only recently been moved to the department, and now her Features Editor would question why she'd been promoted at all. She did her best to hide the panic ready to send her into a frenzied state.

"Some new picture assignments came in, so I'll take those and then call it a day."

"Sounds good. Let me know if you need any feedback on your big story." As usual, his shirt was untucked, and his hair in need of combing, but nobody on staff judged him by any of that. Ben was a talented writer and dedicated to the paper. He maintained high expectations but was also willing to offer his assistance to meet them.

She loved being part of his team and didn't want to disappoint him so she nodded, acknowledging his offer, then continued packing up her laptop and camera bag. With a wave over her shoulder, she hurried down the hall, anxious to avoid any conversation about her story and the fact it wasn't coming together yet.

Even if they took away her position in this department, she rationalized, they would keep her on board as the staff photographer, and probably let her keep her weekly Hometown Pride page as well. They would certainly do that. A sense of dread settled over her as she realized the answer to that was not an automatic yes. Would she be okay if they decided they'd made a mistake by promoting her? Could she quietly return to the city news desk, hoping something of interest might pop up as a story assignment?

If she wanted to keep her job, she had to produce. Translation: She had to make this story work. Translated again: She had to put her feelings aside and focus on the task—even if she didn't like to think about her hometown changing.

The headache was settling in for the long haul as she tossed her bags onto the front seat and steered toward Lake Shore Drive. Rain was forecast once again for later in the day but right now the sun was shining, so there was a chance she could get the pictures she needed.

An ironic laugh escaped her. She would have great pictures, even if she didn't have a story. The laugh faded away quickly, replaced by a sick feeling in the pit of her stomach.

Chapter Three

Madison carefully framed the image before snapping two photos in quick succession. The lighting was ideal, and the shimmer of the lake served as a perfect backdrop. The fresh air lifted her spirits, and she no longer felt the pain of a headache as she took a moment to slowly roll her head, enjoying the release of her earlier stressors. She took a deep breath and raised the camera again. With each click, she was already considering the layout. As much as she wanted to use the photos for her next Hometown Pride, she'd probably need these to augment one of the articles in the series.

She recalled the shock when Marty came to her that day last year, praising her eye for beautiful photos and his belief readers would appreciate seeing more of them, too. Pictures and captions. Every Sunday. All she had to do was capture the people and places that she loved so much in her hometown. It was a dream assignment from the Laurel Lake Times Editor-in-Chief that quickly moved from a three-installment trial to a regular assignment.

The thought brought a smile as she looked at the expansive scene before her from her perch on the hillside, across the road from the lake. The spot gave her the perfect vantage point from which to capture the water, alive with ripples, as well as the newly constructed pier system. The construction company had been busy, getting the public marina finished just in time for the busy summer season. She continued to snap photos, capturing the improvements to the parking lot, the ramp, and the new docks.

The old public landing had been used for decades by local fishermen to put their boats into the lake. As more tourists discovered the pristine beauty of Laurel Lake, and more and more recreational activities became popular—skiing, wakeboarding, floating pontoon parties—improvements were needed. These newest developments for the docks were particularly necessary because of increased boat traffic to what used to be a small burger joint only accessible by land but was now a beautiful lakeside bar and restaurant with its own intricately designed boat docks. The Dockside Bar and Grill was now accessible by water so boaters and landlubbers alike could enjoy it. Sometimes it was hard to tell if the many changes represented progress, or an invasion into their quiet lakeshore life.

Resting the camera on her lap, she closed her eyes, feeling the warmth of the sun on her face. Growing up in Fairview, she'd spent her childhood on this lake, loving every moment of ice cream melting down her hand as she played in the sand, skipping stones with her dad in the early mornings when the lake's surface was like glass, and spending lazy afternoons with her friends on beach towels as their skin turned golden brown. She could almost smell the sunscreen and hear their carefree laughter. Before her thoughts skipped ahead to Carl, she opened her eyes, ready to continue her picture taking.

Raising the camera to take a few final shots before the clouds could steal her sun, she paused, watching as a white Ford pickup pulled into the parking lot at the same time an obtrusive, gray-rimmed cloud threatened her perfect lighting. Her opportunity was about to disappear.

"Darn it!"

Mumbling to herself, she scrolled back through the photos to see if she had captured enough or if she'd have to plan another afternoon for the shoot. Slightly miffed but slightly more curious, she watched as the man climbed from the driver's seat. His back remained to her as he pulled out his phone and snapped pictures of the water and docks. She raised her camera, capturing a picture of the man taking a picture. It struck her as amusing, despite her annoyance.

It was obvious the lighting wasn't going to get any better and the man didn't seem to be moving his truck anytime soon, so Madison decided to wrap the session, carefully placing her camera back in its case on the front seat of her jeep.

With one last glance at the intruder, she turned her vehicle toward the center of town, taking a left onto Water Street and angle parking directly in front of Poppy's Diner. The charm of Water Street made her momentarily forget about the changes down on the lakefront, and she sat for a moment, admiring the old storefronts. Although some of the businesses were bought and sold, and some renamed, they were still the heart and soul of the old downtown she knew and loved, their facades old-fashioned, rustic, and some quite weather-worn but still beautiful. She hoped they would stay untouched, quaint, and charming in their own way, even as the rest of her town was ever-changing, modernizing, and expanding.

She smiled at childhood memories of racing Patrick up and down the street, waving to the shop owners, and then dashing over the sidewalk, down the sandy slope, and into the cold water. The initial shock took their breath away, but they laughed and screamed with the rest of the kids as watchful parents stood nearby, their eyes on all of the children, prepared to scold anyone acting out or misbehaving—no matter who they belonged to. Madison missed those carefree days.

The red awning of Poppy's Diner danced in the breeze, making a crackling sound above to welcome her. For most people, this would always be the Fairview Diner, but when it came under new ownership, it was bequeathed its new name. The reason Patrick changed the name was not because he disliked its previous name, but to pay homage to the man responsible for opening the business decades before.

Madison pushed the door open, the tinkle of the bell announcing her visit and making her smile. Her own grandfather had placed that gold bell above the door back in 1955. She knew that to be true because a framed black and white photograph depicting him on a ladder with the bell in hand, smiling broadly, was hanging just inside, next to the quaint window seat. Alongside the photo was another frame, this one holding a newspaper article highlighting the opening of a new downtown restaurant and its proprietor, Prescott "Poppy" Keller.

The only other adornment on the walls made her flush with pride. Framed and matted photographs of some of her favorite pictures of Laurel Lake were displayed also. Maddy had presented the framed photos she had taken as a gift to her brother when he took over as the owner. Her parents loved them so much, she made copies for them as well.

"Hey, Poppy," she whispered to the man in the photo as she walked by, on her way to the counter.

The off-season meant the restaurant served only until 3:00 with the locals enjoying the relatively quiet breakfast and lunch hours. As soon as Memorial Day weekend arrived, however, the diner, and all the rest of the Water Street businesses, would be bustling with activity. The population of Fairview almost doubled during the summer months, with every cottage, cabin and hotel room in use and spare bedrooms in homes becoming potential rentals for young people who showed up around Memorial Day and disappeared after Labor Day, having made good money as lifeguards, waitresses, and at countless other summer jobs. It didn't matter if they were vacationing or working, visitors sought the resort lifestyle of the Laurel Lake area.

"The grill is off," a voice carried from the back.

"Well, that's good because I hate your cooking anyway. It's just me," Madison answered, laughing at her own joke as she set her purse and camera case on the counter. "Is the coffee still hot?"

She didn't wait for an answer, slipping around to help herself to the contents of a lone pot still on the warming plate.

Patrick walked through the swinging door, a towel over his shoulder and his glasses on his forehead. His apron held evidence of a lunch hour behind the grill, colorful splatters and smears abundant on the once white fabric. He reached down to untie the strings at his waist, his frame so thin he had to wrap them around his body twice. He slipped it over his neck, tossing it onto a nearby chair.

"If there's enough, pour me a cup, too." He pulled his glasses down into position over his eyes as he read a label on a package he'd carried from the back. "Why do they make the expiration dates so tiny on these things?"

Madison reached for another cup, filling both with the still-steaming dark brew. "Maybe you should admit you're turning into an old man. What are you now? Thirty-two? The eyesight goes first. I'm afraid your hair might be next. Then you'll *really* look like dad!" It was true. Patrick and Brent were readily identified as relatives, with similar facial features and the same height. They even gravitated toward the same style of glasses. Patrick was lucky enough to still have a full head of light brown hair. Their dad, however, wasn't as fortunate, good-humoredly joking about his own receding hairline. "It receded all the way to my back," he loved telling people. "And some of it is hanging on to my chin for dear life." That was true, too. While he had very little hair remaining on the top of his head, their dad had a hairy back and a full beard. Patrick either preferred to be clean-shaven or was unable to grow a decent beard. Nobody ever asked him.

Madison took after their mother with her dark blonde hair and petite figure. She was thankful for the genetic genius that made that all work out.

Patrick pretended he was about to snap her with the towel, opting instead to take the cup she held out to him.

"You look like you could use something stronger than coffee."

"Piper kept us up last night. I think she had a nightmare. Can a two-year-old have nightmares?"

Madison shrugged, holding back her laughter. "You're asking *me*?" She opened the small under-counter fridge and pulled out a carton of coffee creamer, pouring a generous amount into her cup. "I was hoping she'd be here." The elementary school let out at 3:00 and Mya usually picked up Piper from daycare and dropped by the diner to see Patrick before taking her home. There was something extra special about spending time with her toddler niece, making her forget all the troubles of the world.

"Mya took her directly home from Wee Ones for a nap. I'm guessing they're both sleeping right now." He used the towel to wipe off his glasses before putting them back on the top of his head. "Lucky girls." He checked his watch and then walked over to lock the door, flipping the sign over so CLOSED was displayed through the window. "She's really looking forward to the end of the school year and spending full days with the Piper Monster."

Madison smiled at that. "She's the cutest monster I've ever seen." She moved around the counter and sat on a stool, pulling her camera from the bag to get a look at the pictures she'd just taken. The glistening water was captured almost perfectly. She'd hoped for a couple more, though, as the sun filtered through the incoming clouds. The effect would have been stunning. But that hadn't been possible. The last shot included the white pickup truck, bringing a scowl to her face.

"Something wrong?"

"No. I missed out on a couple good shots because some guy parked in the marina lot just as I was trying to finish the dock project pictures."

He leaned over her shoulders, squinting at the image displayed on the tiny screen of her camera and then pulling his glasses down for a better look. "White pickup? It might be that guy who's renting the Clough house right now. Tall, reddish colored hair?" With a laugh he remembered, "He wanted an iced latte. I told him I could give him a cup of black coffee and some flavored creamers...and lots of ice cubes, of course. I'll give him credit. He thought it was funny."

Her brother stubbornly refused to "clutter the counter" with an espresso machine, staunchly sticking by his belief that good old-fashioned brewed coffee was the best option for his customers. "I'm glad someone appreciates your sense of humor. I didn't talk to him or get close enough to really see him. He just managed to block my last shots." She took another look at the picture and shrugged, pretending she wasn't seeing the stranger's broad shoulders and muscular arms. "Whatever." Setting her cup down, Madison spun around on her stool to face her brother. "I can help if you want."

"Really?"

"I am free labor for one hour. Tell me what you need." She took her cup behind the counter and put it into the small dishwasher they used to run light loads.

"Thanks, sis. I appreciate it." He smiled as he took her by the shoulders, gently pushing her through the swinging doors, past the grill and into the combined kitchen and workroom. "You can start by washing these." He spread his arms in a "ta-da" flourish.

The stack of pots leaned precariously close to the edge of the counter and Madison sputtered, an excuse to leave at once forming on her lips. Even as she turned to protest, her brother was busy pulling cartons of paper napkins from a shelf to stock the dining room. She sullenly donned an apron and started running hot water into the sink. She'd gotten herself into this one. "You owe me," she shouted toward the front, but he simply laughed in response.

As Patrick moved back and forth between the rooms, he hummed quietly to himself. On one trip through, he paused, his arms laden with boxes. "Hey, did you hear from Natalie, yet?"

"She'll be here the second week in June."

"So will I finally get to meet that husband of hers?"

"Nope. Byron isn't coming with her because he has some conference he's going to." She turned from the sink, suds dripping from her hands. He gestured for her to stop making a mess. "I'm excited. I have a ton of stuff planned for us. I can't believe she hasn't been here since her...since she moved to Minnesota. It's just so out-of-the-blue that she decided to come back now." A smile played across her face as she returned to her task. "Maybe she's ditching Byron and moving back here. If that's the case, he has no idea how happy he's made me."

"Byron has no idea how happy he would make *me*. Just think, I'd get an extra pair of hands around here. That, my sister, makes me one happy restaurant owner."

She ignored his mocking tone. "And what, exactly, makes you think she would want to help out here?" This time she kept her hands in the suds but turned her head to give him her best raised eyebrow along with the query.

"Come on, Mads." He looked at her with feigned wide-eyed innocence and gave her an exaggerated shrug. "She worked here as a high school kid. Why in the world wouldn't she want to re-live those magical times? Seems like a no-brainer to me."

"I see. Using the old nostalgia hook. Good one."

Even as she mocked him, in her heart of hearts, it was what she wanted. She would give anything to have the whole gang back as if they were all still in school together, a small group of friends who did everything together. She was swept back in time, moments so precious she felt her chest tighten with the memory. They had been such close friends, and they were supposed to stay that way.

Lazy summer days on the lake and long quiet falls and winters defined their existence. And then things happened, and some of them left and never returned.

"Are you okay?"

Madison took a deep breath and plunged her arms back into the suds, shaking away the thoughts. She'd been swept away by the very same memories she'd accused her brother of using to his advantage. They were all adults now, and they couldn't go back in time.

"Of course. I'm trying to figure out how to break this to you gently. Natalie won't be working while she's here. And even if she had a spare moment, there's this new-fangled thing called the internet, you see, so she could do her own job remotely. I hardly think she'll be at your beck and call on this visit. Sorry bro."

"Okay, okay, I was just kidding." He paused in the doorway, turning back again to add, "Sort of. If she even *hints* at wanting to pick up a shift, you are *not* allowed to dissuade her. Remind her how much *fun* the ice cream window is." He punctuated the statement by whistling a circus calliope tune and dancing a silly jig as he left the room.

Alone again, Madison pushed away the memories and worked through her schedule in her head. An appointment with Shelly was next. Her face warmed at the thought as she remembered Armando's comments, trying to convince herself she didn't make the appointment because of him—that she'd been due for a trim regardless of his comments—but he was probably right. She had given her hair as little attention as possible. Throwing it into a ponytail every morning was easy, and she liked to think it made her look like someone who didn't have to "try."

What it really meant was she didn't have anyone to impress.

Shaking her head to stop the path her thoughts were determined to pursue, which undoubtedly meant thoughts of Carl, she forced herself to think about the rapidly approaching summer.

Summer did, as Armando said, mean there would be the potential for new people to meet, but hadn't that been the case every year? What made her think this summer would somehow be different? She knew the answer. The season had nothing to do with it. She hadn't yet made room for anyone else in her heart because Carl still resided there.

She pulled herself out of her reverie she'd once again so easily slipped into and glanced at the clock above the sink. She had just 27 minutes left to help her brother.

"Hey Patrick?" she waited a moment and then tried again.

"Patrick?" There was one way to make her feel better when she felt the earth shifting under her feet, like it was now.

"What?" His muffled voice told her he was storing items in the open spaces below the dining room counter.

"Do you have any leftover pie or cake? I'm going to stop by Grandma's later and I'd like to take her a treat, if you have something."

He returned to lean against the doorframe. "Is that all I'm good for? Good grief. Just because a guy owns a restaurant everyone assumes he has food to spare." He grinned at her, his good humor accompanied by just the right amount of sarcasm was what endeared him to everyone and kept customers coming back. Possibly even the one who was given coffee, creamer, and ice cubes in place of an iced latte. Madison hid a smile over that one. It was quite clever of her brother. She should probably give credit to her brother's good food, too, but she didn't want to give him a big head.

"If you are going to make me beg, I'll just buy something from the grocery store. I'm sure it'll taste just as good as yours."

"Okay, okay, I get it. I'll send a slice of Dutch apple pie for her —but you have to tell her I made it." He paused, then added, "Unless she says it's dry. Then you can pretend it's just a store-bought pie."

"Fine," she answered with a roll of her eyes. "I'll still be her favorite no matter what." They talked about their beloved grandmother as if nothing had changed. Sometimes it just felt better to pretend.

A short time later, Madison finished washing the last pan in the stack, grabbed a water bottle from the mini-fridge in the closet-sized office at the back of the restaurant, and said goodbye to her brother. She left her car parked where it was but dropped her camera case and the container of pie on the front seat before walking the short distance to Belle Chic.

Like so many of the quaint storefronts on Water Street, the salon had a storied past. This building originally housed a barbershop, so when Shelly took possession several years earlier and found the red and white striped pole in the back of a storage cabinet, she returned it to its rightful place in the window. Madison guessed Shelly hadn't shaved a single customer in her professional life, but it was nice to see the piece of Americana on display.

Shelly kept busy, not only styling clients in her shop, but also spending two mornings a week at the Laurel Lake Senior Care and Memory Center providing services to the residents there. Madison knew Grandma Ruth saw Shelly for a weekly shampoo and set appointment.

"Hey, doll," Shelly met her at the door, wrapping her in a hug so tight, Madison was sure she could feel Shelly's underwire bra dig into her own chest, but she happily endured the embrace. Pulling back, Shelly reached out to run her hand through the end of Madison's ponytail. "When I saw you walk in, the light behind you was so perfect I had a vision of how I'm coloring your hair today."

"Coloring? Whoa. I thought we were just doing a trim today—you know, an inch off the length kind of thing."

"A trim? Darling, summer is around the corner. We are going to lighten and brighten you—get you summer ready. It's a whole vibe thing. Sit down."

She hesitated, giving Shelly a sideways glance. "Have you been talking to Armando?"

"Armando? Why would I be talking to him?"

Madison laughed nervously. "Never mind. Nothing too drastic, though. Please, Shell?"

"You have to embrace a little change now and then, kiddo." She paused to squeeze Madison's shoulder. "Just relax. I promise this will be completely painless."

While there was no pain, within moments there were pieces of tinfoil covered with goo clinging to her head and powerful chemical smells permeating the air. She wondered if it was too late to rip off the cape and run for her life. This was nothing short of terrifying. Change did that to her.

Reminding herself to breathe, Madison tried to concentrate on Shelly's stories, which were always in abundance, instead of focusing on what was happening to her head. They talked about the upcoming summer season, progress on the marina project, the twins born to the Kensingtons, and the very small number of houses sporting FOR RENT signs yet. That was a sure indicator to locals that a busy season was about to begin.

"Your grandmother is the sweetest angel on earth, Madison. All she ever talked about was you and your brother—but mostly you. I don't know if she was just tired or what, but the last couple visits she couldn't remember my name. She kept asking who I was." She squeezed Madison's shoulder. "I'm sure it's hard for your family."

Perhaps because she wasn't expecting the topic to be brought up, or perhaps because her grandmother's rapid decline was more pronounced of late, Madison felt a burning behind her eyes.

Shelly patted her shoulder, handing her a tissue. "Sometimes these chemicals burn my eyes, too, love."

Madison nodded, dabbing at her eyes, and grateful Shelly was more than capable of filling a silence.

Even when Shelly finally announced it was time to rinse and then led her back to the chair for a cut, relaxing turned out to be easier said than done, as each snip of the scissors made Madison's heart race. The buzz of the blow dryer was just beginning to rattle her brains when Shelly finally spun the chair around to show her the results.

"Oh," Madison said, watching her hair move in the reflection as she turned her head, attempting to see herself from various angles. "Oh," she repeated.

"After all that, I get an 'Oh'? Come on, Madison. There's got to be more reaction than that. Something? Anything?" She gave Madison's shoulders a little shake. "Snap out of it, honey. Tell me the truth now." Concern crossed her face. "Do you hate it?"

Madison shook her head slowly, placing a reassuring hand on Shelly's arm. "I was afraid I'd look...*different*. I look..."

"Lighter and brighter—exactly as I said." Her look sent a clear "I told you so" as she clapped her hands and added, "You had me worried there for a minute." She pulled the neon yellow cape from Madison's shoulders and gave it a shake before folding and placing it over the chair next to her. "*Now* you're ready for summer." She took a broom from its hook and swept pieces of hair into the vacuum system built into the wall, a loud sucking noise filling the salon as bits of hair disappeared into the opening. Madison watched, wishing it was that easy to dispose of other things in life—like the bad memories plaguing her.

Madison's attention returned to the mirror as she continued turning her head from side to side, admiring the way the subtle warm, honey blonde highlights played against her naturally dark blonde hair. "It's perfect. Thank you, Shelly."

"Now you'll be ready to meet some...what do you kids call them? Let's see...oh yes, a hottie. He'll be here for the season and then..." She stopped sweeping to lean on the broom, her eyes dreamy as she stared out the window toward the lake. "There's nothing like a summer romance. I think that's why I loved *Grease* so much. What a great movie. Summer loving." She sighed and then finished straightening, humming a tune from the movie as Madison continued to stare at her reflection.

She looked the same and yet different and for a moment, she felt unbalanced, memories of previous summers marching through her head.

Shelly's voice cut through her reverie. "I almost forgot about the golf course." Madison pulled herself back to the moment, meeting Shelly at the counter to take care of the bill. "You heard they're looking for a buyer, right?"

With a wave of her hand, Madison dismissed the comment. "That rumor recycles every couple of years. The Thorsens will never sell."

"We'll see," Shelly responded, giving her yet another crushing hug. She started to say something else and then stopped herself. "Get out there and enjoy that new hairdo."

Madison felt a strange sense of renewal as she slid behind the wheel, adjusting the rearview mirror so she could look at herself. The truth was obvious to her. Despite the pretty hairstyle, the nice car, and the beautiful home—all those good things—she was, in essence, the most put-together basket case in Fairview.

Swinging out of the parking space, she took the long route, turning onto Lake Shore Drive. While the quaint Water Street businesses maintained the charm of decades past, the houses along Lake Shore Drive hadn't fared as well. Significant renovations and remodels to many of the original homes meant there was no consistency to the blocks she drove along now. It wasn't unusual to find a 1950's cottage next to a contemporary ranch home, or even a stark, modern architectural style. More and more properties had been purchased and the old houses torn down in the name of progress over the past fifteen years or so.

The changes broke her heart a little.

On a whim, she turned left at the next intersection, heading toward the Lakeside Cottages instead of taking the turn toward the Center. It would do her good to see the most historic part of town right now—and a reminder that not everything had to change.

As she rounded the corner that would bring her to the edge of the Erikson property, Madison's heart jumped in an uncomfortable two-step. It took a moment for her brain to register that directly in front of her, on the grassy section separating the Erickson property from the golf course, a surveying crew was putting away equipment, the two men returning to their truck parked on the roadside just ahead. All the exuberance she felt earlier came crashing down, and she heard a loud roaring in her ears. With a sinking heart, she realized maybe, just maybe, this time it was more than a rumor.

Chapter Four

A SPRING WREATH OF WOVEN PINK AND YELLOW flowers adorned the door to room 312. The placard reading Ruth Keller in dark stenciled letters included a red sticker. The director let them know he'd added that detail, a reminder to staff that the resident occupying the room was in some "early stage" of Alzheimer's, which could mean just about anything, given she hadn't been deemed "severe enough" to require a move to the memory care wing just yet. They all knew the significance of that sticker. As had become her habit of late when she stood at this door, Madison took a deep steadying breath, preparing herself for whatever awaited her on the other side. The decline had intensified, the disease somehow choosing a trajectory far more rapid than the family could have imagined.

Inside the one-bedroom apartment-sized unit, she would find her grandmother's furniture and keepsakes, her photographs, and knickknacks. What she was less likely to find was her grandmother —the grandmother she grew up knowing and adoring.

Anxiety built like a pot of water on the cusp of boiling—little bubbles of worry popping up and disappearing, but threatening to roll over her in all-consuming waves. She could blame it on the surveying crew she'd just seen, but the feelings had more to do with the mystery of which grandma was on the other side of the door. One would have a slackness in her mouth, and eyes that couldn't quite focus for minutes at a time; the other would greet Madison with a ready smile of recognition. She desperately hoped for the latter as she gently knocked, pushed the door open, and stepped inside.

Madison had read enough to know it was only going to get worse, but for her grandma's sake, she smiled and carried on as though nothing was wrong. Grandma Ruth rocked slowly in her chair next to the window. Madison searched her face in the darkening room, preparing herself either way. The tell-tale light was in her eyes. Her grandma was still there.

She set the slice of pie in its plastic to-go container on the counter before stepping into the living area and leaning down to kiss the wrinkled cheek turned toward her.

Madison fought the urge to mention the surveying crew, concerned it might upset her grandmother to learn the golf course would be changing hands. The course had been an integral part of the community for all the years she and Poppy ran their business. Then again, there was a chance Ruth Keller might not even remember there was a golf course at all. Alzheimer's was a terrible thief, stealing away great swaths of moments and memories and then sometimes stingily returning them in oddly timed bits and pieces.

"Hey grandma, are you enjoying the view?" She sat across from the old woman, taking her hand to gently rub as they looked out the window together.

Strategically situated on a small rise, this wing of the care center provided a partial view of the lake. A scattering of fluffy white clouds drifted across the horizon, and lilacs were just beginning to add color to the bushes across the sidewalk.

"Is it warm out today?" Her voice was raspy, perhaps because she hadn't used it very much today. When she first moved from her house to the Center, she participated in all the activities— bridge club, exercise class, and even the music ensemble. She watched movies with her friends and spent time socializing in the downstairs salon or out on the patio in nice weather. With the disease progressing, she was no longer doing anything social. The early onset Alzheimer's she was first diagnosed with hadn't seemed too terribly bad. Now that it was progressing more rapidly, they could readily see the changes to the woman they all adored.

"It's light jacket weather. It was cloudy before, but I think we'll have a nice sunset tonight. Do you want to take a walk, grandma?"

Ruth shook her head "I'd like to just sit here. I'm fine right here." She patted the arms of her chair. "Is it getting cold out?"

Madison ignored the fact they had just covered the weather. "As long as you're comfortable, we'll just sit right here. I have something for you." She held up the plastic container, snapped open the cover, and held the pie out to her. "Patrick sent along a treat from the diner—Dutch apple. Would you like to have it now?"

A cloud seemed to drift across her face as though she was trying to put the pieces together—pie, Patrick, diner—and then the cloud disappeared, her eyes lit up, and she clapped her hands like a delighted child. "Ooohh. You should warm it up. And bring...bring a...uhm...something to eat it with and a napkin."

Fork, grandma. The word is fork. Madison wanted to fill in the missing word but was hesitant to draw attention to the fact she couldn't remember the name of a simple utensil. Instead, she did as her grandma said and soon the sweet aroma of the dessert wafted from the microwave oven, bringing an unexpected hominess and nostalgia to the small living space. Reaching into the silverware drawer, her hand hovered over something unusual. Glancing over at her grandmother, she reached into the drawer and pulled out a toothbrush. Her heart sank as she battled tears. She would slip it back into her grandma's bathroom before she left.

She delivered the warmed slice to her grandmother's eager

hands, while a déjà vu moment swept over her—the countless times she had been on the receiving end of one of her grandma's homemade goodies. The desire to have one of their old, easy conversations was overwhelming, and Madison girded herself against the ensuing ache. The chasm between them was widening. She stifled the urge to reach out and grab her grandmother to keep her close, even though it would serve little purpose. Ruth was already drifting farther away from them with each passing month.

Madison watched as her grandmother raised a forkful of pie to her mouth. Did it take her back to a time she made the dessert at the diner day after day? She couldn't ask her. It might very well be there was no memory attached at all and it was just the simple task of biting, chewing, and swallowing. Her own head reeled with the countless moments they'd shared. She blinked rapidly, determined to maintain a happy front.

"Your flowers are beautiful." Madison distracted herself by inspecting the vase full of blossoms she instinctively knew had to be one of her mother's designs. It was a piece of art, strategically placed flowers and greenery arranged in perfect balance.

Ruth carefully chewed the bite she'd put in her mouth before responding. "Your mother is a sweet girl, Madison. Such a sweet girl. Brent is a lucky man. I was trying to remember how long they've been married, but I..." She gave an almost imperceptible shrug.

It was rare for a single day to go by without someone in the family paying a visit and they compared notes regularly, convinced she was still more lucid than not, and still unsure if that were the truth or simply wishful thinking. There was no denying she was sliding into a confused state more frequently, but still able to return, suddenly recalling events and incidents with surprising acuity.

Using hindsight, they tried to pinpoint how long ago the earliest symptoms began, but they couldn't come to any consensus. Their guesses ranged from seven years to perhaps ten. Ruth had been active socially, still coming and going whenever she wanted, living with what they all saw as minor inconveniences of the aging process. (After all, who didn't forget where the keys were now and then?) Eventually, they realized it was more than simple forgetfulness. There had been no diagnosis, however, until after she'd made the move to this new home. Brent and Nina wanted her to live with them when it became evident the house was getting burdensome for her, but she shocked them all by announcing her desire to move to the care center, insisting it was better to be with her friends who'd already made that move. They couldn't be sure if she was getting worried about her forgetfulness or if she really was looking forward to the social aspects of moving to this senior community.

"They are celebrating their 35th anniversary next month, grandma." She moved the flower arrangement to the windowsill to give it a bit of the rapidly waning sunshine. "They had Patrick three years after they married and he's almost 32." Madison hoped she was providing enough detail to trigger her grandma's memory without making her feel worse for having forgotten. The last thing she wanted was to add more confusion to her easily addled thought processing. It was difficult to find the right balance.

Madison looked around the small living room, eyes falling on two picture frames, each holding a Hometown Pride section of the newspaper. She recognized them as her first two submissions for the special weekly assignment she had been given last year. Her heart swelled, knowing how much she was like her grandmother with their shared love of Fairview. And now her grandmother was on the cusp of losing all her wonderful memories of their special hometown.

"Thirty-two. That's right. Nina looked like a princess. And I remember Liz dancing with Chuck. Everyone thought they were getting together, didn't they?"

"That was long before I was born, grandma, so I don't know." Madison said this gently, never quite sure how to respond to the slips in memory of this magnitude. It was possible she could gently prod for clarification once her grandmother seemed a bit sharper.

A look crossed Ruth's face, and she held the pie plate out to Madison, most of it still uneaten, her appetite nothing like it used to be. "But they weren't a couple, were they?" Her hands fluttered nervously, and she glanced around as if surprised by her setting. Just as quickly, the confusion left her face, and her eyes were again bright. "Make sure you tell Patrick how good the pie was. I'll have the rest of it tomorrow so you can just put that in the refrigerator. Make sure you cover it completely, so it doesn't dry out." She stood slowly, shuffling to the loveseat, and arranging herself among the pillows there.

Madison smiled at the litany of instructions as she put the pie away. There were so many little things she would miss as her grandma slipped further away. The thought made it difficult to breathe as she eyed the toothbrush on the counter. It was like looking at a children's book. Can you see what's wrong with this picture?

She pulled her camera from her bag, anxious for a distraction from the overwhelmingly sad thoughts. "Look at how nice the marina is looking, grandma. Grandpa would have loved putting a boat in there, don't you think?"

Her very voice held all the love she'd had for the man as she turned her eyes back to Madison, a warmth and lightness in her face making her look years younger. "Your grandpa. Oh, how he loved to fish. And I'd fry them up nice and crisp on the outside." She laughed thinking about it. "We never ate that pickled herring Agnes made. Oh goodness, that was horrid." She added something under her breath, too quiet for Madison to hear.

"What was that grandma?" She leaned closer, again taking Ruth's hand in her own.

"I don't think that's right. Chuck and Liz. I think I was mistaken. They weren't a couple."

She looked to Madison for some reassurance she was remembering events correctly.

"I'm not sure." It was entirely possible a 35-year-old Liz could have danced with someone named Chuck at her parents' wedding, but she had no way of knowing. Desperate to distract her, Madison's eyes landed on a box on the bookshelf. "Do you want to work on a puzzle? I think Patrick got you this one for your birthday." She walked to the shelf, holding up the box to show her grandmother the scene of an English garden with flowers of every hue growing in window boxes and winding up wooden trellises. "Mom would love this one, wouldn't she?"

"Chuck." Her voice was quiet as she once again tried to remember something that seemed to slip away from her. The confusion in her voice was painful. "Where is Chuck?" Her fingers played with the material of her blouse, agitation growing.

"Sorry, grandma, I don't know." She hesitated, then decided to help bring some clarity to the conversation her grandma was intent on having. Reaching over to rest a hand on her grandmother's she waited a beat before diving in. "I don't remember Chuck's last name, do you?"

Ruth gave her a funny look. "You don't know? He used to sit at the counter every morning."

Unsure how to respond, Madison tried to hide her confusion. Her grandmother hadn't been able to work at the diner on any regular basis for almost 15 years now, so she was likely talking about a time that stretched back in her memory far longer than before Madison was old enough to help on weekends. As much as she wanted to ask more questions, she could tell it was upsetting Ruth.

It was happening rapidly now. She would call her parents later to fill them in on tonight's memory lapses.

But Ruth wasn't finished. "He was heartbroken when she started dating that other boy. Oh, goodness, what was his name?" She pulled her hands free from Madison's, raising them to her face as she tried to bring back the memory. "I can see his face. He was always smiling, showing off those dimples. Poor boy. He died over there, and nobody seemed to care. Those poor boys shipped off to Vietnam. They were never treated right if you ask me."

Madison was even more confused as the memory—or her grandma's version of a memory—became more convoluted. She didn't know the characters in the jumbled play acted out in her grandmother's mind and now, she knew whatever it was happened decades ago.

Leaning closer, Madison took her grandma's shaking hands from her face and held them in her own. "It's okay if you don't remember. You can tell me about it later. I'd love to hear the whole story. You'll remember it."

"I'll have to call Agnes. She'll know their names." She stopped fussing momentarily, sitting quietly to look in her granddaughter's eyes. "You look so pretty. I just know you'll be a beautiful bride. I'd like to rest now. Will you help me to my bedroom?"

Madison put her hand under Ruth's elbow as she shuffled the few steps to her room. "There you go," she murmured, tucking the sheets around the tiny frame. Her grandmother wanted her to be happy, and in her mind, that meant marriage and babies. Madison wasn't sure when any of that would happen, and she certainly wasn't going to inform her grandma she wouldn't be walking down an aisle anytime soon. The thought was interrupted by a gasp.

"Gordon. His name was Gordon. I remembered." She pulled the sheet up to her chin and rested her arms on top, crossed at her chest, a look of triumph on her face. "You can sit here with me for a minute."

"Of course." Madison sat in the chair close to the bed, one hand resting lightly on Ruth's arm. Her skin, paper-thin, was spotted, lined, and wrinkled, an intricate roadmap outlining the trials, tribulations, and celebrations of her 88 years on earth. Madison rubbed gently, thinking about all the years of work her grandmother had put in at the restaurant helping Grandpa Poppy, and how lonely she had to be since burying him all those years ago.

"Agnes Carlson had her eye on your grandfather, too." She didn't open her eyes, but a smile played on her lips. "She was prettier than me, but he liked my coffee cake better than hers. I never told her my special ingredient. I kept that a secret."

Madison's head was spinning from the rapid change in topics, and this time she didn't try to make any sense of who her grandma was talking about.

"You always made the most delicious cake, grandma, so I'm not surprised." For some reason, Madison felt tears behind her eyes, caught up in the nostalgia, and how quickly everything changed in life. With a swift movement, she wiped them away, afraid her grandma might open her eyes and see her crying.

Ruth's eyes remained closed. Just when Madison thought her grandmother was asleep, the woman murmured, "But she was still my best friend—even after he picked me." Her words were coming out slower and softer as she drifted toward sleep. Madison had to lean in closer to catch the last part. "I didn't tell her the secret ingredient. I was a good secret keeper. I kept hers, too. Such a delicate matter."

After a moment of quiet, Ruth let out a sound that could have been a sigh or perhaps a soft snore. She wouldn't be sharing more stories—real or made-up—on this visit.

Madison watched her grandma sleep, overwhelmed by a sadness that had everything to do with the vitality rapidly slipping from this special lady she so adored. *Please stay with me, Grandma. Don't get lost inside there. I need you. I can't lose anyone else. I need to know you're still here.*

Thinking back over their odd conversation, Madison considered the marriage comment, which certainly hit a tender spot in her heart, whether her grandmother knew it or not, but that wasn't nearly as troubling as the realization her grandmother wanted to call someone who had been dead for several decades.

Chapter Five

"It was just a survey crew. That doesn't automatically translate into them selling it. Maybe they plan to do some improvements along that side of the property. It could be a lot of things, honey."

Her dad's words, meant to reassure her, only served to frustrate her more. "Selling it would change *everything*." She paused mid-step, a look of horror crossing her face. "And what if a new owner decided to make it a private course? *That* would be a disaster."

Brent Keller touched his daughter on the shoulder as he continued past her to the deck box. "And that's why they wouldn't make it a private club. I think the Thorsens will do what's in the town's best interest. They're good people and they care about Fairview. Relax." He smiled, motioning for her to help him take the cushions from the box to place on the patio chairs. "I told your mom we could leave these out, and lucky for me, she's just smarter than I am. They would have gotten soaked through in yesterday's rain. I'm going to keep that gal around."

Any other time she would have paused to acknowledge his comment and bask in the happiness of her parents' relationship. Not everyone was fortunate enough to have such a loving couple setting an example for the family. But today, she had distractions compounding, leaving her off-balance.

The loud cry of gulls drew her attention to the lake, and she had a sudden urge to take off her shoes, open the backyard gate and make her way down to the shore. It would feel good to dig her toes in the cool sand, feel the small rocks under her feet, and shiver at the chill of the lake water lapping against her ankles. The moment passed, and she returned to feeling on edge.

Madison let her dad draw her into a hug. "I know the golf course means a lot to you. It'll always be there. Don't worry." They stood side by side for a moment, looking at the lake stretching before them, interrupted by the sound of the patio slider opening.

"I think they're here," Nina announced, gesturing for them to hurry inside. Nina beat them to the front door by a couple steps and she swung it open. Family dinners were always fun events, but with the addition of Piper, they were taken to a whole new level.

The little girl's squeal rang through the house, the sound sending Houston scrambling from his spot on the sofa to hide under a bed in a room far from the tiny noisy human invading his quiet space.

"That poor dog will never get used to her voice," Nina laughed. "You can bet he'll be back as soon as she starts dropping food on the floor though."

Patrick and Mya struggled to get through the doorway, loaded with a dessert plate, diaper bag, and the wiggling 18-month-old Piper as six additional arms were extended to help with the baby and all the accoutrements. Through all the commotion, Piper smiled her toothy grin at everyone before reaching her arms out to her grandpa.

"Come here, my little Pipe-ster." She allowed him to snuggle her close, giggling as he gently rubbed his beard against her face.

Patrick laughed, more than happy to give someone else a chance to spend time with the ball of energy. "That poor kid is going to have an identity crisis. She has no idea what her real name is."

Turning accusatory eyes to her husband, Mya added, "Maybe you could stop calling her Pooper?"

"I can't help it. Have you smelled what she leaves us in her diapers? We need to get that girl potty-trained!"

Brent tickled her belly, making her squeal once again. "Just as long as she keeps calling me Papa, it's all good." He held her high above his head, pretending to let her slip, but catching her and pulling her tightly against his chest. "We sound like an act. Piper and Papa. They'll come from all over the world to see us," he said, in a dramatic circus master voice.

"More Papa," she answered. He obliged, lifting her into the air once again.

"That's not how it works these days, dad." Patrick reached over his dad's shoulder to wipe some dried-on food from his daughter's face. "You simply post a video of the two of you being cute and you'll become overnight internet sensations. That's the wonder of social media." He couldn't quite keep the sarcasm from his voice.

Brent rolled his eyes in agreement. "Yep, I'll pass." The toddler was anxious to get down and find something else to hold her attention for a while. "Let's just be a regular grandpa and his beautiful granddaughter without the fame."

"Good plan," Mya nodded, bending to set the diaper bag on the floor and re-fasten Piper's sandal. "We already know she's the cutest kid in the universe without millions of people giving her a thumb's up." She demonstrated with her own thumb pointed upward before turning her attention to her sister-in-law. "You look fabulous, Mads. Did you get a haircut? I feel like I haven't seen you in ages."

"Just a trim," she smiled, taking the cake pan from Patrick's hand, pleased with herself for styling her hair instead of throwing it into a ponytail. Madison shifted the pan to one hand and put her other up to her mouth as a shield, before stage whispering, "And some magical coloring potion."

Mya reached a hand up to touch Madison's hair, nodding in approval. "It's beautiful."

"I needed something lighter and brighter, according to Shelly."

"Sometimes I think I should cut all of this off."

Madison's eyes flashed with horror. "No! Your hair is always perfect." It was true. Mya's long dark hair shimmered, a cascading wave any time she moved her head.

"I agree, Mya. But I'm sure you'd look great no matter how you wear it." Nina held her arms out to Piper. "Come by grandma. My little lady is getting so big." She squeezed the toddler and kissed the top of her head.

Piper's large dark eyes perfectly matched her mother's, and it was looking more and more likely she'd have her mom's thick, black hair as well. Animatedly babbling a mile-a-minute, she looked around the group. Everyone pretended to fully understand each word, when in truth, they caught an occasional word here and there. Madison looked to her brother and sister-in-law for translation from time to time, but most of it was some randomized variations of dada, mama, papa, doggie, and something that sounded like banana. Nobody was quite sure if Piper's name for grandma was banana or if she was referencing the fruit.

"I'll take the hamburger patties out if someone else can grab the rest of the stuff from the kitchen." Brent broke away to make his way to the kitchen, followed by the rest.

They scrambled to fill their arms with buns, salads, chips, plates, and everything else they needed, as Piper toddled along behind, continuing her nonstop chatter. Although rain had been prevalent most of the weekend, Memorial Day dawned warm and sunny, and perfect for the family's traditional cookout. Patrick returned to the kitchen to get the highchair, situating it between two of the chairs at the patio dining set.

Brent put his black chef's apron on, its bold stenciled lettering claiming him to be "The Great Grill Master," and started placing the seasoned patties on the grill. He readily admitted Patrick was the food expert in the family, but when it came to his grill, he was the king reigning supreme. "Does everyone want cheese?" He surveyed the group, counting the nodding heads. "Perfect. You'll all be getting heaven on a bun before you know it."

He was right, and their chatter paused momentarily as they all tucked into the meal. When he was finished, Brent put his napkin over his face to entertain Piper who was getting antsy to be freed from her chair to explore. Madison soaked in the moment, wishing her grandmother were there, too. She used to join them for these events, but over the past year there were fewer and fewer jaunts from the care center, and the family felt the gaping hole left by her absence without mentioning it.

"I was starving." Patrick offered Piper a bite-size piece of watermelon. She squeezed it between her fingers before popping it into her mouth and holding her hand out for more, pink juices dripping from her chubby fist.

Madison grinned, nodding toward the doorway where the face of a Shih tzu was squashed up against the screen on the patio door, watching them cautiously. "Houston is dying to come out and scavenge."

"You can let him out." Nina watched Madison open the door to the excited dog, who shied away momentarily as Piper squealed in delight once again, then cautiously approached her offering of watermelon. Nina handed the dog a bit of burger when he sniffed the melon with disdain. "I can't even remember when we did our last family dinner. We've all been so busy. Hopefully we can settle into a routine again."

Brent gave her a funny look. "You do remember we're heading into the summer, right? Since when do our routines 'settle' enough for us to do *more* together between Memorial and Labor Day?" He added air quotes for emphasis.

Nina grinned ruefully. "I can dream, can't I?"

"I think I'm in pretty good shape. Thank goodness I have

Sandra as my weekday waitress. She could run the whole place if she had to. I have three high school returnees from last summer so I should be able to slip away now and then. Tino is ready to take on more responsibility. He'll be helping me train the new group of hires."

"And let him do the scheduling, honey. Give him the chance to prove himself."

Patrick grimaced. "I know, I know. It's not easy giving up that control, but you're right. He deserves the chance. I'm starting out with six new hires because you know those kids tend to leave as soon as they realize how much fun their friends are having while they're working. If I start out with more, I can give them fewer shifts, and maybe they'll stick around." He shrugged, the formula for running the diner sometimes more luck than planning. "If that doesn't work, maybe I need to find a few foreign prospects."

Back in the late 1970's, the small businesses along Water Street could no longer compete for the small number of high school and college kids looking for jobs, so they worked with the Chamber of Commerce to start a program that encouraged foreign students to spend the summer in Fairview. It was touted as the perfect opportunity to practice their English, learn about American culture, earn some money, and enjoy summer in a resort community. It worked. Young people flocked to the area from Europe, South America and even some African nations.

When it became evident there was a shortage of places for them to stay, the Chamber took the bold step of convincing locals to open their homes to these travelers, mostly free of charge, creating a unique cultural experience on both ends.

In the 1980's a shift in the economy became impetus for locals to earn a little cash by charging a nominal rental fee for students to stay in their extra bedrooms, unused cottages, or garage apartments. Wait staff, lifeguards, golf course greens keepers, and many other positions available during the busy summer months were filled by these young world travelers, and locals earned a bit of extra cash from the rent they charged.

As the economy slumped further, residents started filling the jobs themselves, decreasing the need for foreign workers. Even young people living in Brookfield, 35 miles from Fairview, became interested in working whatever job was available to them. When the economy improved, the struggle to find help returned with a vengeance but there was also far less interest from around the world to fill the jobs.

Madison couldn't figure out why everyone didn't want to work in Fairview. If they had to have a summer job, it might as well be a fun one on the lakeshore. She had researched the history of the program and its current iteration in one of her journalism courses. Many residents still rented out their spare rooms or entire houses to visitors, whether they were working summer jobs or vacationing.

Mya gave Patrick's arm a pat. "It would be nice to have you around more. We could take Piper to the beach together. She would love that."

He nodded, crossing his fingers to emphasize his hope for the plan. "And I'm still convinced Natalie is dying to take on a shift or two during the few days she's here." He grinned at his sister, waiting for her reaction to his ribbing, but she was lost in her own thoughts. He nudged her gently. "You must be excited to see Natalie. It's what, two more weeks?"

"That's the plan. Once she drops Byron at the airport to send him off to his conference, she'll drive directly here." As excited as she was for Natalie to return to Fairview, Madison was anxious to move to another topic she couldn't get out of her head. "Did you two hear anything more about the golf course? Is it really for sale this time?"

"You're giving yourself wrinkles with all that worrying. You don't have to solve the world's problems, Madison." Mya's words were a momentary calming salve.

"Not the world, I know, but can I try solving Fairview's?" She sighed, wishing once again everything could stay the same for a while. Even as she gave her sister-in-law a reassuring smile, a familiar ache rose in her chest. Everything was always changing. Her grandmother's health was failing. Her family couldn't find time to be together as much lately. And what about Fairview? Why couldn't it stay the same? She gripped her chair, as if that action could stop her from reeling out of control.

"Something is definitely going on this time." Patrick took the potato chip bowl to help himself before passing it along. "I think the Thorsen family lost interest once their kids moved away. Last year, some of us noticed that the course wasn't as groomed as it used to be."

Brent leaned back in his chair. "I'd agree with that. I guess it could be for all kinds of reasons other than a lack of interest, but if that is the case, it will be better for the course if someone comes in to breathe life back into it. It's too nice to let it go downhill." He ate the lone chip remaining on his plate.

Piper let out a string of syllables, so all eyes turned to her, putting discussion about the fate of the course on hold momentarily.

But Madison wasn't ready to let it go. "I was telling dad that if new owners come in and make it a private club, it'll hurt every business."

"I'm telling you, kiddo, I don't believe anyone would buy it for that reason." He stood, surveying the remnants of their meal. "I'll get some of this cleaned up before we bring out the dessert." Nina started to rise, but he leaned over to kiss the top of his wife's head. "You stay here and relax. I've got it."

Nina and Patrick began chatting about their expectations for the busy summer season ahead on Water Street while Madison and Mya took Piper to play on the lawn.

"Something else is bothering you, Madison. What is it?"

Madison looked into Mya's dark eyes, remembering when her entire family had descended upon Fairview for the wedding four years ago. Mya's parents, brothers, aunts, and cousins were all in attendance, their soft-spoken warm ways charming and inviting, letting Patrick know they welcomed him into their tight-knit group—along with his entire family, too. Mya was a beautiful bride, connecting the Kim family to the Keller family, and in that warm, inviting way, she made Madison want to share some of the burden on her heart.

"Someone I haven't seen in a very long time is planning to be here for the 150th. It's a person who brings back some bad memories." What she wanted to say was the past she had masterfully managed to keep a comfortable distance behind her was about to come crashing down on her, leaving her flattened and unrecognizable.

"Oh." She bent, once again re-fastening the Velcro strap on Piper's sandal. "I need to get you some new shoes, little one." She turned her attention back to Madison. "Will you have to see her while she's here?" Mya's calm, rational approach would have been helpful in any other scenario, but Madison couldn't find a way to avoid the inevitable with Becca.

"I don't think I'll be able to avoid her entirely." She hadn't seen her since the week after the...the accident because Becca left for New York immediately following the funeral, somehow able to put the entire tragic mess aside as though nothing had ever happened. Madison carried it daily. Her chest felt heavy with grief, and she squatted down next to Piper to hide her trembling hands as well as the tears threatening to reveal themselves. "Look, Piper, a dandelion."

She held the bright yellow weed out to her niece, watching her stick her nose into it as if it were the sweetest smelling flower on the planet. Piper grinned broadly then toddled away in search of more of the yellow treasures.

Mya touched Madison's arm, speaking softly. "You should never let another person dictate how you feel, Madison. She can't be that important. I'm here any time you need someone to talk to. Don't ever forget that."

Madison could only nod in response and then excused herself, needing a quick visit to the bathroom to compose herself. She returned to the patio in time for the fudge cake Mya made for the occasion.

Nina waited until everyone finished eating before quietly clearing her throat to get their attention. "Your dad and I want to talk with you about Grandma Ruth."

The very air around them seemed to change, the shift almost physical, as the animated conversation of moments before was replaced by a heavy silence. Brent started to speak, stopped, swallowed hard and then looked around the table at his family.

"We're meeting with the center's director next week." Brent covered Nina's hand with his own. "His recommendation is to start the process to move her to the memory care unit."

Piper whined, so Mya gently wiped the sticky mess from the toddler's fingers and lifted her from Patrick's lap. "I'll take her in the house and get her cleaned up so you can talk." She leaned over to kiss Patrick's cheek.

Quiet again settled over the group.

Brent cleared his throat. "She's getting confused more often now. We've all seen that. She has amazing caregivers there, but they aren't trained to deal with memory care patients." The move meant leaving her apartment to live in something more like a hospital room with limited space. He rubbed his temples, suddenly looking tired. "I think it's better if we talk to her about it while she's still lucid enough to understand what's happening. She should help make the decision."

"Honey, maybe we should wait to discuss any of this until we've met with Greg and get a better understanding of his timeline."

"We need to be prepared." They nodded in agreement. For years they saw it creeping in, an uninvited stranger coming to inhabit the woman they all loved. "Yesterday she told me she tried to call Agnes, but the line was busy all day. She told me to drive over to the house to make sure she was okay."

Nina picked up where he left off. "Agnes Eriksson died before Poppy did, so we know her processing is getting worse."

"Agnes Carlson." Madison said it almost under her breath. "She told me she needed to call Agnes Carlson. Was that her maiden name?"

Brent nodded. He squeezed his wife's hand, and looked around the table. "This is going to mean another big change for all of us."

After cleaning up the last of their lunch, they readied themselves for a pontoon boat ride on the glassy clear lake. They tried to find the celebratory mood of earlier but fell short. The touch of the sun on her upturned face felt deliciously wonderful, but Madison couldn't completely let go of the chill that had crept into her heart.

Sleep was impossible. The illuminated face of the clock changing numbers only served to agitate her more. Every part of her being had been forced to look back in time, blinders pulled away, leaving an eyes-wide-open view of how her world collapsed around her. It had been ten years, and she still couldn't fit what transpired into a neat little package to be tucked away and forgotten, meaning it was very much present in her heart and mind.

Pushing off the covers, she slid out of bed and padded across the hall to the guest bedroom. It was all set for Natalie, and she was looking forward to having company, someone to help ward off the emptiness she was suffocating under tonight.

Despite living alone, it was rare for Madison to feel this depth of loneliness. Most of the time she felt the warm presence of her grandparents wrapped securely around her, but tonight, their comforting voices were silent. There was a standing invitation from her parents to move back to her old bedroom should she ever want to, but that wasn't going to happen, even at moments like this when she felt impossibly alone. This was her home. As if on cue, a floorboard creaked below her feet, reassuring her.

Returning to her own bedroom, Madison sat on the edge of

her bed, staring at the closet door before her. Finally, she crossed the room and opened it, pulling out a cardboard file box and setting it on the bed next to her. The manilla envelope was on top, exactly where she'd left it. She turned it over in her hands before unfastening the metal clasp holding it shut. How funny it was, she thought, to keep it clasped, as if that tiny metal tab could keep the contents securely out of mind until released.

Her hand trembled as she ran it over the creased newspaper article she removed from the envelope. Although she had read the headline so many times it was etched on her brain, she read it again, as if needing to see it in print to remind her it was real.

TRAGIC ACCIDENT CLAIMS FAIRVIEW MAN

It was real, and as always, she felt the weight of the words on her entire being, the old, familiar aches all-consuming. She didn't need any additional reminders and her eyes filled with tears as she shoved the paper back into the envelope. Something small was tucked deep inside, and she pulled it out, her trembling fingers holding tightly to the tile, its surface smooth and cold.

Patrick told her it was ivory when they first started playing with the domino set at their grandparents' house. She learned later the creamy white pieces were made of bone. She didn't care what the polished tiles were made of, she loved the near-magic Patrick performed with them. On Sunday evenings they would gather for dinner and while the adults lingered over coffee, Patrick would construct an intricate train of domino tiles, lining them up in the living room, through the hallway, and on into the bedrooms. With all the painstaking care of a well-trained engineer, he stood his little soldiers at attention, each perfectly spaced to fall when it was supposed to. Madison waited impatiently for him to finally give the signal that he was setting the first one in motion so everyone could stop what they were doing and watch.

It always went too quickly and within seconds, the snaking

lines of dominoes had fallen, as if the time and effort Patrick had just expended was meaningless.

She vividly remembered the urge to randomly pull one out before it touched the next, to forestall the inevitable of one hitting against the next, but they were always too fast and she was too mesmerized by the tidal wave to try. Then, before she knew it, the entire carefully crafted lineup of tiles would be toppled, a well-aligned trail of wreckage waiting to be rebuilt. And Patrick gladly rebuilt, experimenting with more intricate designs as more domino sets (*All plastic*, her brother mentioned with a touch of contempt) joined the original set in the cabinet, the adults as impressed with his construction abilities as Madison. He learned to create more obstacles and build structures so he could go up and over furniture. Her favorite was the split design so two lines simultaneously circled around objects, converging at just the right moment every time.

When she cleaned out the built-in cabinets during her grandmother's move, Madison had come across the boxes and boxes of dominoes, and she'd sat on the floor for a moment with them surrounding her, remembering the hours of fun they provided. She dumped all of them in a cardboard box, the clattering and chattering of them banging together echoing through the living room, as if remembering those times themselves. With a Sharpie, Madison wrote PATRICK on the side, and smiled at the thought of how much fun he would have with Piper, building his famous domino trains. Before sealing the box, however, she paused, burying her hand deep inside, turning over piece after piece until she finally found what she was looking for and put it in her pocket.

Patrick sometimes let her be the official starter. His tongue vibrating against the roof of his mouth as a drumroll, he would ceremoniously deliver a tile to her, stretching his palms out to present it. He always used the same one—the blank tile, the one without any dots. *(They're pips, not dots,* she could hear him reminding her repeatedly). The catalyst. He proudly taught her that word. She would take her job seriously, carefully placing the domino on the floor and giving it the gentlest of taps to send it on its devastating path.

Now, sitting in her bedroom, staring at the single tile in her palm, Madison was reminded yet again of how easily things can spin out of control. Something so innocent by itself, if given even the smallest bit of pressure, became the firing pin for something potentially destructive. If only the train worked in reverse—so that she could push the knocked over tiles back up and they would return to their standing, unscathed positions. But it didn't work that way. Once done, most things cannot be undone. She continued rubbing her thumb over the pip-less tile. The starter. The cause of the destruction.

After a few minutes, she put everything back where she'd found it and returned to her bed, pulling the covers up to her chin and letting the tears fall unchecked. Missing everything she could no longer have was more than she could handle at times.

The box didn't hold any of the answers. For ten years she had tried to find them. Only one made sense. The last time she'd seen her, Becca had made it clear. Everything that happened was started by one person. Madison had been the catalyst.

Sleep eventually gave her respite.

Chapter Six

THERE WAS A DISTINCT BUZZ IN THE AIR OF THE Laurel Lake Times that had nothing to do with scoops, breaking news, or deadlines, and everything to do with the new management company. Madison could sense the moment she walked through the door and started toward her cubicle that another change had been made by Galloway Newspapers. When Martin Garvey, the long-time Editor-in-Chief, announced the sale of the local newspaper to a national corporation, he gave the staff fair warning his retirement was now imminent, not having any desire to "sell his soul to a corporate devil."

They all should have been as concerned as Marty. Since the sale, nothing had been the same at the paper. Nuanced changes started immediately, implemented so slowly they didn't seem immediately impactful. In no time at all, the warm working environment the staff had enjoyed was different. A focus on the bottom line took precedence over everything else at weekly meetings, and subscribers were surprised to find their small-town paper now included a national insert. Most didn't care; some found it downright ridiculous. All they wanted was their usual hometown news.

Now, after almost four months under Galloway ownership, the employees wondered what would be next.

"Did you hear what happened?" Wide-eyed, Adele hurried toward Madison as quickly as her swollen belly allowed, speaking in a stage whisper. It was hard to tell if she was out of breath from her current size or her shocking news. "Marty quit. He just *quit*. Yelled at someone over the phone that he was done as of this minute and then walked out. He just *walked out*." She pointed toward the front door, as though it was happening at this very moment and Madison would be able to see his dramatic exit if she looked up quickly enough.

Madison's mouth went dry, unsure what this meant but certain something serious for the newspaper and the job she loved. "Oh my gosh. You saw that?"

"I didn't, but one of the ad sales guys heard it and told me." For a serious news source, they sure enjoyed their gossip, too.

"I wonder what'll happen now." She was talking more to herself than to Adele, but an answer was provided anyway, an ominous response that matched what Madison was feeling.

"Unfortunately, we'll find out soon and I'm sure it won't be sunshine and roses. Let me know if you hear *anything*." She hurried away to commiserate with someone else while Madison settled into her chair and opened her laptop.

It was bad enough they were dealing with the changes brought on by the Galloway leadership, but now they would have to wait and see who would replace Marty given his unexpected departure. Voices carried through the building, wondering, surmising, and hoping for the best while expecting the worst. It had been the nature of the beast to date.

"I sure hope they go with Ben."

"Ben wouldn't want to be Chief. That would cut into his fishing time too much."

Madison overheard the comments from two women as they strolled past her cubicle, their laughter drifting away once they turned the corner and continued out of earshot. Everyone had an opinion.

They were a small staff of full-time writers, with a wide range of support staff, part and full-time. Madison was unable to think of anyone, other than Ben, who might be ready to step into Marty's shoes, but she hated the thought of losing her Features Editor.

While nobody knew for sure what might happen in terms of a new Editor, they all could be certain of one thing. This turn of events would mean a visit from Gavin Maves. That fact was indisputable, and now it was a matter of *when* he would grace them with his presence, making them all feel somehow inadequate—a bunch of country bumpkins who had nothing in common with the real journalists with whom he was accustomed to working.

Galloway Newspapers, whose holdings included local and national newspapers, had made enough changes for all of them to know they were no longer the small-town paper they were just a few short months ago. And the biggest change had come in the form of Gavin Maves, one of the company's regional managers, who had inserted himself in the workings of the paper, whether they needed (or wanted) him.

Madison did not begrudge Marty his decision to leave, but her stomach knotted all the same when she thought about the changes that would be even more profound now that they no longer had their staunchest supporter as a buffer. In some ways, she had been on edge ever since Galloway took over, waiting for a proverbial shoe to drop, and now it apparently had. Galloway could do anything it wanted, and the staff would have no say. If the corporate offices brought in some "outsider" as the Chief, any last remnants of their hometown paper would disappear completely—like so many things in Fairview.

They didn't have to wait long to learn more. An email indicated they would have a meeting the next morning. Madison did her best to shut out the gossip, but its continuous buzz made that impossible.

Madison checked her watch. 9:45. She would be joining the rest of her colleagues in the conference room at precisely 10:30. Her stomach was a knot of nervousness, and attempting to get any work done was close to fruitless. She checked her watch. 9:50. With a sigh, she turned her attention back to her monitor, but the words blended together as she read and re-read the start of an article before her.

She would miss everything about Marty—barrel-chested, broad shouldered, balding, and as rosy cheeked as a department store Santa Claus—and the way he ran the paper like they were one big happy family with a single mission. Since Galloway took over, the family atmosphere was slipping away, and the mission seemed to have changed. She heard more complaining than laughing.

Trista interrupted her thoughts, sidling up next to her chair and dropping a stack of files she'd been carrying on the desk, prepared to add her own worries to the scrambled mess in Madison's head. "I am going on record here and now to say I'm not happy with Marty for bailing on us."

Nodding in agreement, Madison reached over to close her laptop, not even pretending anymore that she could be productive. "And now they're sending Gavin Maves to tell us what's going on." A mild shudder ran through her at the thought. "I don't like that guy at all." She knew that everything about Gavin Maves was wrong for Fairview and for the newspaper.

Adele reappeared out of nowhere, crowding into the now claustrophobic cubicle with her baby bulge protruding under her blouse. "Have you heard anything new? All of this is making me nervous. Maybe I should be happy I'll be on maternity leave soon. I don't think it's going to be fun around here." Her face broke into a sudden smile. "Of course, maybe they'll hire some hottie as our new boss." Both Madison and Trista looked at Adele, pregnant and madly in love with her firefighter husband. Her face flushed dark pink as she quickly added, "I mean, for one of the single girls."

"That leaves Madison, I guess." Trista flashed her engagement ring, as if they had not been exposed to it enough in the past six months since it had been placed on her finger. "If he's not married, you could be looking at your future husband, Madison Keller."

Madison's face burned hot and red. "I'm not interested, but thank you, ladies," she said quietly. "And don't you think you're being quite sexist? What if our new Chief is a woman?"

It worked to shut down the part of the conversation Madison was most uncomfortable with. They were as bad as her family, pressuring her about her dating life, which was completely non-existent. Attempts in the past had been few, far between, and feeble.

Trista and Adele walked away together, leaving Madison alone to face the slow passage of time. At exactly 10:25, she made her way to the conference room, a nervous smile plastered on her face as she took a seat, arranging her skirt under her and watching the door.

Trista gave her a nudge as she took the seat next to her at the table. "You look really nice today." She appraised her further. "No ponytail. Is that lip gloss? Why are you all dressed up?"

Hiding her flush, Madison laughed, reaching down to take a notepad from her bag. It was true. She had been paying more attention to her wardrobe and hair lately, taking to heart the notion that meeting someone might take a bit of effort on her part. "I'm visiting my grandmother after work and she's a stickler for dressing properly." It wasn't entirely untrue. It felt good to spend a little time on her appearance. She just wasn't sure who she was doing it for. Trista gave her a funny look, about to say something else, but she was interrupted by Adele grunting next to her as she lowered herself into the chair.

Rubbing her large belly, she looked at her two work friends. "It's not easy being the size of a small elephant," she whispered loudly, and then let out a soft groan. "Ugh. Are you kidding me? I've got to pee again. I better not miss anything." She clumsily made her way from the conference room as the general din continued.

Madison focused her attention on the notepad before her, drawing random swirls across the page. She couldn't say exactly why she felt so out of sorts, but she was pretty sure it had something to do with Gavin Maves, who would be walking through the door at any moment. The first day he'd breezed into the offices, she'd found him to be...unpleasant. She couldn't pinpoint what it was, but something about him rubbed her the wrong way. He had moved from Tampa Bay to Chicago, so how he found himself working in little Fairview, a far cry from his usual big-city environments, was beyond her ability to figure out.

The feelings hadn't changed, she realized, as he appeared in the doorway, stopping to greet Ben with a handshake. She watched him take his place at the front of the conference room, knowing she had no real reason to dislike the man, but for some reason, she did. In a strange way, he was the polar opposite of Marty. Tall, hollow-cheeked, and painfully thin in his stylish skinny jeans, he had a way of looking through them instead of at them, constantly running his hand through his dark hair. As soon as he pushed it back from his forehead, it fell right back in place, as though he'd perfected the cut for exactly that effect. Some might consider him good looking, but she didn't.

He cleared his throat, a signal for everyone to stop chatting amongst themselves. Adele squeezed through, causing just enough commotion for him to look their way, and Madison quickly averted her eyes.

A hush returned and Madison missed the usual fun banter they were used to at meetings. Marty had maintained a casual, jovial mood. It had slowly disappeared in the past months.

"If we're all settled now, I'll get started. Thank you for taking time to show up."

"You mean we had a choice?" The muttered response came

from someone seated against the wall behind her, and Madison recognized the voice as Stan's, their sports reporter. It was then she realized what she was feeling wasn't exclusive to her. She could clearly sense it now, a simmering slow boil, as the staff recognized the small changes they'd already experienced were probably nothing compared to what was on the way. Marty hated Galloway enough to leave a job he loved. That didn't bode well for the rest of them.

If Gavin heard the muttering, he didn't let on, continuing with his prepared speech to the staff. "By now you know Martin has chosen to leave the paper. Filling his shoes will be no easy matter, as I'm sure you can all understand." More quiet grumbling followed the comment, and once again, Maves ignored it, going on to enumerate the many good things happening since Galloway took over operations. Then he told them the last thing they wanted to hear.

"I'll be running things until we find a replacement. I scheduled a meeting with all editors for later today and we'll go from there. Our plan is to hire a replacement no later than August 1. I'll be around on an as-needed basis until that happens." He looked around the room at the gathered staff, rubbed his hands together and gave what appeared to be a half bow. "Thank you for your time. I look forward to working with all of you...and turning this paper into a better version of itself." Although he smiled at the group, Madison noticed his eyes didn't reflect any warmth.

He walked out the door, leaving the staff to murmur among themselves as they gathered notepads and bags, making their way toward the exit.

"That was pretty anticlimactic," muttered Trista, watching others move toward the door.

"I thought there'd be snacks."

"It wasn't exactly a celebration, silly."

Jolted out of her thoughts, Madison realized Adele was talking to her. "I'm sorry, what?"

"Don't you think he could have sprung for donuts or something? Marty always treated us when we had meetings." Adele turned her disappointed face to each corner of the room, as if expecting some sugary treat to have magically appeared. "I would have settled for some cookies."

"You are *always* thinking about food. I'm afraid the days of treats are behind us now that there's a new sheriff in town." Trista pretended to pull six-shooters from holsters at her side, firing them and blowing the imaginary smoke away before re-holstering the make-believe weapons.

"Shut up, Trista. You would be thinking about food all the time, too, if you had a human being growing inside of you." She stood, breathing heavily with the effort caused by her seventh month of pregnancy. "Crap," she groaned. "I have to pee again."

They stood, ready to leave the now empty conference room. Trista patted Adele's back. "You go to the bathroom. I'll dig up a Twinkie or something for you." Madison continued past them to her cubicle, not sure how to feel about the meeting.

―――

The stress of the morning was offset by some good news. To her great relief, she had done well enough on her first feature to earn a second, lifting a bit of weight from Madison's shoulders. Somehow, she had managed to make the history of the cottages and their current owner interesting enough to earn another shot at a story. She didn't realize how worried she had been until that moment Ben handed out new assignments.

Madison looked over the list of photos needed for various stories, but her focus was on her new feature. Writing about the golf course would bring up some memories she preferred to keep at bay, but she was lucky to get an assignment.

After captioning three photos for a 4 p.m. deadline and finishing a working outline for her next feature, she packed up for the day. She still had a list of things she wanted to accomplish before going home, and once home, she planned to dive into some note-taking for the new story. She was riding on a mini-high.

Despite all the anxiety of the morning, Ben had been reassuring. A collective sigh of relief filled the conference room after the features desk meeting. At least Ben was still on board with the paper's mission pre-Galloway. Maybe she was overreacting to the potential changes at the paper. They still had a singular goal to put out a good newspaper, no matter who was at the helm.

She decided ice cream with her grandma would be the perfect way to celebrate her small success.

Madison drove out to the Shop and Go on the outskirts of "old town." The delineation between the two sections of Fairview could not be clearer—a state highway literally split the town in half. Crossing the highway meant having a choice of big box stores, their lots always full of cars as shoppers sought deals at Walmart or Home Depot, or lunched at any number of fast-food options. Madison was grateful "progress" had not spread to "old town." She preferred the old mom and pop shops closer to home. Located just west of the highway was the grocery store owned by Frannie and Mason Rivera. They carried everything from camping and fishing gear to convenience and grocery items.

Most residents of the lakeshore did their shopping at the Shop and Go to support the Rivera family instead of crossing the highway to get to the fairly recent additions to the expanding town. Those same people also preferred the gas station, car dealership and furniture store on the west side. The town's growth spurt, sprawling rapidly east, was shortening the distance between the lakeshore and the neighboring town of Brookfield more each year. The subdivisions boasted large homes with three-car garages and backyard pools. The area was markedly different than the part of Fairview Madison grew up knowing, with the cottages and modest homes that lined the streets that all seemed to lead to the lake.

The year after she graduated from high school, the "great transition" occurred. That's what her brother and his friends called it and it seemed to catch on for most of the old towners. That was the year the Fairview Secondary School closed its doors. The school had housed both middle and high school students because the small lakeshore community population couldn't support two separate buildings. As the population grew, with subdivisions cropping up almost overnight, the need for new, larger schools was born. After major renovations, the original building, the combined school attended by the Keller siblings and generations prior, became an elementary school combined with the district administrative offices. Both the new high school and the middle school were built east of the highway—in "new town." Just one year after that, another elementary school was added to that same area. It was impossible to get together with classmates without someone lamenting the fact that their youth was somehow taken from them because their high school was no longer there. The transition had stolen something special from them.

Progress, they were reminded. Madison had decided long ago that progress didn't always translate into something better as far as she was concerned. She sometimes felt almost desperate to hold on to any last piece of the Fairview in which she was raised, old-fashioned shops and all.

Her love of taking pictures of everything she'd come to know and love about her hometown—the lakeshore, the quaint businesses on Water Street, the places that meant something to her because of the memories they held—created a sense of stability for her. It was a good thing she had those photos, because much had changed, and she had difficulty remembering what her town had been like even though she'd witnessed the baby steps of those changes with each snap of a photo over time.

She wondered if Natalie would even recognize the town when

she saw it again after ten years. The thought sent a wave of excitement through her. Natalie was coming home.

Standing in front of the freezer, she scanned the flavors until her eyes landed on the perfect one. The Shop and Go had her grandma's favorite brand of maple nut ice cream, so she took a quart, adding it to the basket. Despite its rocky start, it was shaping up to be a good day after all.

The good feelings that had ballooned during the afternoon began to deflate as she sat in the parking lot. From her Jeep, she took in the sprawling complex that was the Laurel Lake Senior Care and Memory Center. The various wings extending from the administrative offices in the center made it look like a giant insect with splayed legs. As much as she loved seeing her grandma, her heart was heavy as she anticipated the differences she'd see in her each time. The memory care wing was at capacity, so even though the director said she was ready to be moved there, that was impossible until a room opened for Grandma Ruth. In some ways that was comforting, but it was still putting off the inevitable.

Her current apartment in the assisted living wing was spacious enough to hold several of her favorite furniture pieces from her house. She had a "kitchenette," living room, bathroom, and bedroom. The familiar atmosphere of her house was still evident here. Up until recently, she hadn't spent a great deal of time in her apartment, as she joined fellow residents for games, movies, and outings, and she ate her meals in the large, bright cafeteria. It was only in the past several months she'd stopped the activities, and now, her meals were brought to her on a tray three times a day as she slowly lost the ability to socialize with her friends.

Right now, her grandma had one of the best rooms at the Center, with a view of the lake when the trees weren't in full summer foliage. That would change if she was moved to the other wing. Madison corrected herself. At this point it was clearly *when*, not *if*. There would be no view of the water, and soon, no memory of the years she'd enjoyed on the lakeshore.

Madison's heart broke at the thought of what was ahead for Grandma Ruth.

After the morning meeting, she'd spent time reading through archived issues of the paper, unable to focus on any real work, and was left with an overwhelming sense of nostalgia. Life was sweet, simple, and perfect in the past, Madison decided, staring at the broad smiles on the faces of citizens photographed over the past decades. She wouldn't describe it as reckless abandon, but they exuded a sense of pure joy, contentment perhaps, in living their lives, quietly and simply. Her thoughts wandered to her grandma who had seen so much change over the decades of her life in Fairview and should have been Madison's go-to historian. But now those memories were slipping away. What would she hold onto the longest? Madison hoped it was her life with grandpa.

What would Carl have held onto as a favorite memory?

That thought jolted her back to the moment. Snapped out of her reverie, she realized the ice cream would start melting if she didn't get it inside. Grabbing her purse, camera, and the plastic grocery bag, she made her way inside, hoping Grandma Ruth was having a good day—a day filled with wonderful memories of happier times. Madison knocked gently and then let herself in, pulling out the carton and holding it up for her grandmother to see.

"You brought ice cream. How lovely." Ruth, her white hair perfectly styled, rose unsteadily from the rocking chair, taking baby steps toward the cupboard. As she pulled two bowls out, she asked, "How's Carl, honey?"

Madison froze. The question startled her, especially since she had just been thinking about him a few minutes earlier. She couldn't remember the last time Carl's name would have been brought up for any reason, and her grandmother's mention of him was unsettling. She placed a scoop of ice cream in each bowl and followed her grandma to the small kitchen table.

"He's the same, grandma. Always the same. Did you get your hair done today? It looks wonderful."

"A very nice lady did it." She'd forgotten Shelly's name again, but Madison didn't fill in the blanks for her, opting instead to change the subject.

"How's the ice cream?"

"Good. I've had this kind before. It's very good."

They sat in silence, the only sound the scraping of the spoon against the bowl as they finished the last of the treat. Madison rinsed the bowls and then pulled out her camera, flipping through pictures until she found what she'd been looking for. There was less sharpness to her grandmother's mind tonight, and she hoped to bring her back to the present. "Look. These ducklings hatched yesterday. They're so cute, aren't they?"

Ruth pulled the camera closer, squinting into the viewfinder. "Oh, my goodness, look at that. Your papa used to take you and Patrick down to the dock to feed the ducks. Do you remember?"

"I've seen pictures of doing that with Grandpa Poppy, but I don't really remember since I was so young." She'd been only four when Grandpa Poppy died. It was difficult to separate real memories from those created by looking at old photos. It could be confusing even to her, so maybe pictures weren't the best way to help her grandma, but she still had to try. "Do you want to look at more pictures I took this week?"

Instead of answering the question, though, it was evident Ruth was stuck on unscrambling whatever memory had been triggered, knowing she didn't have something quite right. "Do you think Liz was back home then? Maybe she fed the ducks with us." The confused expression crossed her grandmother's face once again, the look becoming all too familiar to Madison, as though her grandmother was far away, the light disappearing from her eyes. "No, she came back after Papa died to babysit Brent. Oh, that's not right either, is it?" Her hands twisted in her lap, signaling her growing agitation. "I didn't tell you her secret, did I? I promised I wouldn't."

"It's okay, grandma. You never told me any secrets. Never."

Madison was struck by the strangeness of wanting so desperately to help her grandmother hold onto precious memories when she herself was trying desperately to keep some at bay.

She sat with the old woman's hand in her own, waiting for the fog to lift and for her grandmother to re-join her in the moment. There would come a time when she wouldn't return, the disease taking her away from all that she knew and had been. Madison found it hard to breathe, but she held tightly to the hand, as though she might be a portal through which her grandmother could retain the memories of her life.

Chapter Seven

THE DIM LIGHT OF THE REFRIGERATOR PROVIDED A soft glow in the dark kitchen as she dropped the leftovers on the shelf and closed the door. Going out for pizza and beer was fun, but her grownup friendships could never compare to her childhood friendships with Becca and Natalie. They had called each other forever friends.

Forever had an expiration date, apparently.

She filled a glass with water and slid the patio door open, the night still warm even as dark descended on Fairview. Sighing softly, she sat in one of the lounge chairs on her deck, leaning back so she could watch the stars.

Maybe growing up was overrated. The three of them spent so much of their time together talking about being grownups. They should have kept enjoying the moment for what it was. Why didn't someone tell them that then?

The summer after third grade, the three of them spent hours in the lake, perfecting handstands underwater and then pretending to be mermaids, turning summersaults until they were too dizzy to stand up. They wore matching hairbands as they ate ice cream cones and giggled at the teenagers sneaking kisses when they thought no one was watching.

The summer after fourth grade, the three of them spent hours on beach towels making friendship bracelets out of embroidery floss, braiding, and weaving different colors together, vowing to never take them off—even when they became grownups.

The summer after fifth grade, they walked arm-in-arm on the beach, looking over their shoulders to see if any boys noticed them in their new two-piece swimming suits. They had sleepovers, staying up all night to talk about what it would be like to be in middle school, high school, college. All their plans included returning to Fairview to live on the same block after they married, and have kids who would grow up together and become best friends, just like them. They decided they would each have two—a boy and a girl. It had seemed so simple then.

The stars shifted overhead, seemingly dancing in the sky as she continued staring, and then blurred, her eyes watering from not blinking, or from the vivid memories.

She reached out her hands, almost feeling Natalie take one and Becca the other. They would race to the end of the dock to jump into the lake, never letting go. Looking at each other under water, they didn't have to speak to convey entire worlds of conversation with one another. Then they would break through the surface, laughing, droplets of water on their eyelashes glittering in the sun like diamonds.

Those were the easy times. She was all grown up now and neither of those friends lived on her street—or even in her state. They grew up to be very different than they so carefully planned.

She was here. She was living out at least part of their grand plan. And now she had to write a story about the golf course. Everything about the golf course made her think of Carl.

Carl.

The summer after junior year, she was just getting into the swing of her summer routine, spending three mornings a week at the Fairview Diner waitressing, one day a week at the flower shop helping her mom, one day a week helping her grandma with yardwork and errand running, and every afternoon at the beach.

Weekends were family time. When she and Patrick weren't working diner shifts, they were with their parents, boating, cooking out, or taking day trips to visit family.

Meeting Carl shook up that routine.

When the good-looking young man walked into the diner, *Carl* stitched on his Fairview Golf Course polo shirt, Sandy, the weekday waitress, gave her a jab in the rib. Wiggling her eyebrows, she loudly whispered, "He's cute. You wait on him, honey," leaving Madison red-faced and mortified as she prepared his to-go coffee order.

She had off the next day, but found herself keeping an eye out for him the next. He didn't disappoint her, showing up a few minutes earlier than he had the first day, and finding opportunities to make small talk as he sat at the counter, eating a full breakfast order. "You weren't here yesterday," he commented, and she found herself blushing, happy he had noticed.

One week later, she invited him to join the group of friends hanging out on the beach that weekend. "I'll have to work all day Saturday, but I'll swing by the pavilion after to see if anyone is still there."

Madison made sure she was still there. It was only the second time she felt a flutter in her stomach when talking to a boy.

She shouldn't have thought of him as a boy. Two years her senior, Carl was ambitious, career-driven, and very serious. Madison found every excuse to hang out with him. And the timing couldn't have been better because she was, for the first summer *ever*, without her two forever friends.

Natalie was working as a counselor at the church camp her dad ran. She had been looking forward to it for years, but had to wait until she was old enough. Next summer, she would do her first international mission trip.

Becca was away at a prestigious acting camp—yet another indulgent gift from her now-divorced parents. She masterfully manipulated them into giving her expensive gifts, playing one against the other in a tug-of-war for her love.

Their absence left Madison with plenty of time on her hands that she filled with Carl.

His free time was limited, but he gave it all to Madison. Even when he wasn't working at the course, he was talking about golf. She was impressed by his commitment to his career goal.

"So, why do you want to be a golf pro?"

"I think it's the versatility. I can give lessons, operate the business side of the course, manage the employees, oversee merchandise..." He had paused, smiling at the endless possibilities.

"And which part do you want to do?"

"All of it." He had graduated from high school the year before and was taking business courses. He was anxious to learn as much as possible that summer working with the grounds and greens crew. "I want to learn every aspect of the job here. And in the fall, I go down to Florida for a training program."

His passion for golf made her take stock of her own future and what she wanted to do with it. She was on the swimming team, but wasn't planning a future around swimming. Writing for the school paper was probably the closest thing she had to a passion.

"What do you like about being a newspaper writer?" His question gave her a brief pause. Nobody had ever asked her that before.

"I get to observe life. I like documenting that we were here in this time and preserve something for future generations."

He hadn't laughed at her or questioned her. Carl had nodded and said, "I get that."

As excited as she was to have the new feature assignment, anxiety crept to the surface, and that had everything to do with Carl. She couldn't let her emotions get in the way of her professional obligations. But it would not be easy. It was because of Carl that she studied journalism in the first place.

Nothing more had come up about the golf course, so Madison determined it had all been another rumor. If the Thorsen family was looking for a buyer, they were certainly not doing it publicly. She was relieved she wouldn't have to incorporate any of that detail into her golf course sesquicentennial story.

Madison read through the notes she had gathered, and then reviewed the photos she was able to find in the paper's archives. Obtaining stock photos of the course from 1970, after the Thorsen family purchased the business and started major updates and improvements, was easy, but she didn't have any from its earlier days. The library archives were another possibility. If that didn't work, she had a backup list of people who might have access to pictures from when the course first opened in the 1950's.

She had already scheduled an interview with the course manager, and would have an opportunity for picture taking. The story would almost write itself, she figured.

Madison leaned back in her chair to stretch, a smile crossing her lips as she realized she was finding her niche as a features writer after all, and it felt good. But right now, she needed a break. Pushing away from her desk, she took her water bottle and started down the hall.

The "break room" wasn't much of a room at all, but a niche set in a corner near the end of the main hallway with a sink, microwave, and refrigerator. There was barely enough counter space for the coffee maker and a plate of whatever goodies someone might have brought in to share. There were no treats today, which meant nobody felt generous or, just as possible, anything brought in earlier was long gone.

She filled her water bottle at the cooler standing at the end of the counter, glancing over her shoulder to sneak a look inside the glass-enclosed offices of the Editor-in-Chief. From his office, the Chief had a view of the entire floor of writers and staff, a watchful eye ever on them should they slack off. Marty never watched over them too closely, but she had a feeling Gavin would be more than happy to be their task master. Hopefully he was diligently working on bringing in a replacement for Marty because his very presence made her uncomfortable.

At his desk just inside the suite, Gavin was pinching the bridge of his nose with his thumb and forefinger. As she watched, he abruptly stood, picking up his stainless-steel water bottle and striding toward the door.

Madison pretended she hadn't been watching him, and started back to her desk, but not in time to avoid greeting him. Even though he had been their regional manager for almost four months, she had never had more than a brief hallway "hello, how are you" with him, and she was fine keeping it that way.

"Madison Keller." He pointed a finger near her face. "I believe I met your brother yesterday."

Disappointed that she hadn't been able to escape quickly enough, Madison turned and smiled at him, noticing the scent of his cologne didn't really fit him. It was woodsy, like he had just come in from a hunting trip or a long nature hike. Gavin Maves probably didn't even like being outside.

"You must have visited Poppy's Diner. I hope that wasn't your first time there." It was almost painful to be pleasant to him, but she was determined to make the effort. "He has the best coffee in town."

He held his hands up, defending his answer. "I'm an espresso man. I've learned that if I want it done the way I like it, I need to make it for myself, so I travel with my own machine." His tone was markedly snobbish. "But I did order a scone there. It was tasty."

Madison wondered if that was code for *if I have to be stuck in this hick town, I guess I can't have high expectations.* "Are you staying at The Waterford?" Armando would be full of gossip about this big-city guy if he were staying at the boutique hotel he managed, and Madison would get an earful the next time she ran into him whether she wanted to hear it or not.

"I'm at the Hilton. It's spartan at best, but it serves its purpose." He shrugged, again letting his disdain for all things small town be clearly known.

"The Waterford would have been a lot more charming. But I'm always a sucker for the character of old town."

His brow furrowed. "Old town?"

"Sorry," she smiled then, her way of saying he may think he was classier than the rest of them, but they could all appreciate what they had in Fairview, and she was happy to fill him in on some local history, even if he probably couldn't care less. "Those of us who've been around for a while sort of divide the town in half—the old section and the new section. The old part is really what we're celebrating with the sesquicentennial. East of the highway was developed within the last decade or two. That's new, as far as we're concerned."

"I see. How long have *you* been in Fairview?"

"Me? My whole life." She sipped her water, studying him closely. He was once again wearing black skinny jeans, this time with a yellow shirt under his black sport coat. He had an air about him, a swagger she found unappealing. Despite her feelings for him, she continued, compelled for some reason to make him see there was more to Fairview than small-town hicks. "We are 'old towners' through and through. My mom owns the flower shop on Water Street a few doors down from Poppy's. My grandparents ran that diner for almost 40 years, but my brother owns it now. He renamed it Poppy's just a couple years ago, in honor of my grandpa." It was impossible to keep the pride from her voice.

"And your dad? Let me guess. Does he run the local hardware store?"

Her face reddened as she realized he was clearly mocking her. The water cooler gurgled next to her. "He's a dentist. I should probably…" She gestured down the hall in the general direction of her desk.

"It makes sense that you do the Hometown Pride thing. You probably know everyone in town. How long have you been here at the paper?" He didn't seem in any hurry to refill his water and return to work, but she couldn't shake the feeling that their conversation wasn't entirely friendly.

"I started in ad sales and copy as soon as I graduated from college, but I also did two summer internships here while I was still in school." Madison didn't mention the fact that she didn't start college directly out of high school. There were blanks she had no intention of filling in for him and the desire to escape this conversation altogether was becoming more pronounced. "Since I was just promoted to the features desk a few weeks ago, I better get back to work before someone decides to demote me." She turned to make a getaway, but he wasn't finished.

"Personnel changes go through me. I think you're safe—for now, anyway." He chuckled at his joke. "Your sesquicentennial opening story? It was good." His words didn't fully match his expression, and once again, she noted a coldness in his eyes. He took another drink, refilled his water bottle, and started toward his office, adding over his shoulder, "It was a pleasure talking to you Madison. Stop by my office if you need anything."

She watched him walk away, assured she would never 'need anything' from him. And the conversation had been anything but a pleasure for her...and probably not for him either.

The thought was interrupted by a chiming sound, so she set her water bottle on the counter and pulled her phone from her back pocket. "Hey young lady!" Her mom's cheerful voice filled her ear. "Do you feel like a late lunch at Poppy's?"

For a while, back when everyone was keeping a close eye on her, lunch dates with her mom were as frequent as twice a week. As Madison started to regain her footing after the accident, she could tell their watchful eyes were filling with relief instead of the worry they previously held.

"I'm in," Madison responded. "Can we make it 1:30? That gives me time to wrap up a couple things."

She ended the call with a smile, but it disappeared quickly

when she realized Gavin was standing in his office doorway, watching her.

Madison told her mom about the strange encounter with her boss. "Some of the women there are practically swooning over him. He's a good dresser, very GQ, and I'm sure if you like the urban, gaunt look he would be considered good looking, but I find him...I don't know...creepy?" an exaggerated shudder coursed through her body.

Nina watched her daughter closely. "He hasn't...you know... made any passes or anything like that, has he?" Concern was etched deeply in her face and Madison laughed, quick to erase her mother's anxiety.

"Oh no, it's nothing like that at all. It's more of a plotting kind of thing. No, that's not it either." Her forehead creased as she tried to come up with a description for her boss. "He so obviously doesn't fit in here. He looks down on all of us like we're... uneducated. Uncouth. He doesn't *want* to be here."

"I hope you're misreading him. I know him by sight, but I haven't spoken to the man. He *is* a good dresser." She changed the subject quickly, her tone bright. "Do you think you'll have a date for the Sesquicentennial dance?"

Caught off guard and almost choking on her bite of BLT, Madison wiped her mouth with her napkin, staring at her mom in disbelief. "Since when did you join the 'Madison needs a date' coalition?"

"It was just a thought. I mean, there must be *someone* in this town you would consider dating. And the dance is going to be quite the event." She leaned in, seemingly searching for something in her daughter's eyes. "It's time to move on, honey. You can't live in the past."

There was an almost unsettling hope in her mother's eyes. Madison hated disappointing her but opening herself to a relationship didn't feel right. She was ready to rattle off a whole list of reasons why meeting someone right now was not in the cards—too busy with the paper, visiting Carl, helping at the diner and flower shop, visiting Grandma Ruth. And there was always the possibility her dad needed help with something. She didn't know what, but there must be *something*. Excuses were easy to come by.

"I plan to go, but I'll be quite date-less, thank you very much. I hate to change the subject," she rolled her eyes at her mother, "but I am changing the subject. I can't stop thinking about grandma. What happens when she doesn't even recognize us anymore?" There was a catch in her voice, and she blinked rapidly to prevent tears from spilling out. It was devastating, watching her slip a little farther away with each passing week.

"All we can do is keep using the suggestions Greg gave us to help maintain her memory for as long as possible. We'll keep visiting her, showing her pictures, telling all the great stories of her life." Nina picked a French fry from her plate, dipped it in ketchup, then changed her mind, setting it back down on her plate. "Your dad and I...we know that time is coming. We will do what we have always done—be strong for each other. That's what family is all about."

Madison slowly nodded. She of all people knew how important it was to have a family rallying around in time of need, a shelter from any storm, large or small. "It's happening so fast now. I want so desperately for her to hold onto her memories, I feel like I'm almost force feeding them to her. I'm so afraid of that day when she doesn't know who I am."

"We all are. When that happens, we remember *for* her. We remember how wonderful it has been having her in our lives." She spoke quietly, despite the fact the restaurant was almost empty now. "Your bond with her is special. She needs you more than ever to hold onto the memories for her." She wiped away her own tears. "We will be the keeper of her memories, Maddy."

Nodding silently, tears slipping down her cheeks, Madison looked at her mother. "I know you're right." She didn't tell her mom how hard she tried to forget some things while desperately trying to hold on as tightly as possible to others. She pushed thoughts of Carl from her head. If she opened that door even a crack, she'd be unable to close it and they had enough emotion spewing onto the table already.

"We will find the strength when the time comes, honey." She smiled through her tears. "You have *always* been strong."

Patrick strolled to their table, pulling out a chair, flipping it around and seating himself on it, his arms resting on the top of the chair's back. "What the heck, you two? You're going to chase business away looking so sad. You look like you've lost your best friend."

Madison looked around the almost empty dining room. "I think you already did that with your lousy cooking."

He put a hand over his heart, a grimace on his face. "Oh, ouch. Could one of you pull this knife out of my heart, please?"

"You two," Nina laughed. "It's a good thing you love each other."

"Seriously, is everything okay here?"

Madison rolled her eyes at him. "We're fine. Don't be such a worrywart."

He pulled a rag from the front pocket of his apron, rubbing at an imaginary spot on the tabletop as he spoke. "Your boss stopped by. Strange guy." He shook his head, finally looking at his sister. "He was on his phone with somebody, talking about how the mayor is making Becca Ristow the parade marshal and they are doing some big program at the pavilion to present her with the key to the city or something. I didn't catch all of it, but he was talking loudly enough for everyone to hear it."

Madison stared at her brother, mouth agape. "Are you serious?"

"I'm just telling you what I heard."

Any hope she had held onto that she could avoid Becca while she was in town, was now dashed. If her boss was talking about it, the paper would cover it, and she would be unable to avoid an interaction of some kind.

"It would be nice if you could somehow find a way to mend this. You, Natalie, and Becca—I mean—you three were so close." Nina handed her empty dish to Patrick, wiping the crumbs from in front of her with a napkin, completely unaware of how painful all talk of that friendship was to her daughter.

It was true, they *had* been close. They were like a strange Fairview version of Charlie's Angels. The dark blonde Madison was the shy one; the red-headed Natalie was the smart one; the petite brunette Becca was the pretty one. They were always together. Nothing was supposed to come between the three forever friends.

But something did.

Madison finally broke the silence. "A lot happened. We'll see."

Nina patted her daughter's hand. "Good. Now get out of here before your brother puts you to work."

Patrick gave them an innocent look. "Like I would ever do that."

Even as she laughed along with them, Madison felt a terrible sense of dread. She was not ready to face Becca, and despite what her mother believed, that friendship was far too broken to ever be mended.

Chapter Eight

MADISON WOKE TO THE SOUND OF BIRDS NOISILY chattering outside her window, but the cheerfulness of their music was lost on her as a heaviness had taken up residence in her heart. Her usual Saturday morning routine, weather permitting, meant walking or biking to the diner to have a cup of coffee and a fresh muffin or scone, checking in with her family to see if they needed her help on any projects, and then visiting her grandma. She usually found comfort in the routine, but it was a luxury she couldn't enjoy today because she had made up her mind it was time to visit Carl.

It was a drive she used to make at least once a month, but now there were stretches of several months between visits. She wasn't sure what compelled her to keep making the trip, but for now, she also didn't know how to entirely stop. As was her habit, she listened to an audio book for the two-hour drive, intent on keeping her mind from wandering. It sometimes worked, but today, deep in thought about too many things, she had no idea what she'd been listening to.

No story was compelling enough to sweep away memories of Carl. She pictured him taking her hand and showing her his favorite spots on the course, each with its own spectacular view of water or foliage. His blue eyes lit up as he talked to her.

Missing the sparkle in those eyes was a physical pain and she pulled off the highway at the next exit, needing a moment to catch her breath. For the rest of the ride she listened to music, doing her best to drown out memories.

Sara pulled the door open on the second knock, stepping back to let Madison into the small, dark entry of the apartment before drawing her into a tight hug. Madison breathed in her scent of lilacs, and for some reason, that saddened her even more, associating the fragrance with a long, leisurely spring walk—an indulgence probably foreign to Sara.

"Oh honey, it's so good to see you. Carl will be thrilled to have company."

Sara said the same thing each time Madison visited. Unfortunately, Carl wouldn't be thrilled. In fact, she had to assume he didn't know her at all.

"Sorry about the mess." As usual, Sara looked frazzled and disheveled, at the same time vibrating with an energy that completely contradicted how exhausted she looked. "I'm working on a wedding gown and four bridesmaid dresses right now so there isn't space for anything else in this room."

She was right. The living room, long ago transformed into her workroom, housed a sewing machine, cutting table, and two mannequin fitting forms. Making sure Carl had around-the-clock attention meant the apartment was home, workshop, and care center all wrapped up in one.

One mannequin was draped with a light pink jersey material and the other had pinned to it the beginnings of a white beaded bodice. A hand-sketched drawing of a gown was attached to the wall behind the form, the only direction Sara needed to create exactly what the bride had in mind.

"This is pretty," Madison whispered. She gently touched the beading with one finger, wondering what it would have been like planning a wedding, and maybe even asking Sara to make the gown. She shook the thought from her head, then turned to smile at Sara. "I don't know how you do it." She looked down the hall, nodding in the direction of the bedrooms. "I'll go say hi to Carl. And I'll take him for a walk, if you'd like."

"I'm sure he's feeling neglected but..." She didn't finish, instead gesturing toward the material and mannequins. "He's watching a movie."

Madison moved through the living room, past Sara's bedroom to the room at the end of the hall. The television volume was low, and she didn't know if he was seeing the car chase on the screen or not, but he was a captive audience for the action scene regardless since his wheelchair was parked directly in front of it. Besides the bed with its side rails and the TV stand, the room held little. A large mobile with sea creatures danced in the air above his bed, as if he were a baby and not a grown man.

"Hey, Carl."

His head, drooping to the side, raised and bobbed before settling back onto his chest. A palsied movement of his left arm suggested an awareness of her presence, but Madison could never be fully sure. The fingers of his right hand curled inward like claws. The sight of him took her breath away momentarily, just as it did every time she visited. Somehow, she always hoped to see the old Carl, even though that was impossible.

She turned off the TV and stood in front of him, smiling, despite the fact she was crying inside, and straightened the collar of his polo shirt.

"You always did look good in blue, you handsome thing. This color perfectly matches your eyes." She wouldn't allow herself to think about how those eyes had once looked deeply into her own, able to see right through to her very soul. They stared straight ahead now, unfocused but still the beautiful blue she remembered so well. "I thought we'd go for a walk." Stepping around him, she deftly took the handles of the wheelchair in her hands, used her foot to release the brake, and backed up to turn the chair around, maneuvering down the hallway the way she'd just come.

Sara held the door open as Madison urged the chair over the low threshold, and they bumped forward awkwardly until they reached the sidewalk.

His head lolled to the side, staccato guttural noises escaping him. Madison wanted desperately to distinguish actual words, but no matter how hard she tried, it was futile. Sometimes, after a visit like this she'd lie awake at night, making up entire conversations—the kind they used to have. When she was with him, though, she had a one-way conversation, usually repeating the same things she said the previous visit and even the one before that. It was difficult to keep coming up with topics when only one of them could do the talking—or have new experiences to talk about.

"You wouldn't recognize the lakefront. Remember that dock we sat on to feed ducks? It's gone now. When we were kids, Natalie, Becca and I used to watch the clouds from the end of the dock. We saw entire worlds in the cloud shapes." The memory brought a smile to her face, but she had to fight back a sob trying to escape. She missed her forever friends. "That dock is gone now. They replaced it with a huge new one with about 20 boat slips. The hamburger place all the kids went to after football games is gone too. Well, it's not actually gone. It reopened as a fancy bar and grill with its own slips so boaters can get there now. They are going to be busy this summer."

She missed Carl, despite the fact she was with him right now.

But for all practical purposes, he wasn't.

Had she known she had so little time with the Carl she knew before… Tears stung behind her eyelids, and she fought to keep her voice natural and steady. The Carl in the wheelchair was the one she'd known for almost ten years now. The other one, the *real* one, she'd known for such a brief moment in time, she wondered if he'd been real. But she knew he was. And she had ruined everything they had and were.

"You won't believe who's coming back to Fairview to visit. I knew you couldn't guess. Natalie! She's staying with me for a few days. I can't wait to see her." She could almost hear Carl laughing at some of the antics she had shared with him about those days when they were just a bunch of silly kids. "I would give anything to have her move back to Fairview, Carl. I haven't had a best friend since that summer." That was true. She had work friends and a handful of classmates who had also remained in Fairview, but none of them could take on the role of Natalie or Becca...and certainly not Carl.

"Piper is getting big. Maybe when she grows up she will own the diner. Another generation of the Keller family. Crazy, huh? I think I told you it's not called Fairview Diner anymore. Patrick and Mya changed the name. He thought it would be a special tribute to my grandpa, you know, even though that wasn't his real name. He was Prescott Patrick Keller, but everyone called him Poppy. Patrick was close to him."

At the corner, she stood for a moment, a quiet settling over them once she stopped rattling off the same old news she shared every visit. Sometimes it was easier to fill her head with noise so her heart wouldn't feel just how broken it was.

It was time to go back to the apartment complex. Sara and her husband Bob used to live in a brick house with ivy climbing trellises and flowers cascading out of window boxes. Madison knew that because she visited that house in Brookfield once with Carl. Sara made chocolate chip cookies and Bob showed her Carl's golf trophies.

After the accident, they sold the house and moved to Milwaukee to be closer to the trauma rehab center. While Carl was in the hospital for months on end, bills piled up to astronomical amounts, and then Bob died of cancer just two years after they moved. The small apartment was all Sara could afford. Bad luck and then more bad luck seemed to stick to the family.

But part of it had nothing to do with luck, really. It had everything to do with her...

Madison spoke softly now, more to herself than to Carl. "Do you miss your old house, Carl? I'll bet your mom does. She would never say that, though, because all she cares about is making sure she can take care of you. It must be hard in that tiny apartment." She wondered if he knew what had been left behind—if he had flashes of memories of growing up in the nice house in Brookfield, golfing with his dad, spending time in Fairview, and falling in love with her.

In some ways, it was comforting to say whatever was on her mind, even without a response. She pushed the chair forward.

Madison looked down at the head bobbing before her in the wheelchair. The strong, independent young man she'd known was a shell of himself. She walked along in silence for a while, struggling to say the next part.

"Don't you wish you could go back in time? I do. I would go back in a heartbeat, Carl. I know exactly what I would do. *Nothing*. I would keep my big mouth shut. If I had done that in the first place, you wouldn't have gone after Jared and you'd be okay right now. Jared would be alive and you would still be my old Carl."

She didn't bother to wipe the tears rolling down her face.

"Every time I see something else change in Fairview, I lose a little bit more of you. Everything that was a part of us is disappearing, Carl. Pretty soon I won't remember how wonderful it all was then. I wish you were still there."

Madison hiccupped, sucked in a shuddering breath, and tried to pull herself together. Crying in public was embarrassing enough but it would be absolutely humiliating if someone stopped to check on her. She was grateful for the quiet street as she headed back toward the apartment.

"It's hard, Carl. I don't know how…" She looked up at the blue sky, a reminder that some things stayed the same. How many times had they all floated on their backs in the lake, looking up at that same sky or spread a blanket on the beach, shoulders gently touching as they looked at clouds drifting slowly overhead?

Natalie and Becca moved away. Carl wasn't Carl anymore. Her grandma had a terrible disease. "I don't know how to let go of any of it."

It was *all* too much at times.

Chapter Nine

"Do you think we'll ever get kissed?"

Natalie was staring at herself in the mirror. They were at Becca's house, experimenting with her mom's eye shadow, being careful not to leave a mess or she would know they had been into her makeup.

Becca cleared her throat and looked at the reflection of all three of them. "Justin kissed me."

Natalie and Madison stared, open-mouthed. Becca might as well have said she was flying to the moon that night.

"We're supposed to do everything together." Madison said the words without thinking.

"Okay, that's kind of gross." Becca raised her eyebrow at Madison and they laughed.

Her face flaming with embarrassment, Madison muttered, "You know what I mean. You didn't even tell us that you liked him."

Becca's thin shoulders raised in a shrug. "I don't really like him. But he wanted to kiss me so I said yes."

She pulled a pink lipstick tube from her mom's makeup drawer and liberally applied it to her puckered lips. Leaning forward, she kissed the mirror, leaving a pink lip outline on the glass. Nobody said anything for a beat as they stared at the mark, then they all laughed.

"What was it like?" Natalie pushed her glasses up from the bridge of her nose where they perpetually seemed to be resting. "Was it...wet?"

Becca smiled, suddenly so much older and wiser than her two friends. "It was soft and nice. I would probably let him do it again."

They knew for a fact Becca was the first fifth grade girl to get a kiss and it seemed to change their worldview. And it was the beginning of Natalie and Madison living vicariously through their friend. They hooked their pinkies together, swearing they wouldn't tell any grownups about this new level of maturity they were moving into.

Having someone as cute and brave as Becca as a best friend had been somehow special. She was like a pretty doll that all the other girls wanted to play with, but she'd chosen to play with Madison and Natalie. They coveted the time they spent together.

She had no idea why that memory popped into her head.

Madison pulled her photo album out from the bottom shelf of the television stand, paging through years of photos, but stopping for longer moments on the pictures of the three friends. She missed those girls.

Once they were in middle school, they were allowed to go to the high school football games. Madison remembered the first one they went to completely unchaperoned. They walked to the football stadium together, arguing over which of their favorite singers they would go see in concert as soon as they were old enough. Natalie liked Kelly Clarkson; Becca couldn't decide between Gwen Stefani and Avril Lavigne; Madison swooned over Justin Timberlake.

The night didn't turn out exactly as planned. As soon as they were in the bleachers on that warm September night, the varsity team ready for its first home game of the season, three high school boys they didn't know sat in the row behind them, teasing, trying hard to get Becca's attention. It worked. Becca disappeared with them at half-time, leaving her two friends to worry about her, not sure if they should stay in the bleachers or go in search of her. She reappeared when the game was almost over, amused by their worried faces.

"Please, please, please," she'd said, widening her eyes in that practiced, innocent way she had, "don't tell my parents. They would *kill* me." Of course, they would never tell. They were best friends.

When Becca wasn't with them, when she and Natalie whispered about that night, part of them wished they could be as brave and daring.

Becca became even more brave and daring once her parents separated. When they teamed up for a group project in their ninth grade World Government class, Becca not only did little to pull her weight, she never showed up at Madison's house that Saturday to work on it, texting to ask that they not tell her mom. When the assignment was due, and Becca still hadn't contributed anything of substance, she did what she did best. "You *know* I'll make this up to you. Don't tell Mr. Hanes. You know how hard the separation has been for me," she reminded them, eyelashes fluttering, highlighting the glittery shadow she had started wearing on her lids, and adding a newly developed and highly effective pouty lip. (Madison practiced the look in front of her own mirror, but she could never pull off anything close to Becca's look, instead looking like she had a swollen lip). "It's been so hard now that I don't get to see my dad all the time."

They covered for her, because that's what forever friends do for one another.

She did eventually start to turn on them, though, despite their blind loyalty. Becca pushed the limits, taking off on a weekend camping trip with a group of older theater kids, but telling her mother she was staying at Madison's house. When she and Nat confronted her after that stressful weekend, Becca's eyes narrowed, the pretty face contorted into a sneer. "If you're jealous that I have more fun, then that's your problem, not mine. Don't worry. I won't ask you to help me out anymore. Now I know you were never really my friends."

That stung because they *had* been friends. They had been best friends. Becca was the one who had changed. As junior year started, Becca drifted further from them, deciding the drama club kids were more to her liking, and soon, she was just someone who waved from a distance if they happened to catch her eye. Becca started dating Jared that year, and they became the school's dream couple.

Madison wanted to blame everything that happened on Becca, but the accident, when she was being perfectly honest with herself, was probably more her fault than anyone else's. Pettiness, stupidity, revenge... They all have consequences. She learned that the hard way.

Chapter Ten

MADISON STOPPED BY THE DINER FOR LUNCH THE NEXT day, opting for one of her favorites—a chicken salad sandwich. Patrick still used Grandma Ruth's recipe with perfectly seasoned chicken and just the right balance of walnuts and grapes to enhance the flavor. She downed it quickly, anxious to get to the golf course for her appointment with Sean Fitzpatrick, the new course manager.

She was killing two birds with one stone by stopping at the diner. It was true she needed lunch, of course, but she also wanted to ask Patrick if he knew this Fitzpatrick guy, but so far there hadn't been a lull in the activity at the restaurant and she didn't want to disrupt his busy lunch hour.

Glenn Draper had been the manager at the course for as long as she could remember, so she was surprised to learn he was no longer there, and even more surprised that the typical small town gossip train had not already roared through, spreading the news far and wide. Patrick wasn't prone to spreading gossip but he tended to hear a lot more than he usually let on. He probably had already met the new guy.

Madison crumpled her napkin, letting it fall on top of her plate. Sandy, still the faithful daytime waitress, moved closer, setting the coffee pot that seemed to be an extension of her arm on the edge of the table as she chatted. "It's busy in town. Summer is upon us, Madison. Summer is upon us." She nodded knowingly. "Can I get you anything else, dear? How about a piece of apple pie?"

"I'm good, thank you, Sandy." Madison couldn't remember a time the plump, rosy-cheeked woman hadn't worked the daytime shift. She could be counted on to show up every weekday—except for the two-week Florida vacation she took every January, returning with just enough color from the southern sun to turn her face an even deeper shade of pink than it already naturally tended toward. "It looks like the lunch rush is slowing a bit so I'm going to poke my head in back to say hello to Patrick."

"You do that, honey. And tell your parents hello for me, too. Your dad saved my life last month." She held her hand to the side of her mouth. "That old tooth got abscessed and finally needed to go." The bell jangled and she was off, coffee pot at the ready to greet the newest customers, setting the pot on a nearby table to draw the newcomer into a tight hug.

Madison stepped through the swinging doors, past the grill and into the kitchen, surprised to see Mya coming in the back door of the diner. "Mya, don't tell me Patrick has you working afternoons now that you're done teaching!"

"Heavens, no!" Mya laughed as she set her purse down. "What a nice surprise, Maddy. Did you take the afternoon off? Please don't tell me *you* offered to work today."

"Heavens, no!" She mocked her sister-in-law. "I didn't have time to eat breakfast this morning, so I treated myself to lunch." She looked around, lowered her voice, and talked behind her hand, drawing Mya into her confidence. "His chicken salad is out of this world, but if Patrick asks, I'll tell him it was mediocre at best."

The walk-in freezer door unexpectedly opened, and Patrick stepped out with an exaggerated shiver. "I thought I had that organized, but apparently not." He leaned forward, giving his wife a peck on the cheek.

"Brrr. You *are* cold. If you're trying to hide from the world, I'm sure there are warmer places." She cupped his face in her hands, then kissed his lips. "That should warm you up. Piper is at a playdate, so I thought I'd drop in to offer my help with anything you might need for later." She turned back to Madison. "They're training two new high school kids tonight on how to close. That's always fun." She turned a stern face to her husband. "And you *will* let Tino take the lead on this," she waved a finger in Patrick's face, "or I'll drag you out of here. Better yet, I'll hold you captive in the walk-in."

"I get it, I get it." He held his arms up in surrender.

"I just wanted to let you know I'm taking off, but we should all get together while Nat's in town."

"This one," Mya poked him in the chest with a finger, "keeps telling me he's going to trust Tino to take on more responsibility, so we should be able to get away whenever we want. Isn't that right, sweetie?" There was a clear challenge in her voice.

"I'm a changed man. You'll see." He pulled her into his arms and pretended to nibble her neck as she squealed and struggled to free herself.

Madison laughed at their antics, wondering if she would one day have a special someone at her side, and it wasn't until she was almost to the course that she realized she hadn't asked her brother about Sean Fitzpatrick.

A handful of vehicles were in the lot when Madison pulled up to the Lakeview Golf Course pro shop. It was impossible to ignore the feeling in the pit of her stomach. Everywhere she looked she saw reminders of Carl. He should be here right now, managing this course, living out his dream, and maybe, just maybe, planning a life with her. It took almost physical effort to force the thoughts away.

A young man watching a video on his phone looked up as she walked in, and then quickly put the device on the counter, not saying anything by way of greeting as she approached, and his eyes wandering to the screen even as she closed the distance between them.

"I'm Madison Keller with the Laurel Lake Times." She pulled her credentials card from the camera bag slung over her shoulder, but his eyes had already strayed back to the phone. Waiting for him to make eye contact, she continued. "I'll be taking some photos on the course today, and I'm meeting with Mr. Fitzpatrick." She was pretty confident this kid had never read one of her articles or even looked at the pictures in one of her Hometown Pride sections of the paper.

"Okay. He's not here right now. You know how to drive one?" He jerked his head toward the wall of windows through which she could see carts lined up. He was more interested in returning to his video than showing her how to operate one, so he looked relieved when she nodded. "Okay, you can take number four." He drifted away from the counter, staring at his phone, already forgetting he had been interrupted in the first place.

"Thank you." Madison had no idea what she was thanking him for given his lack of interest in assisting her. Carl would have been outraged over a golf course employee so clearly disinterested in his job. (*Sacrilege!* She could almost hear him whispering in her ear.)

She carefully avoided the golfers on the course as she rode around, snapping pictures of the fairways, greens, and foliage. The holes featuring lake views were especially captivating. She took far more pictures than she would ever be able to use for a Hometown Pride edition, and was already planning to print some to share with her grandma.

The cart seemed to have a mind of its own, steering directly toward one of her favorite places on the course, her heart weighted by the memories even as she anticipated the spectacular view. Madison stopped the cart on the path and climbed the small mound. With each step, grief became more palpable, and her unease grew, as though the very earth below her was moving, leaving her unsteady and unbalanced. The knoll's vantage point would provide the best photo opportunity, but she didn't raise her camera.

This was the place. Carl had taken her hand in his on this very spot. Involuntarily, the fingers of her left hand moved, as though reaching for his, remembering how magical the moment had been, their fingers entwined so naturally it was difficult to tell where she ended and he began. They shared something special—something more than a summer romance—and she feared she would never feel that way again.

Lost in her memories, she jumped when a man's voice broke through the silence. "Are you getting what you need?"

Clawing her way back to the present, Madison turned, shading her eyes from the bright sun but still unable to see the person behind the voice. She forced her lips to cooperate, hoping they were doing something that would pass for a smile. The voice was too friendly to be that of the young man from the pro shop so she assumed this was Mr. Fitzpatrick.

"I am, thank you."

The man left his cart, taking long strides to reach her side. He was tall, probably a bit over six feet, dwarfing her 5'3" stature. His reddish-blonde hair curled slightly at the ends, and a sprinkling of freckles across his nose gave him a youthful appearance even though she guessed him to be in his early thirties. It was his eyes that caught and held her attention though, sparkling emerald-green pools in the bright afternoon sun. Staring at the gold specks in them, she had a sense she was falling into their depths. The thought took her by such surprise, making the moment suddenly awkward.

"Sean Fitzpatrick, interim course manager," he said by way of introduction as he stopped directly before her, the wide smile making the freckles dance. His easy manner proved he was clearly unaware of her discomfort. "You must be Ms. Keller."

Madison took his extended hand, his warm and strong in her own. The memories she'd been lost in moments before continued to swirl around her, whispering in her ear and taking up space in her very being. It was easy to feel Carl here, in this place he so dearly loved. But this wasn't Carl before her.

"Madison Keller," she said, the sensation of Carl standing next to her evaporating into thin air at the same time she realized her hand had been in Fitzpatrick's a beat longer than necessary. She quickly pulled it away, filled with an emptiness so deep she had to remember to breathe. "I was expecting to talk to Glenn Draper when I called about the interview. I didn't realize he no longer works here."

She and Patrick had taken lessons from Glenn years and years ago. There had been no great talent for golf in either of the siblings, but the pro had been patient with them nonetheless. When it came to whipping his summer staff into shape, Glenn had far less patience. Carl told her numerous stories about his high standards and expectations.

"Yeah, some changes came about when Glenn was offered a job in Orlando."

Madison was busy pulling a notebook and pen from her bag, hoping the focus on the interview would keep thoughts of Carl at bay for a while. "It sounds as though the opening came up quickly. How did you hear about it?"

"A friend contacted me...thought I'd be interested." He raised his hands in a "ta da!" "I was between jobs so I made the trip to Wisconsin."

As she looked at him, a realization hit Madison, and she blurted, "I've seen you before. You drive a white pickup."

If he was taken aback by her observation, he hid it well, nodding; in fact, he seemed amused—evidenced by the sparkle in his eye and his boyish grin. "Do you work for the DMV, or the newspaper, Ms. Keller?"

"Please, call me Madison." Embarrassed, she explained. "I was photographing the marina for the paper a few days ago and your truck...well, your truck blocked my view. I recognized you..." She stopped, about to say she recognized him from the pictures she had taken of him—and looked at several times afterward—but that sounded very stalker-like no matter how she tried to phrase it in her mind. She recovered as best she could. "I recognized you."

"Oh, man. Sorry about that. I never would have interrupted your work had I known. It's a beautiful lake and sometimes the view is so breathtaking, I can't help myself," he admitted. "I have to stop what I'm doing and take pictures."

Carl would have done the same thing. He was, in fact, the one who ignited her love of photography. He also would have given anything to manage this course once he finished his education. But this wasn't Carl before her now and one difference was obvious. It might have been Carl's dream job, but Sean Fitzpatrick was simply filling in between other stints. Her stomach twisted once again. Try as she might, she couldn't stop a new feeling from taking root; a sense of resentment rose from somewhere deep within her.

On some level she recognized none of this was Sean's fault. It wasn't as if he swooped in and stole Carl's job away, but reasoning with her emotions was a struggle. She reminded herself to breathe and then responded airily. "You're forgiven. I'm running out of wall space to hang all the prints I've made of my photographs of the lake, so I get it."

They stood side-by-side, looking at the lake from the hill on the far side of the 12th green, but Madison remained distracted, thinking about Carl, his hand reaching out, warm and possessive, claiming her as his own. She jumped when Sean spoke.

"I wasn't sure what you might need today, so I told Jackson to have a cart ready. Hopefully he took good care of you."

She considered telling him that Jackson had been anything but helpful, but she kept it to herself. Maybe he already knew and was working on it. Or maybe he didn't care. She busied herself with the notepad. "Is that S-h-a-w-n or S-e-a-n?"

He laughed, and his entire face lit up, the freckles dancing once again. "The only way a good Irish grandda would allow it to be spelled. S-e-a-n."

"Oh, are you *from* Ireland?"

"I was born there, but my parents moved us to the states when I was little. My dad wanted to make his fortune here—the American Dream, you know—but my grandda still lives in Cork." He shook his head. "He's a feisty old bugger and Irish through and through."

"Feisty grandparents are the best, right?" It was nice to have found some common ground with the man as she forced herself to relax and do her job. "The paper is running a series of articles to highlight aspects of the town. As I'm sure you know, we are having a blow-out sesquicentennial celebration next month. The golf course is one of our featured topics because of its long history. I know you're new here, but I'm sure you have some insights to share on what's happening these days."

Madison purposely kept her introduction vague, hoping he might share news of a pending sale or something else to satisfy her personal curiosity, even if she couldn't use it in the article.

"FORE!"

The shout startled them at the same time a ball flew dangerously close to her head. Sean's response had been to reach out and pull her toward him, using his own body to shield her from the errant ball.

"Are you okay?"

She was shaken, but she couldn't honestly tell if it was from the near miss of the ball whizzing past her head or the strong arms of Sean Fitzpatrick drawing her close to protect her.

A moment of embarrassment followed as she found her footing, adjusting the camera strap around her neck. He cleared his throat as she breathlessly proclaimed she was fine, the heat in her face giving away the awkwardness she felt.

The sound of laughter reached them before the cart appeared. Two men, oblivious to just how close the shot had come to causing serious injury, drove over the knoll in search of the ball. The driver slowed enough for his companion to scoop it from its resting place, a precarious move that left them laughing even harder as the cart tilted dangerously. As they swung around and the passenger righted himself, Madison got a good look at their faces, but neither looked familiar.

Sean shook his head, muttering under his breath, "*Idiots.*"

They watched as the cart moved around them and back to the path, disappearing over the rise and toward the next tee box. "I'm fine catching up with you later if you need to go deal with that." She remembered the days of taking lessons from Glenn, and the level of intolerance he had for "golf course tomfoolery," as he called it.

"I'll talk to them later." He waved his hand dismissively in their direction.

For some reason, this infuriated Madison. How could he not care about their lack of respect for the game, the course, or other players? Something about the whole situation rubbed her the wrong way. If the course ended up on the market it would be because people like Sean Fitzpatrick simply didn't care enough. Carl would have cared. Anger swept through her unbidden. Why couldn't he do his job? She looked from her notepad to his face, a silence settling between them.

"Well, if you have any questions I can answer, be sure to let me know. Otherwise, I'll leave you to your picture taking."

Madison had no desire to get any additional information from Sean Fitzpatrick. As far as she was concerned, she had seen and heard enough to know he was no Carl.

The interview was over. She would get any information she needed about the course in another way. As she marched away, her foot caught on a clump of grass and she almost lost her balance. She didn't look back to see if Sean had witnessed her clumsiness; instead, she seated herself in the cart and drove back toward the pro shop.

But even as she watched the course disappear in the Jeep's rearview mirror minutes later, she couldn't stop thinking about the way those strong arms felt wrapped protectively around her.

Chapter Eleven

"Your article was wonderful, honey. I get such a thrill seeing your byline in the paper."

Madison's face flushed with pleasure. "Thanks, mom." She scowled. "My stupid boss cut almost half the story, though."

"Well, it was still good. Most people have no idea the course has been here since 1947. Very informative. You'll have to show me the other half of the story."

"Whatever." She shrugged and forced a smile, pretending Gavin's actions had not hurt her feelings at all. "It was probably boring."

They were working side-by-side, storing pails of red and white carnations in the cooler for the local VFW members to place at the Fairview Cemetery on Flag Day. Madison had gladly accepted her mom's request for help because she needed something to help pass the time. Natalie was due to arrive in a matter of hours and she was beside herself with anticipation.

"Have you heard anything about the new course manager?"

Nina slid the last pail into place and they stepped out of the cooler. She reached behind her back to untie the apron and slip it over her head, "I knew they were getting someone new." She stared contemplatively into space, tapping her finger on her lips as she puzzled over who would have mentioned it. "You know what? I think it was Liz Erikson. In fact, I know it was," she said, triumphant that her memory had served her well. (They all seemed to test themselves in strange ways since Grandma Ruth's diagnosis).

"Liz was shopping for flowers?"

"No, I ran into her at the hardware store. I don't remember how it came up, but that's definitely where I heard the news that Glenn left."

Liz again. It struck Madison as funny that her name kept popping up lately. "He's not doing a very good job, I'd say. In the short time I was there I thought he let a lot of things slide that Glenn would have been all over."

Her mom gave her a curious look, but Madison didn't give her a chance to say anything else as she picked up her keys. "I have to run. See you soon, mom." She blew her mom a kiss as she walked out. Her mom knew her too well. She wanted to bring up Carl, thinking it was good for Madison to talk about it. That wasn't going to happen.

Natalie stepped out of the SUV and Madison almost bowled her over, wrapping her arms around her as though she would never let go. Nat was home. Madison had waited over ten years for this.

Natalie held her at arm's length, the first to break the silence. "You look amazing, Mads. Your hair! Oh my gosh! I can't remember the last time I saw you with your hair down." Although they had seen each other about a year ago when Madison visited them in Iowa, it still felt like forever.

Madison's face reddened. "Oh, stop," she managed. She turned to the SUV, opening the back door to pull a bag out. "My stylist told me a little highlighting would make me 'lighter and brighter.' I've been ditching the ponytail lately." She put her hands in the air as if she were a movie star awaiting her closeup. As she shook her head, the late day shimmer of the sun captured the subtle highlights. "Everyone seems to love it."

"And by 'everyone,' I sure hope you mean at least a few of the male persuasion." Although she was clearly teasing, her look was one of hope.

Rolling her eyes, Madison pretended to check the time on her watch. "That was quick. My love life came up in less than three minutes of your arrival. I'm betting that is some kind of record." Even as she reacted in that faux-offended way, an image of the handsome, green-eyed course manager flashed through her mind, making her heart skip a beat. His arms had been so strong around her, keeping her from falling... She shook him away, taken aback by her own foolishness. Sure, the guy was physically attractive, but he had zero other qualities of interest to her. "Let's not talk about that right now." She picked up the overnight bag Natalie had set on the driveway and changed the subject. "You look tired."

Natalie nodded, slinging the laptop case she had taken from the front seat over her shoulder. Her auburn hair was cut shorter than she wore it in high school, and she'd put on a few pounds and gotten contacts, but aside from that, Natalie hadn't changed a bit.

"Byron is off playing with the tortoises, right? Or is it something to do with plate tectonics? I get all that science stuff mixed up."

"I know. I know. He may be a science nerd but he's *my* science nerd." She rubbed her neck, moving her head slowly back and forth. "Driving is hard on the body. Any possibility we can squeeze in a spa day?"

"I happen to know someone who'd be happy to schedule that —and join you, of course."

Despite Natalie's protests, Madison grabbed two small suitcases from the back, noting three plastic bins tucked up against the back seat. "Are you sure you're only staying a few days?" She pretended to be weighed down by the bags. "This is easily enough for a month, I'd say. Tell me the truth. Did Byron kick you out and this is your subtle way of saying you plan to stay here forever?"

"Sorry to disappoint you, but I really did pack this much for a short visit." She waved her hand at the boxes. "Those are some things I need to drop at my great-aunt's house. I really had no idea what to bring because the weather is always crazy here—and you wouldn't tell me what you had planned for us." She started to say more, then stopped.

Madison noticed her hesitation. "Everything okay?"

"Absolutely. Of course. I'm just totally exhausted, that's all. After a good night's rest, I'll be a new woman."

"That's a shame. I kind of like the woman you are right now."

"I almost didn't recognize the exit. Fairview has really grown in ten years. You have a Walmart now!"

"I know. How can anyone live without *that*? Come on. I can't wait for you to see what I've done with the house."

Natalie stood next to her in front of the bungalow Madison's grandparents had proudly purchased shortly after they married. The veranda, shaded by the roof overhang, was the perfect place for the canopied porch swing Madison added once the house became hers. It had been close to heartbreaking for her to replace the two ancient rocking chairs her grandparents had used for decades. She wanted to have them fixed, but they were beyond repair, and ready to be put out to pasture. As her dad hauled them away, she fought back tears, a piece of her grandparents disappearing forever.

Madison led the way up the steps, pleased to hear a gasp behind her as she opened the front door, motioning Natalie through.

"Oh, Madison, this looks amazing!"

At her heels, Madison laughed. "You really need to work on your vocabulary. Not *everything* is amazing."

"Okay, maybe not everything, but your hair and what you've done to this house—definitely amazing."

"Thanks. It was all easy stuff. My mom helped me take down

the curtains and install blinds. That helped a lot. We moved about a half million knick-knacks to grandma's place. Oh, and we painted, too." Sadness threatened to engulf her as she thought about her grandma moving to a different room soon. Would she still have space for her favorite things from home? Would she even remember them? Madison forced the thoughts aside. "I picked out smaller pieces of furniture so that makes the rooms look bigger."

Natalie left her bags in the foyer and wandered through the house gifted to Madison by her grandmother not long after she moved to assisted living. "Hopefully Byron and I will be able to buy a house one of these days. For now, we are perpetual renters. You are so lucky, Madison." She plopped onto the sofa, kicking her sandals from her feet. "That's more like it." She continued looking around. "This is just adorable, Madison. Does your grandma like living at the Center?"

"She seems..." Madison searched for the right word, finally finishing her sentence. "Content, I guess." Her brow furrowed. "I don't know. It's hard to judge now that she stopped socializing. She had all kinds of activities she was doing with friends, and she used to take day trips whenever someone offered a ride. Now that the...the disease is getting worse, she stays in her room most of the time. She mostly just sits and stares out the window." She stopped, blowing air out of her pursed lips. "Can we talk about that later? I'll fill you in on everything. Promise."

"That's topic number two you've put on hold. I'll run out of things to talk about soon."

"Very funny. Come on, old lady. Let's get you settled."

They collected the luggage and Natalie followed Madison into the guest bedroom. "Is it weird that this used to be your dad's room?"

"I stayed here for weeks to help Grandma when she broke her hip and I never once even thought about that. Thanks, Nat. *Now* it's weird." Madison rolled her eyes, laughing.

"Sorry." She bit her lower lip as she turned to face Madison. "I have something to confess. When you first told me you were moving into this house, well...I couldn't picture you in it at all. For some reason I remembered it as dark and small and...old." Natalie put her hands together. "I'm begging you to forgive my initial judgement. I had no idea you had an eye for perking up an old house."

"Ouch! You thought that? It hurts." She laughed, understanding fully that not everyone wants to live in their grandparents' house. Madison was an exception. "At first, I was afraid to change it, as if it was an insult to grandma or something. But I've been working on making it mine. She wanted me to have it and enjoy it so that's what I'm doing. The backyard was her favorite place to be, with all her flowers and trees, so I'm trying to maintain them like she did."

"It looks amazing...oops...I mean, it looks fantastic? Stunning? I've got it! Breathtaking."

"Good Lord, Nat. A moment ago, you had one word for everything and now you've swallowed a thesaurus."

"I have a foggy brain, I guess. Probably the long drive." Again, she seemed on the verge of saying something else, but stopped herself. "Cut me a little slack and offer me an iced tea."

"You do what you need to do to settle in, freshen up, powder your nose, shower, or whatever. I'll get the tea and we can sit outside." She gave her shoulder a playful nudge and then swung back to wrap Natalie in another never-want-to-let-go hug. "It's *so* good to have you here, Nat." Tears of pure joy threatened to spill from her, but she laughed them away, saying, "I'll go prepare your shockingly spectacular, stunningly thirst-quenching iced tea."

Natalie shook her head and smiled, shooing Madison out of the bedroom.

Years dropped away, leaving Madison feeling like a kid again. They first met two decades ago in Mrs. Gray's kindergarten class where they became fast friends on day one. Becca moved to Fairview later that year, and that's when they became an inseparable group of three.

A lightness filled her as she prepared a tray with tea, crackers, and cheese. When Natalie joined her on the patio a short time later, they sat in silence for a moment, wrapped in warm memories. From a distance, the sound of kids laughing carried on the gentle breeze and a dog barked excitedly. Madison wished she could hold onto this moment forever.

The silence didn't last long.

"You've done a great job with your grandma's flowers. I had no idea you possessed such a vividly green thumb." She reached over to pick up Madison's hand, pretending to inspect it. "Nope. I don't see it. Do you have a sexy gardener who comes by to tend to your flowers, my dear?" She wiggled her eyebrows and glanced provocatively at Madison.

They laughed easily, although Madison wondered if this was yet another way to start a conversation about her non-existent love life. She let it go. "Sometimes it's hard to believe we have been friends since kindergarten."

"That is kind of amazing." As an afterthought, she added, "Is Mrs. Gray still around?"

Madison's eyes widened and she laughed in disbelief. "How funny! I was just thinking about her a few minutes ago. They moved to Florida when she retired. Remember, her husband was an engineer for the water plant? Their son, Gary, is the Associate Principal at the high school now and his wife teaches with Mya."

After a brief stunned silence, Natalie murmured, "Good Lord!" She closed her eyes momentarily, then continued. "Every now and then I can almost forget how much everyone knows about everyone else's life around here." She studied the cracker she'd been about to eat, then set it down on the napkin in her lap. "Sorry. That's a demon I still have to conquer. Small towns can be really nice until they become a little…a little too small."

Madison started to speak and then stopped. What Natalie and her mom went through was beyond horrible and she would never wish it on anyone, but she wanted desperately to make Natalie remember how wonderful Fairfield had been—and could be—if she ever decided to return. Instead, she changed the subject.

"How is your mom doing?" Madison could picture the round-faced, red-headed Mrs. Richter, bustling about in her brightly colored dinosaur or lollipop-decorated pediatric nursing smock, always smiling. It was better remembering her that way instead of the Mrs. Richter with the haunted look and red-rimmed eyes, a shell of a woman after her husband's death.

"Good. She plans to stay in Africa as long as they want her." Nancy Richter sold her house in Minnesota and joined an organization that helps kids with disfiguring diseases. They sent her to Africa. "We do video calls when we can, but it's not easy with the internet access there—or should I say the lack thereof? I'll have a chance to..." She stopped short, suddenly interested in her glass of iced tea. "Did you make this from tea bags? It's delicious. Mine never turns out like this. Do you want some more?"

She didn't wait for an answer, instead, hopping out of the chair and going through the sliding door to the kitchen. Moments later, she emerged with the pitcher.

Although ten years had passed since the days they were inseparable, Madison still knew her friend well enough to know she didn't want to talk about her mother right now, or perhaps better said, her mother's reasons for leaving the country, so she changed the subject, hoping they might land on a topic that wasn't off-limits to one or both. When had their lives become so complicated? Madison thought about it a moment until a safe subject came to mind. "Do you remember Liz Erikson?"

"The strange lady who owned the Cottages, right? Remember how she'd sit at the counter and glare at us when we would come in to shoot pool with the renters' kids?" Natalie did a perfect imitation of a cranky Liz Erikson. "She put in all that fun stuff and then yelled at us for 'all that racket.' And then one day, just like that..." she snapped her fingers, "...she got rid of it all—the foosball, pool table, the popcorn maker..." Her laugh was ironic.

"I swear she hated kids. I'm not sure why she had all of that in the first place if she didn't want anyone having fun. So weird!"

"Seriously!" Madison had to cross her legs so she wouldn't pee herself from laughing so hard. This was the sense of humor she remembered, loved, and missed terribly. The moment's lightness faded quickly. "I needed that. Everything here has been kind of gloom and doom. I told you my grandma's memory is slipping badly."

"I'm sorry, Madison. I know how close you are to her."

"The doctor gave us some suggestions to keep her mind active. The only problem is, I don't know how far to push her."

"What do you mean?"

"She keeps mentioning a secret. At first it was about a secret ingredient in a recipe but then it became a secret Liz's mom told her. I'm guessing it was about Liz." Madison picked up her glass, wiping the condensation from the side with a finger as she chose her words. "I wouldn't give it any thought but every time she talks about it, she gets upset. Then I don't know if I should let it go or press her to say more, to help her remember. Grandma called it a 'delicate matter.'"

"And now you're curious." Natalie nodded thoughtfully. "I can see why this would be a conundrum for you. It might be therapeutic for her to work through the memory or it might agitate her more if she can't remember."

Madison leaned forward, setting the glass on the patio table. "But a part of me really wants to know what it is." She continued. "It's this whole tangled web. She wants to know where Chuck is, and then she mentions some Gordon who 'died over there.' Somehow, they are all connected, and something about it is bothering grandma." She finally took a deep breath and sat back in her chair before continuing. "But it's almost impossible to know anymore what's a real memory and what might be made up. She needs to move to a different ward at the Senior Living Center as soon as a room opens." She struggled to get the last words out, and they were barely a whisper. "I'm afraid she won't even remember me soon."

"Oh honey, I'm sorry." As darkness settled around them, Natalie took her friend's hand, offering the only comfort she could. They were no strangers to grief and pain but for a moment, the softness of the evening was a blanket protecting them from the tragedies of their past.

Chapter Twelve

On Saturday morning, Madison awoke to the sound of birds chattering outside her window. A rare sense of things being okay with the world settled over her, making her excited to face the day. She took a quick shower, pulled her hair back in a ponytail and left a note for the still-sleeping Natalie. *Biking to Poppy's to pick up coffee cake. We'll have breakfast on the patio.* The early morning chill in the air would rapidly transition into the warmth of a perfect June day, and the lakeshore would be buzzing with activity. Still caught up in the nostalgia of the previous evening, Madison could almost believe she was back in her pre-driving years, pedaling to meet up with Natalie for whatever summer adventure they had planned, which invariably meant hanging out on Water Street, at the beach, or on the docks. The thought made her smile as she rode the short distance to the diner.

Although she hoped she was early enough to beat the worst of the crowd, Poppy's was bustling with activity, so she waited on a stool at the counter until the waitress had a moment to spare. "I'm not in a hurry. Don't worry, Kayla" she assured the frazzled teenager. Madison briefly considered going behind the counter and helping herself but figured that might be insulting to those patiently waiting to be served. She waved to a couple people she knew.

The fishermen were long gone, usually the first to arrive as the doors opened at 5:30 so they could fill up before hitting the lake for the day. Families usually came in later, planning on a late breakfast or brunch to hold them over as they spent the day on the beach. The ice cream window would see a steady flow of visitors once it opened at eleven. Patrick ran an impressive business.

A loud crash disrupted the general din in the dining room, followed by a gasp and cry of "Oh no!" Every patron, including Madison, turned to see a dismayed Kayla standing over the trayful of now ruined food and broken dishes at her feet. After a beat, Kayla pulled her hands from her face, burst into tears, and ran into the back.

Without hesitation, Madison grabbed a bus tub from behind the counter and began picking up broken dishes, apologizing to nearby diners and trying to make light of the situation. It was easy to remember the first time she'd dropped someone's breakfast, no matter how badly she wanted to forget.

She handed the tub to a skinny, pimply-faced teenager who was serving double duty as a dishwasher and busser. He tucked his head shyly and mumbled something under his breath.

Tino, his dark hair pulled into a tight man-bun atop his head stood with a spatula raised in his hand as she pushed through the swinging doors to the grill. "Madison! Thank goodness! What the heck is going on out there?" He couldn't wait for an answer as about two dozen eggs were in need of his attention. He flipped them two at a time, and then brushed melted butter over the sizzling hashbrowns before turning his attention back to her.

She answered his question with one of her own. "Where did Kayla go?" Madison pushed open the door to the kitchen, glancing toward the employee bathroom. It was unoccupied. "I think I should talk to her."

"She left," the skinny dishwasher said, without emotion, jerking his head in the direction of the back door.

Tino's eyes darted frantically between the grill, the busy dining room and Madison, as panic turned his already flushed face a darker shade of red. "Why didn't you tell me, Ryan? That's just great! Sorry. It's not your fault. Forget I said that. I won't have another server coming in until 9:00. I mean, even if I called Lacy now, she probably couldn't get here any sooner, but I guess I can try her." He glanced at his watch, unsure which way to turn, his entire demeanor radiating confusion. Ellie, the weekend prep cook and kitchen assistant was shaking her head at the whole situation as she continued buttering toast and English muffins, and then mixing more pancake batter, patiently waiting for Tino to put eggs and hashbrowns on plates. "I can't believe I'm asking this, Madison, but could you help me out here, please?"

Madison was already pulling an apron over her shorts and t-shirt as she nodded, taking charge. "Call Lacy." She pointed to the tub still in Ryan's hands. "And whatever that order was, you need to make it again. I'll let them know it's on the house. Ryan, put that down and get the mop bucket." She grabbed a rag, returning to the dining area to finish cleaning what was left of the mess on the floor. A quick scan of the five booths and six tables gave her an idea where to start. Four men, dressed for golf, were tucking into their eggs and sausage at the counter, so she knew she didn't have to worry about them immediately, and the booths held locals who were used to sitting over coffee well after their plates were cleared. She headed toward the booth nearest the door, coffee pot in hand.

"Don't you go throwing food on me, young lady," a white-haired man good-naturedly teased as he waved her over. "Can I get my check?" Madison smiled, picking up his empty plate, and teasing right back.

"Looks like you didn't leave any food on your plate for me to throw at you, George."

He laughed a big belly laugh, hoisting himself from the booth and rubbing his well-fed mid-section. "That I didn't. Tell you what..." He pulled a $20 bill from his wallet and handed it to her. "This more than covers it. Keep the change." He was still smiling as he walked away, loudly acknowledging acquaintances as he made his way to the door. Madison continued to the next table to check on the diners.

The bell jangled as he left, sidestepping another man just entering who barely acknowledged George's "Pardon me." Out of the corner of her eye she saw the newcomer walk toward one of two remaining stools at the counter, turning first to give the wet spot on the floor a disdainful look. Already annoyed at his attitude, Madison took her time getting to him.

"Coffee," he told her without looking up from the phone he gripped in his hand. "Black." As she poured, he looked up momentarily and she thought he looked familiar, but his attention quickly turned to the again-jangling-door, raising a hand in greeting as someone she *did* recognize walked to the empty seat.

"Ms. Keller," Sean Fitzpatrick said, giving her a curious look, "I see you've expanded your horizons even more. Working for the DMV and the newspaper didn't quite fill your days, huh?" His eyes sparkled with amusement, and she was again pulled into the depths of green pools.

The other man was concentrating on his phone again, his fingers tapping rapidly, oblivious to their conversation. Madison still couldn't place him, but was certain she had seen him before.

"This is my brother's place." Flustered, she almost toppled the glass of water she was setting before him. "I'm just helping out this morning."

"All in the family. That's the way it should be." He nodded as if in approval, then smiled and added, "I'll have a coffee, please." Fortunately, Tino shouted, "Order up!" so she hurried to get the hot breakfasts out to customers, still confused over how she felt about Sean Fitzpatrick.

Madison continued to pour coffee, carry out plates of food, and bring some semblance of order to the chaos she'd somehow managed to find herself in. At the counter, Sean and the other man seemed to be carrying on an involved conversation. As she filled their coffee cups, she noticed a business card with Magenta

Enterprises in the space between their cups. She had no idea which of them it belonged to, but she didn't have time to think about it further because a bubbly brunette pushed through the swinging doors at that moment.

Madison smiled at her with relief. "You must be Lacy. Thanks for coming in early."

Lacy had already picked up a coffee pot and was glancing around nervously. "Tino sounded so frantic on the phone. What's going on? Is someone else coming in soon? I thought there would be more waitresses on a Saturday morning."

"I'll check with Tino, and I'll be back in a few minutes. Don't worry. Everything is under control here. Table two is about to finish, and they have their check. Table five is on the house. We had a little...incident." She patted the girl on the shoulder reassuringly. "Saturday mornings are fun. You'll see. Everyone is in a good mood and," she whispered the next, "they tip like you wouldn't believe. Just keep their coffee cups filled, stay off your cellphone, joke around with them, and they'll love you." The pep talk seemed to help as the girl managed a smile and started around the room with coffee.

Madison returned to the grill, checking in on Tino. Sweat beaded on his forehead as he deftly flipped four pancakes in quick succession and then pulled a dish from the shelf above to start plating. "I screwed up. Kelly called me last night and said she had to have off, but she didn't find a replacement like I told her she needed to do. I don't know if she even tried. Then my least experienced waitress ended up alone. What a disaster. Your brother is not going to be happy. He warned me that Saturday is the day most likely to get no-shows. I should have been on top of that."

"There's nothing you can do about it now and Patrick doesn't have to know every detail," she reassured him. "Can I get Kayla's phone number? I'd like to chat with her." She'd seen the look of horror on the girl's face and felt a need to reassure her.

He pointed to the small office space in the back. "On that

paper hanging over the desk. I don't know if it'll do any good, but thanks. And thanks again for helping. You saved my butt."

"No problem at all," she responded, even as she continued toward the back office. She punched the number into her phone and stepped out the back door, hoping Kayla would pick up. To her surprise, the girl hadn't left but was sitting outside under the ice cream window. Her knees were pulled up to her chest and she was staring despondently into space.

"Hey, I was just trying to call you."

Kayla picked up her phone to look at the screen and placed it back on the concrete next to her. She wiped her face on her shirt sleeve and sighed. "I can't believe I did that. I feel so stupid." She couldn't look at Madison. "I guess I'm fired, huh?"

"Fired? Absolutely not. If my grandmother fired everyone who broke a dish or two, even her own grandchildren would have been without jobs." She shrugged and dropped to the ground next to the girl. "It's a good thing you got that out of your system at the start of the season. Smooth sailing should be in your future."

"Maybe I'm not cut out for this job."

"Poppycock!" Madison nudged the girl's arm, trying to get her to laugh. "Have you worked the ice cream window yet? That's the best. I love seeing all the little kids changing their minds five times about which flavor they want. It's a hoot. If you quit now, you'd miss out on all that fun."

"I don't know. That was...that was so embarrassing." She looked back at the door, torn between wanting to try again and wanting to run away.

"Some of my greatest summer adventures came from working here. I think you'll love it once you're more comfortable. You weren't supposed to be out there alone, and you were killing it... until you decided to create a mass casualty of pancakes and eggs, of course. The good news is that I don't think anyone even noticed." She batted her eyes in a comical fashion as she shrugged.

To Madison's surprise, it worked. Kayla laughed. "I guess my break is over, then." She stood, pulled her ponytail tight, and started toward the door, pausing before pulling it open. "They're going to laugh at me, aren't they?"

Smiling, Madison started to shake her head and then nodded instead. "Oh, big time! But just joke along with them. That'll shut them up. Oh, and I left your tips in the cup next to the register. You made a killing this morning."

"Really? You want me to keep them?" After a split-second internal turmoil, she simply said, "Thanks."

Madison watched her go back in, but she remained where she was, thinking about her grandmother and how many of these talks she'd had over decades of running the business. Ruth Keller would have said the same things to Kayla, she was confident, because her grandmother had given her something pretty close to the same pep talk once.

She suddenly missed her grandmother terribly.

Her thoughts were interrupted by a text from Natalie. *Where's that breakfast you promised me?*

With a laugh, she replied, *On my way.*

Natalie was going to love this story. As she rose, wiping the back of her shorts, she looked up in time to see the man who had scowled at the wet floor, the one talking to Sean, and she remembered where she had seen him before. It was one of the men from the golf cart. As unreasonable as it might be, her blood boiled and at that moment she disliked everything about him, his partner who had been in the cart, and Sean Fitzpatrick.

―――

"I thought you got lost."

"I've had quite the morning. You're lucky you have any breakfast at all." Her cheeks were red from the bike ride home in far warmer temps than when she left and perhaps because of seeing Sean again. She grabbed a notebook and scribbled a note to herself to research Magenta Enterprises, curious to know what that meant.

A few minutes later they were settled on the patio, finally enjoying their Saturday morning together. As they ate the fresh coffee cake she brought for them, she told Natalie about Kayla's catastrophe.

"My first spill..." Natalie covered her face, a moan turning to a giggle. "Almost an entire pitcher of iced tea down Mr. Calhoun's front. I turned and bumped his chair, and the entire pitcher went..." She made a gesture to indicate a tsunami of liquid crashing down.

"You know my motto: If you're going to have a great calamity it might as well involve your high school principal."

"I didn't think I could ever face him again. His shoes literally squished when he left. I was mortified."

They laughed over their mishaps now, but Madison could remember how embarrassing those moments had been. She rode out another wave of nostalgia, sighing.

Next to her, Natalie spoke quietly. "Wouldn't it be nice if we could take out all the bad memories and leave that much more room for only the good ones?"

"What? And miss out on all this fun? I haven't laughed this much in a long time."

"But it wasn't all sunshine and roses." Madison knew exactly what she meant, but before she could comment further, Natalie had moved on. "So, what's on the agenda today?"

Madison smiled broadly at her friend. "Well, you know that spa day you said you wanted?" She looked at her watch. "You have forty-five minutes to get ready. We have a couple hours of pampering ahead, my friend." Regardless of the million things making her head spin right now, Madison was determined to remind Natalie how wonderful it was to be back in Fairview, hanging out with her best friend.

Chapter Thirteen

By Sunday evening, despite the pampering at the spa, Natalie looked exhausted from their full day of activities the day prior. Madison had topped off the weekend with a BBQ at her parents' house and a boat ride on what Natalie laughingly referred to as the Keller BPB—Big Party Barge. Piper stole Natalie's heart and the two had been inseparable, Piper's little hand constantly reaching for Nat's as she cried, "Look, Natty, Look."

The jam-packed weekend of fun had all been by careful design. With Natalie's visit to Fairview so short, Madison determinedly crammed as much as possible into it.

A tiny piece of Madison was selfishly looking forward to having some time to herself the next day while Natalie visited her great-aunt in Brookfield for lunch. Ben would distribute new story assignments Tuesday, and she had a short list of photos to take, so that gave her a small window of opportunity to take on some of her own research. There was information to uncover on her grandma's behalf and if time allowed, investigating to do on whatever Magenta Enterprises happened to be. She had all kinds of suspicions brewing inside her, but she forced herself to go slowly and not jump to any conclusions.

Madison woke early Monday and was in the process of leaving

a note for Natalie when the guest bedroom opened and she shuffled into the kitchen, her short hair a frizzy mess on one side and flattened against her face on the other.

"Good morning, sunshine." Madison laughed, thoroughly amused at her friend's appearance. "If this is how you look every morning, I can see why Byron dashed off to a conference."

"Do you have to be so chipper in the morning?" Natalie reached up, trying to poof her hair into something more flattering and then gesturing to indicate how useless her actions were. She took a glass from the cupboard, filling it with orange juice she pulled from the fridge. "I didn't sleep well. The bed is great," she was quick to add. "I just have a lot on my mind."

"Everything okay? Do you want coffee?"

"Just juice. Thanks. Everything is good." She plopped herself onto a kitchen chair, taking a long drink of her juice. "Ahhh. That's better. Systems are turning on now. I talked with Byron for a while last night, but I think I fell asleep while he was telling me about the conference." She grimaced. "I'm a terrible wife."

"Well, if you change your mind, I made plenty of coffee. Help yourself. It might help you look less zombie-like. And when Byron dumps your uncaring butt, you can always live with me." Madison smirked at her friend before turning to rinse her own mug. "You're still okay meeting at the diner around 6?"

Natalie nodded, then groaned. "If I can get Aunt Linda to stop talking long enough for me to escape." Her great-aunt in Brookfield had been disappointed to learn Natalie would be in the area and wasn't planning to stay with her. "Thank goodness I was able to negotiate just a lunch date with her. I still have to convince her I want to *take* her out for lunch. I wouldn't be able to handle all that hair." She supported the statement with an exaggerated shudder. "She really is the stereotypical cat lady. I think she had eight or nine the last time I was at her house, but that was over ten years ago. Either they all are long gone, or by now they multiplied exponentially and have completely taken over the place." She followed this up with another shudder.

"Wouldn't be my cup of tea, either. Little dogs are more my speed." Madison stood and stretched. "Tomorrow will be fun. Tonight, we'll go through all the fine tuning for picking up the cake, decorating, blah, blah, blah." Her voice took on a sad note. "And then you'll be leaving Wednesday afternoon."

"Let's focus on happy stuff. The party. They will love it."

It had been Mya's idea to surprise Brent and Nina with a special anniversary dinner at Dockside with the family and a few of their close friends. The four of them were meeting at the diner to go over the final plans for the surprise.

"I know. It'll be fun."

Yawning, Natalie turned her wrist to look at her watch. "Isn't it early for you to be going into work?"

"Early bird catches the worm, you know." She shrugged, not quite ready to share any more details about the real reason for her rush to get there. In truth, she had become more and more intrigued with the whole Liz, Chuck, and Gordon thing. Most of all, it was a great mystery as to how her grandmother fit into the great scheme of things. Natalie would get the full story once she had details to share. Since Monday mornings tended to be relatively quiet at the newspaper, she would have ample time to focus on...she couldn't name it...whatever it was she needed to figure out in order to get to the bottom of the whole mystery.

"Okay, Miss Early Bird. Enjoy those worms. I'll try to make myself look a little more presentable before I head out to Brookfield. Poppy's. 6:00. Got it."

Madison used the short drive to collect her thoughts. Letting her imagination run wild, she had created a number of possible scenarios that could be connecting points between the various players. She was determined to find clues that would put it all together.

She planned to start the morning with a brief stop at the office to upload photos for upcoming stories, edit a couple captions, and then visit the library to look at archived copies of high school yearbooks. She was convinced Chuck and Liz went to high school together. The romantic in her surmised they were high school sweethearts, but what did that have to do with her grandma? And how did Gordon fit into any of it?

A few people might also be able to provide answers. Jenny Whitebird came to mind. She didn't take to gossip, but this was less gossip and more historical research. Perhaps, in a last ditch, desperate moment, she would even think about talking to Liz again. That would be tricky because she didn't know how sensitive the matter really was. Hopefully, she'd get some clarity at the library.

As predicted, only a couple cars were in the staff lot, including the sleek black Mustang belonging to her new, hopefully very temporary boss. Madison was grateful to see Ben's old blue pickup was also in the lot, because the last thing she wanted was to be alone with Gavin Maves. As she filled her bottle at the water cooler, she could see Gavin speaking with Ben inside the Editor-in-Chief's office. By the expression on Ben's face, she guessed he wasn't happy.

At her desk, she pulled up her picture-taking assignments, syncing her schedule with specific events she had to photograph. She had diligently submitted her most recent feature Friday morning and would get the marked-up copy back in order to finalize edits later in the week. She would have to complete the Hometown Pride layout by Thursday. The week would be relatively easy in terms of her work schedule, she decided, opening her laptop.

Lost in these thoughts, Ben's unexpected appearance at her desk startled her, and the water she was about to drink sloshed over onto the papers before her.

"Sorry, Madison. I didn't mean to scare you."

Blotting the droplets with a tissue, Madison laughed. "I didn't hear you. You have an impressive stealth mode."

He shifted from one foot to the other, glancing back over his shoulder, noticeably uncomfortable. "Look, I'm just coming from a meeting and…" He ran his hand over his beard, clearly searching for the right words. "I'm glad I caught you here right away." He cleared his throat and started again. "Look, Keller, Gavin is planning to make some changes in the coming weeks and I just wanted to give you a head's up." Ben couldn't look her in the eye, staring at a spot off to the right of her earlobe. "I know how hard you've been working on your features, and the stories have been good…" He hesitated, leaving Madison with a sinking feeling in the pit of her stomach. She watched him rub his hands across his face again, waiting for him to finish a thought, which he did, all in a rush. "I don't want you to think his changes have anything to do with your writing."

Madison pushed her chair back so she could force her editor to look *at* her. "My writing? What… Why…I don't understand what you're trying to say, Ben." The last came out as more of a question than a statement, and she was horrified to realize she was close to tears. She quickly pulled herself together. "Okay, what are you trying so hard not to tell me, Ben? Am I getting kicked off the features team already?" Although a part of her thought she was saying it jokingly, she braced herself for the answer.

Ben shuffled the papers in his hand, anxious to get away, and not providing the kind of reassurance she hoped for. "He's our acting chief, so whatever he says, goes. I don't know the specifics, but he's throwing some ideas around that could impact your…" He didn't finish, the look on his face showing how much he hated being the bearer of bad news. "He said he'd be announcing the changes in the coming days." He shrugged apologetically. "That's all I know right now, so I'll let you get back to work. It might be nothing, Madison." With a tap on the edge of her desk with his fingertips, and a look that seemed to say he wanted to share more, Ben continued down the hall as quickly as his legs could carry him.

Her heart sinking into her stomach, Madison stared at the monitor, no longer sure how to proceed as she replayed the words Ben had spoken. This probably was no big deal, but the initial surprise rapidly turned to dejection that weighed heavily. Did

Gavin Maves think her writing was subpar? As much as she didn't want to admit it, that had been her worst fear when she was given the promotion, but then she started to believe in herself, casting away those doubts. How foolish of her. Here they were, now, back in full force and ready to crush her.

She wasn't sure how long she sat, but as the initial numbness wore off, she became aware of a couple other coworkers coming in and the hum of activity around her. How could she focus on any tasks in front of her?

Unable to sit still, Madison took a deep breath and pushed away from her desk, suddenly sure what she needed to do. She would talk to her boss in person. He would have to look her in the face and talk about whatever the changes he mentioned were and how they would impact her. If he had issues with her, she wanted to face them, figure out a way to move forward. It was better than sitting here thinking the worst. He was a newcomer here...no, he was a mere visitor here in Fairview, dropping in and dropping little bombs on the staff. Who did he think he was?

Unfortunately, he was already gone, his office dark and empty, and Madison was immediately deflated. What had she been thinking? Confronting him would have been a disaster, and she was grateful Gavin was no longer in the office. She went back to her desk, weighing her options.

The longer she sat and thought about it, the more convinced she was that she would soon be demoted back to the news desk. If she didn't get a story assignment from Ben tomorrow, then she would have her answer. Madison continued to sit at her desk, doing absolutely nothing. Something about Gavin Maves had been off-putting from the start and now she had even more reason to believe he was a bigger jerk than she had first believed.

Trista's voice carried toward her and she frantically started packing her laptop into the bag, not in the mood to socialize with her friend today, but not having enough time to avoid her. "Hey, Mad-dog Keller, I'm glad I caught you. We need to start planning

Adele's baby shower." She stopped short when she caught sight of Madison's face. "Are you okay?"

"Yep. You're right. We do have to start planning, so I'll touch base with you soon. I have to go take some pictures right now," she fibbed, grabbing her camera bag from beside her chair and rising.

"If you need to talk..."

Madison simply waved to Trista over her shoulder. "I'm fine."

The newspaper office had been her home away from home and her coworkers a second family, but at the moment, it no longer felt that way. She had been totally committed to them—her newspaper family—but maybe she would focus on her own family for a while. Her grandma needed her. With a bit of defiance, she pushed open the door and without so much as a glance backwards, walked out into the sunny June day.

Chapter Fourteen

OUT OF PURE HABIT, SHE FOUND HERSELF WHISPERING across the desk, the hush of the library bringing back memories of being scolded as she, Becca, and Natalie sat with heads close together, laughing at everything and nothing.

"I'd like to use the archive room, please," she said quietly, clearing her throat and trying again when the elderly Myrtle Blossom turned her ear toward Madison, indicating she hadn't heard her and then gesturing impatiently for her to speak up. She repeated the request a third time, reverting to a child in this woman's presence.

Mrs. Blossom had been the middle school librarian when Madison was a student there, and she'd seemed ancient then. Now her lined and wrinkled face resembled a jack-o-lantern that had sat out on too many warm fall days, the shrinking mouth, nose, and eyes collapsing toward the center.

"You know the rules." And even though she nodded, Mrs. Blossom repeated every single one of them, loudly and clearly, causing Madison's face to grow warm as the sprinkling of patrons tried to hide their grins. "Make sure your hands are clean. You should use the washroom before you go in. Nothing leaves that room. Sign the book, signifying you agree to the rules of the archive room. Do not reshelve anything on your own. Put items in the baskets on the table or by the door." She paused to breathe finally, eyes big and round in her shrunken face. "Questions?"

"No ma'am, I understand," Madison responded respectfully, feeling like a 12-year-old all over again, almost able to hear Becca and Natalie giggling behind her. Mrs. Blossom took her job seriously. Madison wouldn't begrudge her that, though, because she totally understood. She loved the archive room herself, so she made a beeline for the bathroom to wash her hands before entering the over-stuffed room tucked behind the reference stacks.

The door squeaked as she entered, and as always, the mustiness enveloped her. She thought of it as stepping through a portal to a different time and the smell was the fragrance of memories, old stories, lore, and legend, and most of all, the history of Laurel Lake and Fairview.

Instead of a straight line to the yearbooks, once she'd signed her name in the book, Madison meandered through the stacks, reaching out to gently touch old volumes. Mrs. Blossom was probably right to make visitors to the room wash their hands, she thought, grinning, imagining the trail she was leaving as she carefully touched each book.

A part of her had always been awed by history. The lives lived, good and bad, were documented for all to see, if they just took the time to look. The subjects were mostly long gone, but everything written about them would live on forever. History was not meant to be rewritten—but it could certainly be interpreted.

Madison could never change what she had done—that moment in time when her moral compass lost its true north—but she had done everything possible to atone since then, and maybe there would be a different way to interpret her history. Her chest tightened and she forced herself to put those thoughts aside and focus on the reason she was there.

The yearbooks stood neatly arranged like marching soldiers on the shelf. Madison ran her fingers over the bindings, looking for 1967. She had carefully worked through the math and knew this would be the year Liz was a freshman, so she would begin tracking from that year any Chuck or Gordon who might be in her class—or the classes after her.

Aware that Mrs. Blossom would be watching the room closely, she pulled only one book from the shelf to take to the table, determined to follow every rule so she wouldn't be banned from the room for life. The thought made her smile, but deep down she had an unreasonable fear Mrs. Blossom could make that happen.

Madison carefully arranged her notepad and pen, took a deep breath, and opened the book to take a fascinating journey back in time. The black and white class photos were all very similar. The girls tilted their faces just so, hair piled on top of their heads in an updo or cascading down their shoulders, pearls or crosses hanging around their necks and resting on their sweater sets or turtleneck fronts. Most of the boys sported crew cuts. A few had a slicked back style, reminding her of the way Gavin Maves wore his. (She shuddered, pushing him away just as quickly as the thought of him had arrived). The glasses were heavy frames, obscuring some of the thinner faces. Some smiled; some were serious.

The picture of Elizabeth Eriksson among the other freshmen class members was nondescript. She looked like so many of the other girls in her class, Madison was thankful the pictures were labeled with names. She skipped ahead to the activity photos, not even trying to pick Liz out in pictures, but relying instead on the small print captions listing each name.

When she finally finished with the first yearbook, she had found Liz was in Drama Club, Future Homemakers of America, Student Governance, and Pep Club. Madison stared at the list of activities jotted in her notes, trying to reconcile those with the Liz she knew. Pep Club? Future Homemakers? She couldn't decide which seemed more out of character for the woman she had recently interviewed or the one she remembered seeing around town over the years.

There were four boys named some variation of Charles in her

class—Charles Albright, Charlie McMahon, Chuckie Warden, and Chuck Wilson. She had no idea which of them, if any, might be the Chuck her grandma talked about. Her class didn't have a Gordon. She found one who would be a year older, Gordon Thomas, a fine featured, high cheek-boned boy whose face was almost hidden behind thick, dark-framed glasses. For some reason she saw him as more college-bound than military-bound. Searching the first yearbook left her needing more information. Madison carefully set the book in the nearby basket and returned to the shelf for the next one, excited to continue.

In the next yearbook, Madison found much the same, but during the 1968-69 school year, Liz was now involved in something called the International Relations Club and was on the field hockey team. Her class picture hadn't changed very much, and she wore the same hairstyle in the photo as she'd had the year prior —long hair swept up on her head with bobby pins holding it in place. Again, she barely smiled, but her eyes were bright and lively, as she looked shyly at the camera.

Mrs. Blossom was peering at her from her perch behind the circulation desk when she stood to add the book to the basket, and she fought the temptation to wave at her.

The 1969 yearbook took a noticeable turn, and Madison gasped. Liz was no longer a girl smiling shyly into a camera, but a young woman who was nothing short of beautiful very much aware of the impact she had. This time, Madison was able to pick her out of candid shots included in various sections, without the need for captions. Elizabeth Eriksson had turned into a stunner, she realized. Her hair was chic and stylish, pinned back with a barrette on top of her head with long waves cascading down her shoulders and back, a look straight out of a fashion magazine of the time. Her face radiated confidence and it was evident she was enjoying life in these captured moments.

In one candid toward the back of the yearbook, Liz was smiling broadly at the camera, surrounded by classmates. Madison couldn't remember a time that she saw a smile even close to that on the owner of the Cottages. The Liz in this yearbook was confident, carefree, and happy. Definitely happy.

She set the book in the basket before pulling the 1970 yearbook from the shelf. Excited to see what changes she might encounter in *this* version of the woman she knew, she settled herself back in the chair and pulled her notebook closer. Madison started with the senior pictures, and then, in confusion, paged back through again. She checked the cover to make sure she had the correct year. Turning to the activities section, she searched diligently, looking in every club, organization, and society she'd seen Liz in previously, but it was all to no avail. There was no Elizabeth Eriksson in the 1970 yearbook.

Gobsmacked. Madison couldn't think of another word to better fit her feelings. What happened to Liz? She considered that question on the drive to see her grandmother, wishing she could ask her. Attempting to keep some memories intact, as Greg had recommended to them, she had put together a little gift for her grandmother. Hopefully it would help.

Ruth wouldn't be joining them for the surprise party but Patrick and Mya planned to pick her up Friday evening for a family BBQ, and an opportunity for Ruth to celebrate Brent and Nina's anniversary. As much as they wanted her at the restaurant event, they knew it would be too overwhelming.

To her great relief, Madison noticed the flicker of life in her grandmother's eyes, a telltale sign that part of her old self was still there. She held tightly to that hope as she handed her grandmother a photo album, its cover a country landscape with a lake. Ruth took the book, holding it in her lap. She ran her hand across the top as though trying to draw something from the cover into her being. "It's beautiful, honey. Thank you."

"You need to look inside." Reaching over, Madison flipped the cover, revealing a picture of Grandpa Poppy on the first page.

"Oh," she responded, bringing the book closer to her face to get a better look. "Oh."

"He loved the diner, didn't he, grandma?" The black and white photo depicted her grandfather smiling proudly, holding a spatula in one hand while his other arm was thrown around his wife's shoulders. Her shy smile was partially hidden as her face was turned upward, looking at her husband with obvious pride.

"Oh my, he did." Ruth rubbed her hand over the photo, just as she'd done with the cover. "He loved standing at that grill. But he loved talking to customers more. The regulars wanted him to sit and talk so I had to shoo him back to work all day long. That crazy fool apparently thought the food would grill itself." She smiled, remembering, and Madison was thrilled to find her grandmother in good spirits and able to find joy in the memories the pictures evoked.

Encouraged by her grandmother's response, she prodded her, anxious to have her remember more. "Go ahead and look at the next picture, grandma." After a pause, Madison gently repeated, "Turn the page. I put more pictures in there I think you'll like."

The prodding did nothing as Ruth continued to stare at the picture of the diner's interior. "That's where Liz sat. Was she there today?" She touched the picture, her finger moving slowly over the stool at the counter in the background of the photo, and Madison could sense her grandmother was slipping away once again. "Oh, those boys pestered that girl. She was a pretty little thing, that Liz."

Madison knew that part to be true, even if her grandma's memory was clouded about other things. She had seen the photo evidence. She let her hand rest on her grandma's shoulder. "Liz is busy running her cottage business these days so she doesn't have time to eat out, I guess. Maybe Patrick has seen her there. You can ask him the next time you see him." She reached down again to turn the page, but her grandmother's mind had drifted away, focused on something that happened long ago, which could be real or imagined.

"Chuck couldn't find her either, but I didn't tell him a thing about..." She shook her head so hard, Madison feared she might hurt herself, then stopped as suddenly as she started. "Such a delicate matter." She raised questioning eyes. "Where is Chuck? Why haven't I seen him? Did your grandfather tell him to stay away?"

Once again, Madison didn't know what to say. It was wrong to let her go on about people and events from decades past, no matter how much she wanted to know the secret bothering her grandmother. Madison looked at her grandma, shaken and upset before her, and she wanted desperately to reach inside and pull the woman she knew out, the loving grandma who'd been there whenever she needed someone. But that person was slipping further and further away.

Madison's desire to learn more was strong, but the need to help her grandma find some peace was far greater. She made up her mind.

"Grandma, I'll try to find out what happened to Chuck." She held her grandmother's hand tightly in her own. "I'll find out for you."

It was the only thing she could think of to calm her grandma, but once it was out of her mouth, she started to believe she really should do just that. There had to be someone besides Liz in Fairview who remembered him. She was a journalist. She knew how to research a story. This was no different. Resolved that she could figure out what happened to the young man her grandmother was concerned about, she again offered reassurances.

"I'll find Chuck," she repeated, patting her grandmother's frail hand. Whatever well-kept secret her grandmother held onto was trying to come out. If it would make her feel better, Madison was willing to help her dig back in her memory to find it. She would do anything for her Grandma Ruth.

"He's probably at the golf course. That boy is always at the golf course." She shook her head, a smile crossing her face as she looked directly at Madison. "We can ask Poppy when he gets home from work."

Chapter Fifteen

A STRING OF LIGHTS OVERHEAD BOUNCED IN THE breeze on the patio of the Dockside Bar and Grill. Music poured from the speakers tucked under the wooden trusses of the gazebo. Madison set the cake on the table off to the side, and then stood at the rail to enjoy the view from the restaurant's newly built patio. She could almost smell the faint scent of sawdust in the air as she ran her hand along the beautifully crafted woodwork and again wondered if the shiny new objects were worth the loss of Fairview's past treasures. Treasures was perhaps a stretch in describing the old burger hangout, but it still held a special place in her heart.

The sun was still high above the water, a glowing yellow ball that would disappear over the horizon just after 8:30. It was warm now, but Madison knew she would be grateful for the sweater she'd grabbed on the way out the door. She stood for a moment watching a speed boat in the distance and two fishing boats closer to shore. The lakeshore was well into its busy season, with local businesses reaping the benefits.

Natalie's voice from the doorway interrupted her thoughts. "I have to stop at the bathroom and then I'll get the balloons out of the car."

"Oh my gosh, Nat, you just went before we left home. You must have a pea-sized bladder."

"P-e-e-sized, to be exact. Huh! I crack myself up." She disappeared back through the sliding door into the restaurant.

Madison continued staring out at the sparkling water, enjoying the moment of quiet. She was grateful for the reprieve tonight provided from the jumbled chaos swirling in her head. Since her grandma couldn't provide clarification on the many questions Madison had, she had moved on to investigating Magenta Enterprises, the company name she'd seen on the business card between the two men at the counter. Now she needed a break from what appeared to be bad news for the golf course, and tonight's party would provide that.

Her thoughts were interrupted as a server stepped out on the patio, and Madison looked up to see a young woman smiling warmly. "I'm so happy to see you. It's been forever."

It took a surprised Madison a second to recognize her and then she drew her into a hug. "It's good to see you, too, Gabbie. I thought you moved." Gabbie waitressed at the diner while she was in high school. After graduation, she married her high school sweetheart, a Marine stationed in North Carolina.

"Chip was scheduled to ship out so we thought it might be best if I moved back here to live with mom and dad again until his tour ends. It could be a whole year he's over there and I needed help with the kids."

"Kids?" Madison tried to wrap her head around the kid she used to know being a wife and mom. "Oh man, that's got to be hard on both of you. How many do you have?"

Gabbie raised her hand, two fingers extended like a peace sign. "But some days it feels like double that. They're only 14 months apart so it can be a lot."

And now you're working here. Do you like it?"

"It's *almost* as much fun as working the ice cream window," she responded with a laugh. "Remember when this used to be just a burger place? This remodel job is unbelievable, and we're crazy busy all the time. *This* is the best part of the whole restaurant." She looked around the patio with pride, as though she'd had a hand in designing it. "Anyway, I'm taking care of your party tonight. I'll bring the food out at about 6:30 and set it up here." She indicated a table already covered with a cloth and warming trays. "I see you have a cake. I'll bring a knife and dessert plates. We have the two tripods for your photo displays you requested so you should be set, but if you think of anything else, just give me a holler."

"Is there someone who could help us hang a few decorations?"

"I'll send one of the busboys out in a few minutes." Madison watched her leave, trying to do the math. Gabbie had to be about 24 now, and here she was, married with two kids. Madison couldn't define how she was feeling about that. With no prospects of her own, she would be lucky to start a family by the time she turned 50.

Natalie stuck her head through the door to let her know she was ready to help unload the car. As Madison followed her outside, she said, "I don't know if you remember her, but Gabbie Wendell is working our party. Can you believe she has two kids already? I think she graduated four or five years after us. We are so far behind, Nat. Well, I am, anyway. At least you're married."

Natalie started to respond, pursed her lips as though deep in thought, then snickered. "Is that an open invitation for me to find you a man?"

"That's a hard pass, thanks." She hesitated as they reached the car, and then decided to share. "I did meet someone interesting, though."

Natalie's face lit up, but before she could add anything else, Patrick pulled up next to them.

"We're not done with this conversation," Natalie warned her as Patrick and Mya joined them and together, they pulled decorations from the back of the Jeep and hauled their armloads inside.

Brent and Nina's 35th wedding anniversary celebration called for balloons, banners, and cardboard displays of pictures now resting on the tripods. They'd stayed up late the night before pulling it all together, laughing over old family pictures and even crying over some. And somehow, they'd managed to get everything done. A busboy helped them hang the long Happy Anniversary banner now draped above the food table and bunches of balloons were tied to weights and bobbing in the light breeze.

"How pretty!" Tony and Penny, good friends of her parents, joined her on the patio at that moment, Penny wrapping her in an embrace and then setting the small gift box, beautifully wrapped in lavender paper with a matching bow, next to the cake. "You get the prize for best daughter, hands down."

Tony reached around to draw her into a one-armed hug. "I don't know how you do it, kiddo. When you aren't waiting on tables at Poppy's, you're doing a stint as party planner. When do you find time to write those great stories for the paper?"

She blushed, pleased with the compliment. At least somebody appreciated her work, she thought, wanting to shove that in Gavin's face. Just as quickly, she wondered how Tony knew she had filled in at the diner. Of course, Patrick was aware and greatly appreciative, but Tony had heard from someone other than a family member. Small-town gossip was quick to make the rounds.

"I hope that doesn't make me a Jack-of-all-trades and master of none," she responded with a grimace, before grinning at them. Her parents and grandparents had stressed the value of hard work, and both she and Patrick did their best to meet that expectation. But she could also admit to herself she was driven to work extra hard to make amends for her past transgressions, as if her actions now could wipe away her wrong doings. It was too somber a thought on a celebratory night, so she did what she did well—push the thoughts away until another time. Even though she was anxious to continue researching the past for her grandma's benefit and doing a deep dive into Magenta Enterprises, she compartmentalized them away until later.

She greeted new arrivals, handing out noisemakers to the guests. "Let 'er rip as soon as you see them at the patio door."

"Is there anything else I can do to help?" Natalie surveyed the room, taking in the centerpieces and the cake. "Everything looks so pretty." She smiled, but Madison could see an underlying sadness so she reached out to squeeze Nat's arm. There would never be a celebration like this for her parents, and Madison felt that pain in her friend.

"I think we are all set," Madison assured her. "Patrick and Mya are waiting in the lobby." Her parents believed they were meeting the kids for a quiet dinner. "I hope they like the surprise."

Within the next ten minutes, more of her parents' friends were gathered on the patio and it was almost time for Brent and Nina to arrive. Someone was exclaiming over the pictures on display while another guest commented on how young the couple looked on their wedding day. All of it made Madison smile. Natalie's idea to create a loop of photos on her laptop that would run all evening long had been a good one. There was a lot that could be captured in 35 years, and they'd done their best to make that happen. Set to some of Brent and Nina's favorite music, it would play throughout the evening.

With a final nod of approval, she clapped her hands to get everyone's attention. "I think we're ready. Let's get in place. I hope someone gets a good picture of their faces." With a warmth that spread throughout her being, she wondered if they would be displaying that picture on their 50th wedding anniversary.

The sun bled an orangish red hue over the horizon before dropping like a giant glowing ball below the surface of the lake, leaving behind a tangerine radiance that continued to spread up and out into the darkening sky. The string of lights turned on at dusk and added a soft glow on their faces. Next to her, Patrick stood with his arms around Mya's waist as they leaned into each other, enjoying the last of the sky's spectacular show before dark settled completely.

Mya sighed and Madison turned to her, surprised to see a tear slipping down her cheek. Alarmed, she whispered, "Are you okay?"

"Don't mind me. These are happy tears. You gave them the most wonderful night—and it made me miss my parents." She tilted her head back so she could see her husband's face. "I honestly couldn't be more blessed being part of this family. I'll stop crying now. Promise."

Guests had said their goodbyes, leaving just the three of them remaining on the patio. As predicted, the warm breeze of earlier was turning chilly as the sky darkened around the last streaks of sunset glow. Madison slipped her sweater on, looking around for Natalie, who was probably in the bathroom again. Maybe she needed to see a doctor about that.

Gabbie walked through, gathering empty glasses to stack on her tray. "I hope everyone enjoyed the party."

Patrick shook his head. "We didn't, Gabbie." Seeing the alarm begin on his former employee's face, Patrick laughed as Mya slapped his arm. "I'm just kidding," he said, arms up in surrender. "I'd say they had the most amazing party imaginable. Thank you."

Natalie returned, retrieved her laptop from the table and came to stand at the railing with the others. "Your parents are *still* saying goodbye to some people in the parking lot. I swear, that's been going on for an hour at least."

"We should get going, too, so the babysitter doesn't think we got lost," Patrick said, hugging his sister. "I think we pulled it off, sis."

Madison nodded in agreement. "They were definitely surprised."

Natalie and Madison watched them go, then Natalie turned to her friend. "I know you're dying to spill whatever those beans are you're holding inside."

"I don't know what you're talking about." Feigning confusion, Madison shrugged her shoulders.

"Very funny. Let's start with, 'I met a guy,' and go from there. I'm all ears."

"I'd love to have this conversation right now, but I have to settle the bill inside."

Natalie would be a dog with a bone over this, and Madison already regretted giving her something to chew on in the first place. They moved from the patio to the bar, waiting for Gabbie to bring the bill. "This isn't difficult, I met a guy today …"

A man further down the bar let out a loud laugh as his companion told a story, their voices booming louder as the story progressed.

Madison turned her attention to Natalie. "Okay. I met a guy who might know what's going on with the golf course sale."

Disappointment replaced anticipation on Natalie's face. "Oh, the golf course. I thought you were going to say…you know… maybe you'd met someone who could be like a potential relationship kind of thing. So, all of this is just about the course maybe going up for sale?"

Nodding vigorously, excited to get that ball rolling again now that the party was behind them, Madison held onto what she was about to say as a bartender strode toward them. "I'm just waiting to settle up for the Keller party on the patio." He nodded and walked away, and Madison turned her attention back to Natalie. "I'm serious, Nat. I've been researching the company and they buy up all sorts of nice property…like waterfront property. This guy might be with that Magenta company and I think they want to buy it so they can build condos on it."

Natalie stared at her, but Madison didn't give her an opportunity to say anything, pausing just briefly enough to take another breath.

"But I was thinking about it, and I'm pretty sure they need to get the city council to agree to that change. I think. I still have a lot of checking to do. But if they *do* need some kind of approval, well, I doubt the council would go along with that kind of plan so that means the sale won't go through—especially if the community starts putting pressure on the council. And at the very least, we would buy time to figure out another plan." She was almost giddy in her confidence that the golf course would be spared from the Magenta buyers.

Natalie studied her friend for a long moment, her eyes seeming to search for something in Madison's. Sighing, she finally said, "I'm worried about you, Madison. You're so busy taking care of everything and everybody else, that you ignore the fact you need to take care of yourself. I mean, you need to think about what you want for..."

She didn't have a chance to finish her sentence, because the loud voice of one of the men at the bar carried to them. "I swear he has that old-timer's disease. You know, where you forget everything." Furious, Madison again looked in their direction, seemingly ready to charge over and confront them. Natalie placed her hand on Madison's arm.

"Let it go. They're probably drunk."

Gabbie appeared at that moment, handing the bill to Madison, and taking her credit card. As Gabbie stepped away to run the card, the bartender returned. "That guy at the end of the bar, the one in the blue polo shirt?" He waited for Madison to see the man for herself. "He wants to buy you two a drink."

At once, Madison's face reddened as she recognized him as the golf cart passenger whose ball had nearly hit her—and the same guy who had sneered at the mess on the diner floor after Kayla's mishap. He was beginning to infuriate her.

"That's the jerk that almost killed me," she sputtered to Natalie and then to the bartender said, "Tell him I'm not interested. No. Forget it. I'll tell him."

"Maddy, wait." Before Natalie could stop her friend, she'd stepped around her and was practically marching over to the blue polo shirt clad man, her eyes laser beams of anger.

"I don't know who you think you are, but you've been kind

of a pain in my butt since the first time I saw you." Her voice was becoming high pitched, something that happened when she was upset, but she couldn't control it, not sure if she was more furious about him almost killing her, the crass joking about Alzheimer's, or the fact that either he, or perhaps Sean, was working for Magenta Enterprises.

He held his hands up as if to stop the force of her anger, a smile only serving to enrage her more. "Whoa, lady. I just wanted to buy you a drink. I think my buddy nearly beaned you with a ball at the golf course so I was trying to apologize."

If his words were meant to soothe her ire, he had failed miserably.

"I don't want your drink and I don't want your apology." She leaned in closer to him, attempting to lower her voice, but only drawing more attention to herself. "What I'd really like is for you to leave Fairview and take your stupid ideas about buying any property in this town with you."

In her attempt to storm back to Natalie's side, she caught her foot on the barstool, sending her awkwardly stumbling to maintain her balance. Natalie was staring, mouth agape. Around them, the handful of bar patrons were expressing various levels of amusement and concern over the show they had witnessed. Madison quickly signed the credit card slip.

"Let's get out of here," Madison hissed at her friend, her heart racing as she attempted unsuccessfully to regain some composure, and fully aware her anger was perhaps misdirected. She thought about the business card resting on the counter at the diner, situated directly between Sean and the guy who was now trying to buy her a drink. Based on the scant information she'd uncovered thus far, the company was not in Fairview to do anyone any favors. She wasn't sure who set the business card down and who picked it up, but one thing was crystal clear: One of the two men worked for Magenta Enterprises.

As they hurried toward the door, Madison was certain she could hear the man's laughter. His glee burned a hole through the tough armor she'd pretended to don as she chewed him out, leaving her exposed and vulnerable. How could the Thorsens even think of selling the course?

Her heart raced, making her pulse roar so loudly in her ears she had no idea Natalie was calling her name until she felt her arm being grabbed, swinging her around so they were face to face. Almost immediately, the fury subsided, leaving Madison shaking. Tears threatened to spill from her eyes.

"What was *that* all about?" Natalie still gripped her arms, but slowly dropped her hands to her side, waiting for Madison to compose herself enough to speak.

"That jerk has something to do with... He's going to change everything. There isn't going to be anything left that was a part of..."

"Take a breath, Mads. First, I agree the guy is a total jerk. You're right about that. But if he does work for that company, then he's just doing his job. *This* isn't personal to him." She gestured broadly, including the entire Laurel Lake community in her reference.

Madison shook her head, and this time tears trickled down her cheek and under her chin. Using the back of her hand, she wiped them away. "But it *is* personal. *All* of it is personal." She looked away, biting her lip, trying to figure out how to express what she was feeling. "I need to keep something the same," she whispered. "I need to keep something we all had here somehow. There's not going to be anything left that was all of us together." She was frustrated, not able to express to her friend exactly what she was feeling.

Loud laughter spilled from the restaurant as the door opened and someone stepped out into the cool night. There was the click of a lighter and brief flare of a cigarette being lit.

"Let's go home. We can't talk about this here. Give me the keys. I'll drive."

Defeated, she handed the keys to her friend.

As they drove home in silence, Madison was beating herself

up. The beautiful evening she worked hard to create for her parents had ended with the ugly encounter. The man seemed to appear out of nowhere with every turn she made, taunting her desire to have the golf course remain intact.

What if her efforts to hold onto the past were for nothing? She felt it slipping between her fingers.

"You need to let go." Natalie's voice was firm.

Madison spoke softly as the darkness settled deeply around the quiet lakeshore, blanketing them in its cocoon. "If I let go, who's going to remember how wonderful it used to be?"

Natalie didn't respond. For the rest of the drive, Madison's sniffles were the only sound in the car.

Chapter Sixteen

THE NEXT MORNING, HER HEART RATE BACK TO NORMAL but the ache of something she could not quite define worse than ever, Madison faced her friend across the kitchen table. Although she knew Natalie wanted to talk when they returned from the party, Madison closed her bedroom door, ashamed of her behavior and unable to wade through the emotional quagmire she found herself in, even with the ever-supportive Natalie. This morning, however, she could no longer avoid it.

Madison lifted her coffee cup, looking beneath it, then moved the newspaper aside, in search of something.

"What are you looking for?" Natalie finally asked.

"My dignity. Did you happen to see it?"

Natalie laughed, shaking her head at the joke, and not hiding the relief that everything seemed back to normal this morning. "Cute, Mads."

"I'm sorry I let my emotions get the best of me. Stupid me. I was relieved my family was long gone before my... my outburst, but who am I kidding? Someone will be more than happy to tell them." News travelled fast in Fairview. Someone always seemed to be watching.

"Oh, Mads. You don't have to apologize to me." Her eyes

held sympathy, and something else Madison couldn't quite decipher. "And who cares what anyone else says. You were standing up for something you believe in. Not everyone is able to do that."

"I made an idiot of myself, and yes, I do have to apologize. And now I'm making coffee."

Natalie twisted a napkin around her finger, a partially eaten piece of toast on a plate before her and an untouched glass of orange juice next to it. "Wait. Please..." She gestured for Madison to sit back down. "This isn't exactly the timing I hoped for, but I've wanted to tell you something ever since I got here." She set the napkin down and slid the toast away. "I'm going to tell you what it is, but I don't want you to...I don't know...freak out. You know I love you, and these few days with you have been exactly what we both needed, but I came here for another reason. There's something I have to tell you in person."

Madison lowered herself onto the chair, fear twisting her stomach in knots. This sounded so serious, so ominous, and her breath caught in her lungs. Was something wrong with Natalie? She had no idea how to brace herself for whatever it was Natalie was about to say.

"Byron is happy in Iowa, but it isn't exactly what he thought he'd be doing, so I encouraged him to apply for other positions. Some of them were just dream jobs that he never expected to be seriously considered for, but he decided to try anyway. You know Byron. I would give anything for just an ounce of his self-confidence." She stopped, once again picking up the now shredded napkin and then setting it down again before picking up her orange juice to take a long drink as Madison's concern turned to confusion. Finally, the words tumbled out rapidly as if she had suddenly found the courage to begin. "He told me last night he... he had a second interview and he was offered a position. It was the last one out of all the applications he submitted he ever thought he would get awarded, but he did it." Her face beaming with pride in her husband, she said, "Byron was offered a two-year post-graduate fellowship to teach at the University of Iceland in Reykjavik."

Madison's face lit up and she took Natalie's hand, relief finally allowing her to breathe again. "That is wonderful news! So, you need a place to stay for the next two years. I know you'll miss him like crazy, but you are definitely welcome to stay here."

Confusion swept across Natalie's face momentarily and then she groaned. "Madison, that's not what I'm trying to tell you. I'm not staying here. Byron won't be going alone. I will be moving to Iceland with him."

The news was a gut punch. She couldn't speak, her face on fire, embarrassed over her misunderstanding. Madison opened her mouth and then closed it again.

"Please say something, Mads. Please."

Madison busied herself wiping imaginary crumbs off the table. Finally, she looked at Natalie. "I thought maybe you were ready to come back home."

"This isn't my home, and it hasn't been since I was a kid. We are all grown up now and I need you to hear this." When Madison didn't respond, Natalie pleaded, reaching across to touch her friend's hand. "Please don't be upset."

After a beat, Madison looked at her friend. She was losing someone again, and she wasn't sure how to handle yet another gaping wound. Her voice was strained when she finally answered, "You could have told me that over the phone. You didn't have to come all the way here to tell me you are moving again."

Natalie leaned back in her chair, looking around the kitchen as though trying to find help with what she was about to say.

"Madison, that wasn't even the part I wanted to tell you in person. You are my best friend and I wanted to say this face-to-face." She laughed. "I thought you might even guess it on your own. We're having a baby. I'm pregnant." Her eyes pleaded with her friend to be happy about the exciting news.

Something had happened to the air in the room. Madison tried to take a breath, but her lungs seemed to have forgotten how to operate. Pushing back from the table, she tried again to draw in a deep breath. To her astonishment, a single sob escaped her.

The sense of betrayal overpowered everything else. Natalie belonged with Byron. She was never coming back to Fairview to live. Nothing could ever be the same. There would never be a world in which Natalie, Becca, and Carl were with her again.

She needed to get out of the house, away from Natalie, and as far from the sense of loss that was crushing her, leaving her unable to breathe. Without another word, she strode to the door and walked out.

It wasn't until she heard the door close behind her that she realized she'd run out of the house without her Jeep keys, and she wasn't going back in to get them, so she took her bike from the spot she'd left it, leaned up against the garage.

The need to put distance between herself and Natalie was overwhelming. She saw her at the door, still in her pajamas, hair tousled, looking like she had just lost her best friend. Madison didn't care. Natalie's words had bitten into her flesh, leaving her raw and bleeding.

Pedaling hard, she rode without giving thought to where she might end up, and not caring. Abandoned. Deserted. Left alone once again. Those words tumbled through her head with each spin of her feet on the pedals.

The last time she was deserted by her friend, it had been perfectly understandable. Natalie had to deal with her dad's...situation. She did it by pulling away from her friends and disappearing within herself. That was perfectly understandable. *This* she was doing by choice.

A baby? Natalie was leaving her behind in so many ways. When she could no longer breathe, sobs catching in her throat, she steered down a familiar dirt path. At the maintenance shed of the golf course, Madison stopped and got off her bike, walking off the path to lean the bike against a tree. She continued by foot to her favorite place on the golf course, the familiar knoll. She would be the only one left to remember, and soon, this place might be gone, too.

According to her mom, a good cry now and then was good for the soul. If that were the case, her soul was in great shape by the time she raised her head, drained of emotion for the first time in a while. There was no more anger, no more self-pity, and no more sadness. There was simply a cold, hard truth.

Natalie was leaving again. This wasn't her home, any more than it was Becca or Carl's. Nothing would ever be the same again, just as Fairview could never be the same for her anymore.

Her entire body felt tired as she picked her bike off the ground and started the ride home. She hadn't made it more than a few hundred yards down the path when her foot slipped off the pedal and she knew immediately what happened. The chain had broken.

Madison climbed off, put the kick stand down, and stared at the bike, as though willing it to fix itself. After what seemed like forever, she rolled her eyes, sat down next to it to examine it, and wondered if anything else could go wrong today. Sighing, she knew it was no use. There was no way she would be able to fix it so it would be a long walk home.

It was a good thing she had taken the morning off work, but now it looked like she might not even get to the paper by noon. She trudged along, pushing the resistant bike, wishing she had thought to grab her cell phone on her mad rush out of the house. She made a mental note to herself to do that should she ever again be tempted to make a dramatic exit from someplace.

Finally reaching the end of the dirt road, she started walking along the shoulder of Lake Shore Drive, not sure if she hoped for traffic or not. Someone stopping to help might not be a bad idea, but she knew what a mess she must look. No sooner had she thought it, when she heard a vehicle behind her, tires crunching on the gravel of the road's shoulder as it rolled to a stop next to her.

"Hey! Do you want a ride?"

The last person she expected to see was Liz Erikson in her pickup truck, a baseball cap pulled low over her forehead.

"That would be great. Thank you!"

Liz climbed out to pull the tailgate down and help hoist the bike into the truck's bed. "Your chain is broken." She said it matter-of-factly, as if it was news to Madison. "Where to? Dropping you at a bike repair shop or home?"

"I need to get home." She gave her the address, but Liz simply laughed.

"I know where you live. It's your grandparents' house. I used to babysit your dad there. Your grandma was always real sweet to me." She stopped, having said more than she intended. "I'm really sorry about her...I'll drop you at home." She reached down to turn on the radio, increasing the volume as though the county crop report was the most important information she had ever heard.

Madison wanted desperately to ask her a million questions, but she could read a room—or in this case—the cab of a truck. Liz Erikson had said more than she wanted to and now she would not be saying anything else.

―――

Natalie's car wasn't in the driveway, Madison noticed with relief. She would have to face her friend sooner or later...but for now she was happy it would be later. Unless, of course, Natalie was so upset with her she decided to leave sooner than she had planned. Madison had a hard time believing Natalie would do that to her, though. She was the cool headed, restrained one—unlike Madison, apparently.

She went directly to the bathroom, attempting to wash away the evidence of tears from her face before adding some mascara and blush, brushing her hair, and then pulling a skirt and top from her closet, determined to make herself presentable for work.

Madison's phone was on the counter where she had left it. Three missed calls. She wanted to ignore them, knowing it would be Natalie wanting to talk through what happened, but Madison wasn't ready to do that yet. She was still too busy licking her own wounds.

But the calls were not from her friend. Two were from Patrick and one from her mom. She listened to the message left by her mom. *"We've been trying to reach you, honey. Grandma fell and we are with her at the ER. Everything is checking out okay but I wanted you to know. Call me when you get this."*

All the self-pity disappeared in an instant. She grabbed her keys and raced out the door, making her way to Fairview Community Hospital as fast as she dared to drive. She had been feeling sorry for herself while her grandma was in the hospital. Her heart was in her throat as she found a parking place and ran to the emergency entrance.

Only two people were in the waiting room, and one of them was Natalie. As soon as she saw Madison she rose from the chair, the magazine that had been opened on her lap falling to the floor. She picked it up and tossed it onto a nearby pile before wrapping Madison in a hug. "I don't want to fight with you." She pulled back, gesturing to the counter. "The nurse said she'll take you back to your grandma. Everything is going to be okay."

"Thank you," she whispered, having difficulty finding her voice, and then hurried to see the nurse at the station, her heart in her throat as she followed the middle-aged woman down a corridor to one of the small rooms, the curtain drawn. As she started to pull the curtain back a familiar sound reached her ears.

"Oh my, such a fuss. You didn't have to drag everyone here. This is silly."

Nina was standing at the side of the bed, shaking her head. "Ruth, we are all here because we love you and were worried about you." She turned toward Madison, reassuring her, "At least the x-rays look good. They want her to follow up with Dr. Klawitter tomorrow."

"Thank goodness. I might have to put you in bubble wrap, grandma."

Patrick was in the chair under the window. "I tried calling you a couple times on my way here. I even sent Mya over to the house, but Nat said you weren't home, and she wasn't sure where you'd gone."

"Sorry about that. I went for a bike ride and ended up with a broken chain. Of course, I didn't have my phone with me." She didn't tell them why she had taken off on the unplanned bike ride.

"It's nothing. I hurt my wrist." Grandma Ruth held up a bandaged arm for Madison to see. "I want to go home."

"It's just a sprain and she'll be fine. Luckily, she didn't hit her head."

Madison sat on the edge of the bed, taking the hand that wasn't bandaged in her own. "I'm glad you're okay, grandma. How did it happen?"

"I needed to find the letters. I told you about the letters. I thought the shoebox was on my bookshelf and then I fell over the hassock. That's all." She frowned. "I don't know what happened to that box. Let's go to the house and look in the attic. I was just up there a few days ago but I must have missed them."

Madison looked at her mother and brother, wondering how to respond to Ruth about these letters that may or may not exist. By the looks on their faces, Madison saw they were at as much of a loss as she was, Ruth's thought processing caught somewhere between the past and the present about a memory that may or may not even be real.

"I'll look for them."

Ruth patted Madison's hand and then looked at her daughter-in-law. "I'm ready to go home now."

Nina rolled her eyes in amusement. "It won't be long. The doctor will be here soon to release you."

Madison and Patrick stepped out into the hall to give their grandmother privacy when the nurse came in to check Ruth's vitals.

"I guess I'll have to look in the attic for the box she wants." She groaned. "I hate going in the attic."

"We took everything important out of there before you moved in. I don't think you should worry about something she really doesn't need and that might not even exist. By tonight, she won't remember she was looking for something."

Madison shot him a surprised look. "Even if she doesn't *need* it, I want to try to get it for her. Any time she remembers something from...well, from anytime in the past, I want her to talk about it. It keeps it alive for her."

Patrick shook his head. "I think that's nice, Mads, but you can see how quickly she's going downhill. I'm not sure that prolonging the inevitable will really help." He scrubbed his hands up and down against his face, and she saw exhaustion and sadness there, his comments not meant to minimize his love for Grandma Ruth, but a reaction to the same emotions they all were juggling.

Tears unexpectedly burned behind her eyes. "Let's just say it helps *me*, then."

He wrapped his arms around her, kissing the top of her head. "I'm sorry. I didn't handle that well. I don't know *how* to handle this. Sometimes she's Grandma Ruth and other times..."

"I know. It sucks." She wiped the tears away. "We should update Natalie."

They'd reached the waiting area and Madison, seeing the look of concern on Natalie's face, felt a stab of guilt for the horrible way she'd treated her friend. "She's fine. Sprained wrist." She held her own arm up to demonstrate the location of the injury.

"Thank goodness. I was so worried. I drove around looking for you but... then I came here to sit and wait."

"I appreciate that, Nat." She turned to her brother. "Is dad on his way?"

Patrick shook his head. "As soon as we found out it was a

sprain, mom told him she could handle it. He'll stop at the Center when he finishes with his last patient. Would you like to see her, Natalie?"

"If it's okay, I'd love to."

Madison followed them down the hall, still processing her feelings about Natalie's earlier announcement and the big changes coming to her life. Madison knew she somehow had to accept that they were no longer the inseparable group of kids who'd grown up together on Laurel Lake, but her heart and mind were having a tough time getting in sync over that matter.

Ruth looked up as they walked back in her room, and she smiled warmly at Natalie. "Oh honey. I haven't seen you since the funeral. Come here. Give me a hug. That was such a sad time for you."

Madison was overcome with emotion for both the devastating sadness of her friend's loss and the amazing acuity her grandmother showed in remembering that awful time for Natalie's family.

Natalie patted Ruth's shoulder, thanking her for the kind words as she used her fingers to brush away tears under her eyes. "Thank you, Mrs. Keller."

The old woman continued to stare into Natalie's eyes, speaking quietly, "Secrets are hard to keep, but I kept it."

Panic was the cold blast of a winter wind pushing Madison backwards. How had she not seen this before? The mixed-up timelines and partially remembered details of a secret her grandma was keeping probably had nothing at all to do with Liz. Perhaps Ruth was talking about the secret her own granddaughter was keeping.

Chapter Seventeen

"I wasn't expecting that," Natalie admitted as they stood in the hallway moments later. "I had no idea what to say." When Madison didn't respond, she asked, "Hey, are you okay?"

A deep furrow creased Madison's forehead. "I'm sorry. You can see now why I was hesitant to have you visit her. She slips in and out of...well...awareness, I guess is the best way to put it. That's not the woman we all knew." She tried to keep her voice calm, but inside, she was terrified. It wouldn't take much for everyone to know her secret. Maybe they could already see she was the one whose secret Grandma Ruth had fastidiously kept —until now.

"It's fine, Mads. She didn't mean any harm. That's the disease."

"It's just strange that at first, she seemed to know you and then she thought you were someone else. My guess is she thought you were Liz Erikson. She has been stuck on something to do with her for weeks now. Every time I visit, she talks about her." If she kept them focused on Liz, they wouldn't see the truth about a long-held secret that had everything to do with her.

"Liz? You really think she thought I was Liz? That's a strange connection to make. I mean, I don't look like her or have anything in common with her. I've said it before, and I'll say it again. Alzheimer's really sucks."

Madison wondered whose funeral her grandma was referencing. It could have been Natalie's dad's or it could even have been Jared's. Most of the town showed up for both. The possibility still existed it was the funeral of either Liz's mom or dad. There was no way to know, given her grandmother's scattered thought processing that took quantum leaps between decades with a nimbleness that kept them all guessing.

Madison did her best to hide the anxiety blooming within her. There had been letters, and it was her grandmother who encouraged her to write them.

Patrick came up behind them, putting an arm around Natalie's shoulder. "That went a little off the tracks. I'm not sure who she thought you were." His phone chimed and with a glance at the screen, he stepped away, adding, "I need to take this."

Natalie smiled wanly through the tears brimming her eyes.

"Oh Nat! I don't want you to cry over this. She didn't mean anything by it."

"It isn't what you think. For a second, I thought she remembered me, and everything I went through, but not in that judgmental way that everyone else does, and that felt good. Every now and then I guess I need a good cry. I never got..." Her attempts to smile fell short and she raised her hand, as though she could wave away the bad memories. "But all of that happened a long time ago. I'm fine. I'm not crying because she didn't recognize me. As soon as she mentioned the funeral, all those crazy feelings came crashing down on me again."

Her dad's suicide had shaken the entire town to the core and everything went downhill even further after that. Nobody blamed her mom for needing to get far away from Fairview, but it also meant Natalie would never have a home to return to here.

Taking a tissue from the box on a nearby table, Natalie dabbed at the moisture. "Focus your energy on Grandma Ruth.

Not me. In case you haven't noticed, I've been a little more emotional than usual, and now you know why."

The mention filled Madison with shame for failing her friend. What had she been thinking? She had handled everything terribly wrong. Everything. Of course Natalie would follow her husband, no matter where he decided to go. This would never be home for her. They were starting a family.

Madison's self-pity was replaced with shame. It was completely appropriate for all of them to leave her behind. Carl, Becca and Natalie... It was exactly what she deserved.

Madison lowered herself onto one of the chairs in the waiting room, blankly staring at the institutional gray carpet below her feet. This was all wrong. Her dreams of Natalie rediscovering how wonderful Fairview was and moving back one day had always been a stupid idea. In fact, there wasn't even the remotest possibility. For reasons Madison hadn't allowed herself to understand because she remained caught up in her own issues, Nat didn't even like being back. She had been naïve not to realize that.

"I am so sorry." Madison spoke quietly, still staring at nothing, overwhelmed by the depths of her selfishness. "You're only here because I've been begging you to come. You're here because I guilted you into it. Oh, my gosh, Nat. I'm a horrible friend."

Natalie took a seat next to her, reaching over to cover her friend's hand with her own. "I would do anything for you. Coming here was *my* choice. You didn't *make* me do anything. I love you, Madison. You always were and always will be my best friend." She shifted her hand, wrapping her pinkie around Nat's, and wiggling it the way they used to do when they were little.

"I don't deserve you."

"Stop it." Natalie playfully nudged Madison with her shoulder. "I had to come now. It would have been selfish of *me* to fly off to Iceland without saying goodbye in person." She took hold of Madison's hand, gripping it tightly in her own. "I needed this, even more than I realized. My dad was the selfish one. He took everything away from us—from my mom and me—and I always associated those horrible feelings with this town. I've been scared to come back because I knew being here would bring it all back, but it was time for me to face it and I needed to tell you everything in person. You deserved that." She laughed through her tears then. "You know you're going to have to visit me in Iceland."

Madison laughed along with her, knowing it was true, because she had visited her every time she and Byron moved, so why change now? She turned to look at her friend. "My crystal ball says I will be traveling to Iceland in the next couple years."

Patrick strode toward them, so intent on getting back to work he was oblivious to the emotional maelstrom that had engulfed them. "Let mom know I'm heading back to Poppy's. Tell her to call us if she needs anything."

They watched his tall figure move down the hallway, push through the revolving door, and then disappear into the parking lot beyond.

Natalie cleared her throat. "I know you've been through a lot of stuff, too, Mads, but you always had *this*." She waved her hand in the direction Patrick had just taken and then other way, indicating the room where Ruth and Nina were. "Your family has always been your solid foundation. I don't have that here. Nobody knew how to treat me after my dad decided to… It's still hard to say. After my dad killed himself." She drew in a deep shuddering breath. "I used to be so angry, thinking he was selfish and weak. We never suspected anything. How could he just…I don't know. I'm able to put it out of mind most of the time, but being back here, I have to face it."

"I never saw it through your eyes."

"You wave to people you know and I'm hoping the people you are waving to don't recognize me. Because when they do, they get that look on their faces and I can't go through all of it again. Especially now that I'm a raging pool of hormones."

"You're going to be a mom." Madison said it with a hint of awe in her voice, slowly shaking her head.

They stood, two best friends living very different lives, but forever connected by their childhood together in Fairview—the good and the bad.

"I'm going to be a mom. And you will be the baby's honorary auntie. You're the first person we've told. I guess now I can tell your family, too."

"They'll be happy for you."

"I know." She hesitated, pursing her lips. "Sometimes I miss Becca, too."

Although Madison nodded in understanding, she kept her true feelings to herself. If Natalie knew what Becca had said... She pushed the thoughts aside. Nothing could be gained by revealing how much she did not miss Becca in the least. "We had some good times, but that was a long time ago."

Madison said goodbye to Natalie and returned to her grandmother's room where her mother's look of concern wasn't lost on her. Grandma Ruth was mixing up dates and people more than ever and the need to move her to the memory care wing of the center was becoming urgent now. Acceptance on their part was only half of the matter. The fact they needed to tell Ruth about the move loomed large over them, a dark cloud that could only mean rough waters ahead. Whatever it was about Liz, Chuck, and Gordon caught someplace in her grandmother's mind, Madison was running out of time to help her figure it out.

The day her grandmother suggested she write letters was a decade ago, and such a teeny tiny blip in the long-storied history of her grandmother's life, Madison wanted desperately to believe it couldn't possibly be the letters to which she now referred. It was after the accident, when she felt completely lost—unsure what to do with herself. Natalie had already moved away, Becca was no longer someone she talked to, and Carl was in a medically induced coma. Family was her only lifeline and the opportunity to help her grandma gave her an outlet for the overwhelming sense of loss.

That summer morning in mid-August, when the rest of her classmates were getting ready to move on after graduation, Madison was stuck in a strange limbo, afraid to be far from home and family, struggling with emotions she couldn't get a handle on. So, she sat in Grandma Ruth's kitchen, years before it became hers, caught up in the familiar rhythm of cinnamon roll making she had witnessed time and time again. She watched her grandmother's still-steady hands measure, pour, and stir, all the while humming along with a song on the radio she kept on for company all day long.

She had become introspective after her hip injury, as though she just figured out she was getting old, but her words that day still caught Madison by surprise.

"Sometimes when I'm sad or upset, I write a letter to whoever it is making me feel that way. I never send it, mind you, but it helps lighten the load on my soul." She had looked pointedly at Madison. "You should write to somebody about whatever it is that has you beating yourself up, young lady." She continued adding ingredients to the bowl before her, the steps as familiar to her as the worn path from her patio to her beloved flower beds. As Madison watched that day, Ruth stopped, one hand in mid-air as she was reaching for one of the nearby canisters. Her hand lowered slowly.

"Madison, dear, reach up in the pantry and grab that small box for me."

Madison pulled down a faded blue container with a hinged lid and watched as her grandma wiped her hands on the apron, sifted through a couple index cards, and stopped when she found what she was looking for, a strange look crossing her face.

It wasn't until much later, once the ground felt steadier under her feet and a sense of direction returned to her life that Madison thought back to that day, not because of the letters she had written as her grandmother suggested, but because that day, her grandmother needed the recipe for the cinnamon rolls she had been making most of her life. Madison hadn't caught it right away

—the beginnings of the terrible disease they now witnessed wreaking havoc on Grandma Ruth, because at that time, thinking of herself had taken precedence over everything else.

Even as she tugged the handle on the ceiling in the main hallway, pulled down the ladder, and took the first step up into the attic, she knew she wouldn't find her letters in the attic space—or anywhere else for that matter. Why she had panicked as she did was almost embarrassing now. There was no way her grandmother knew the contents of her old letters, and they no longer existed. Madison had not only written the letters as her grandmother had suggested, but she had later thrown them into the bonfire on the beach during the family's Labor Day picnic a couple weeks later. Her grandmother could only know what she had written if she had snuck a peek, and Ruth Keller would *never* have done that. What had she been thinking? To make up for it, she was more determined than ever to figure all of it out: the letters, the secret, Liz, Gordon and Chuck. She owed it to her grandmother.

She pushed up on the trapdoor and hoisted herself through until she was seated on the attic floor. In horror movies, the attic held terrible secrets, haunting pasts, and sometimes even a bat or two. Fortunately for her, horror had never been her go-to movie genre, so she wasn't terrified about what she might find up there... except for the cobwebs.

The dormer window allowed filtered early evening light to fall across the wooden panel pieces that made up the floor of the attic space. The lightbulb, suspended from the ceiling, had a pull-cord dangling within easy reach. Madison said a quick prayer of thanks when the bulb lit, and her eyes gradually adjusted to the dim light it cast. It was a large space that had once been filled with her grandpa's train sets. Her dad had those set up in his basement now, and as soon as Piper was a bit older, he would share the elaborate set-up with her, as he often reminded them. Madison had vague memories of watching the train circle the track, traveling over bridges and through tunnels, past miniature pine forests and over glassy lakes. She could hear the echo of his laughter as she clapped with glee.

Madison couldn't remember very much about her grandpa "Poppy," but the family talked about him at length, turning her earliest memories into something probably more tangible than they really were. When he died of a heart attack at 68, leaving his wife alone to run the business, their friends rallied around her, helping with the diner until she could find her footing again. And she did. A weaker person would have crumbled under the weight of that loss, selling the business as quickly as possible, but not Ruth Keller. She fought back from her devastating grief to run the diner, determined to keep her husband's dream alive.

Too young to know what was happening, it was only because her dad and grandmother shared the story that she knew how close to giving up the diner they might have been. Madison could hear her grandmother's laughter as Brent told his version of the story. *"When I suggested she sell the diner, she looked at me as though I'd grown a second head."* Her grandma would nod in agreement at this point in the re-telling, adding, *"He seemed to forget that everything he had was because of that diner—including his fancy dental degree—so I didn't think it was his decision to make."*

Madison loved that story. She could picture Grandma Ruth, hands on her hips, chin jutting out the way it did when she was dead serious, putting her dad in his place. She and Poppy had sacrificed long and hard to make the diner a success. They were determined, however, that their only son would do something different with his life. Once in college, he fell in love with Nina and with the idea of becoming a dentist. He ended up with the girl and the degree.

He never again suggested she sell the diner.

And as much as her parents and grandmother initially tried to convince Patrick to do something else with his future, he refused to listen, and it was evident that deep down, she was thrilled that her grandson loved the diner as much as she and his grandpa had.

So, as she planned for her "retirement," a term she laughed at since she had no intention of staying away because as she said, nobody else was going to be in that kitchen fixing *her* famous coleslaw or baking *her* fresh cinnamon rolls. She made a deal with Patrick. If he agreed to complete a business degree, the diner would be his.

Patrick was laser-focused on his goal. And when Mya finished her teaching degree the same year he graduated with a Business Administration degree, he proposed, having no intention of losing the girl he had fallen in love with all those summers past. Although he was only 22, Ruth gave Patrick free rein to run the diner as he saw fit, even before she relinquished it completely. If Brent and Nina were disappointed that Patrick had chosen that career route, they never let on, providing support at every turn.

The timing, it turned out, was impeccable, because shortly thereafter, Ruth took a tumble off her back patio, falling awkwardly on her side. Thankfully, a neighbor was outside gardening and heard her cries for help. The broken hip served two purposes: Ruth was forced to slow down for once and Madison was given an opportunity to discover more about her grandmother than she ever knew before, a gift she still cherished all these years later.

Despite her son's pleas that she temporarily move in with them while she rehabbed her hip, Ruth refused, insisting her home was the only place she could feel comfortable while healing. That's why Madison moved into her grandmother's home, lovingly tending to her in the mornings and evenings. During the day, the rest of the family helped so she could stay in her beloved home. Eventually, it was Ruth who made the decision to move to the Senior Care and Memory Center.

Madison was shocked when her grandma showed her the deed to the house—signed over to Madison Elizabeth Keller. She loved the house, but she had doubts above living there. It was *because* of her grandmother that she loved the house. It couldn't possibly hold the same meaning if her grandma wasn't bustling around the kitchen preparing her mouthwatering cinnamon rolls or singing old show tunes as she was dusting dozens of glass and porcelain figurines on every shelf and surface. Now, after almost three years since she had moved in, Madison could say she did indeed love it.

She stifled a scream as a cobweb dangling from above swept across her forehead. She had been deep in the memories, bombarded one after another, but the cobweb was a reminder that she was supposed to be on a mission to help her grandma, not stroll down memory lane.

"Are you okay?" Natalie shouted from below.

"Just a cobweb. I'm fine. Don't come up here." Now that she knew about the baby, she wasn't letting Natalie do something as crazy as climbing the rickety steps leading to the attic.

Very little had been left behind after her dad and brother helped clean it out when she was preparing to move in. On her right, three stacked boxes were labeled in faded black marker on now crumbling strips of masking tape: DINER RECEIPTS. She didn't bother with those but made a mental note to remind Patrick about them in case he might want to look through them.

A familiar crate was on her right, overflowing with a variety of old ice skates with rusted blades. She remembered it sitting in a corner of the garage when she was younger because the family had used the well-worn skates every winter. Picking up a tiny-sized boot, the leather stiff and cracked, she pictured Piper learning to skate like she did and made a mental note to buy her a shiny new pair for Christmas. She tossed the old skate back in the pile, deciding they were too beat up to donate so she would simply throw them away.

An old cabinet was the last item. The lone drawer was filled with scarves, mittens and stocking caps, sitting unused for as long as the skates had been, as far as she could tell. There was nothing else in the cabinet. There were neither shoeboxes nor letters. It was even possible there never had been any letters. Delusions seemed to be coming faster than ever.

She got too close to the side of the cabinet, a nail catching the pocket of her shorts. The sound of the ripping material was relatively loud in the raftered space, and she glared at the nail and then at the flapping piece of material. After a moment, a smile spread across her face and she shook her head. The little tear was well worth the journey she had just taken down memory lane. Natalie was absolutely right, she realized. No matter what happened in the past or what was coming at her around the next turn, she would always have her family surrounding her.

Chapter Eighteen

Natalie offered to make dinner for them that night and Madison gladly accepted the offer because she still had to run to the office to wrap up some photo captioning and it had already been a crazy day.

"I want to treat you to a home-cooked dinner as a thank you for being such an amazing hostess. And I was thinking we could take a walk later." The original plan had been for her to leave today, but after everything they had been through, she decided to stay one more night.

"Are you just rubbing that whole happy homemaker thing in my face now?"

Natalie's laugh lifted Madison's spirits. They were back to their old selves.

"My cooking isn't exactly gourmet, but I've managed to keep Byron alive all these years." She grew serious then, stirring the sauce on the stovetop. "It will be scary being so far away and raising a baby. I hope I'm doing the right thing."

Madison meant it wholeheartedly when she put her arm around her friend's shoulder and reassured her, "Your home is wherever you and Byron are together. I *know* you're doing the right thing."

After dinner, they drove the short distance to Water Street so Natalie could enjoy one last ice cream cone from the diner. They ordered at the window, and Madison was happy to see a smiling Kayla ready to make their cones. It would have been easy for her to quit; Madison was pleased she hadn't.

They sat at a picnic table so they could people watch, because as usual, Water Street was filled with activity. Families were returning to their cars after a day on the beach, loaded down with beach towels, toys and coolers. The sound of over-tired, cranky kids trailed behind them. Young boys raced along on bikes, shouting to one another. Two girls on matching scooters whizzed by, hair French-braided down their backs. It didn't take long, though, for the quiet of evening to arrive, until only the muffled background noise of someone playing music on the beach, probably around a bonfire, drifted toward them. Kayla waved to them as she locked the window for the night.

"Coming back here wasn't nearly as bad as I built it up to be. When we get back to the states, I want to bring this little one here for a visit." She reached down to pat her belly. "And Byron, too, of course. I think they need to see what a great place I grew up in."

"Wow! I did not expect that to come out of your mouth."

"I've done some serious soul searching. My dad was broken, and we didn't know it. Maybe we could have helped fix whatever it was, or maybe not. But I can't lecture you about letting something go when I spent ten years doing the exact same thing. Forgive me?"

She reached for Natalie's hand across the table as she nodded. "I'm happy to hear that. Really happy. I want to show Natalie Junior all over town—except maybe not new town." She wrinkled her nose and shrugged. "We'll see."

Natalie smiled, but then grew serious once again. "I'm sorry you'll have to face Becca again. I thought you should bury the hatchet, let bygones be bygones, and all that stuff, but the more I've thought about it, maybe it is best to just leave it alone. She pulled away from us. We weren't important to her even after everything we did for her. You...we...don't owe her anything."

Natalie had already moved to Minnesota when the confrontation between Madison and Becca occurred. She only knew what went down based on what Madison chose to tell her, and nothing more. A twinge of trepidation coursed through her body now because Natalie could never learn the truth. "I plan to keep my distance from her, quite honestly. I have nothing to say to her."

Natalie sighed. "You probably both said and did things you regretted, but all of you were still in shock over the accident. Emotions were running high."

Madison concentrated on her cone, finishing it in silence. Finally, she responded. "I don't think talking to her will make any difference." Attempting to lighten the mood, she added, "And besides, she will have her superfans surrounding her all weekend so locals like me probably won't even get close enough to say hello." She crossed her fingers behind her back, wishing fervently for that to be the case.

Natalie's eyes flashed with the sassiness Madison remembered so well from their childhood. "I sure hope you can at least get her autograph for me. She's kind of a big deal now, you know."

Madison held up a hand, playing along with her friend. "Whoa! Don't go getting my hopes up. The disappointment would be too much to handle." They giggled like a couple of school girls.

It was surprising that she could joke about it. For a long time, she pushed every thought of Becca as far away as possible. The pain of that time, ten years ago, could unexpectedly return with such poignancy, she had to remind herself to breathe.

"I wasn't there for you, I know."

Natalie's comment, spoken so quietly in the darkness of the evening, made Madison think she hadn't heard correctly.

"You're kidding me, right? Your dad... Why would you..." She was almost sputtering, trying to put her thoughts into words. She stood to throw her napkin in the nearby trash can. "Please don't *ever* say that again. Please. Are you ready to walk?"

The sidewalk was no longer busy, so they strolled along Water Street, looking at window displays, most of which were already dark. They returned the friendly waves of the few shopkeepers still working. Madison knew all of them by name.

"Mike and Bonnie are building a new house in that subdivision on the north side," she commented, gesturing toward the couple setting up a camping display in their store window. "They're selling that big Victorian home on Sunset Drive." She gave Natalie a poke in the ribs. "You and Byron could buy it. Rent it out until you get back. It's big enough for a family of three, with plenty of room for lots more babies."

Natalie groaned. "No thanks. We already have an astronomical amount of stuff to do before we leave. I will not be adding *that* to the list." She blew her breath out loudly. "Lordy, I can't believe I'm going to have a baby in Iceland." She kicked a stone off the sidewalk with the toe of her sandal. "I have to keep saying it out loud so I can actually believe it. It still sounds crazy to me."

Although it had taken a minute for Madison to get used to the idea of Natalie being pregnant, she was excited beyond words for the couple. "A January baby. Maybe you'll have it on New Year's."

"Anything is possible."

They continued walking, a breeze blowing across the water and cooling them. Madison sighed, content.

By now they had reached the end of Water Street and crossed the wooden bridge to the walkway leading to the public beach. They turned left, a wide expanse of beach stretching before them, remnants of the day's activities scattered about. Half-demolished sandcastles looked like the remains of some archeological dig of a long-lost city. A pair of left-behind swim goggles rested on a rock near the now empty picnic tables. Teenagers were scattered about in small groups, and the smell of cigarette smoke wafted toward them.

After another few minutes of walking in silence, they sat down on the sand, staring across the now dark lake, the fading shades of tangerine, yellow, and red all that remained of the sunset.

"There's one more thing I was thinking about today. I know you don't want to hear this, but I think you should stop visiting Carl."

Madison froze, the good feelings of the last few minutes disappearing. "I don't think I can do that," she said stiffly.

"He was your first love." Natalie's voice was a mere whisper. "But there will be more. You are young and beautiful, but I don't think you're giving anyone the chance to get close, Mads."

She would never let Natalie know what really happened that day. Never. She covered her face with her hands, a sob seemingly coming from nowhere escaping her. "I miss him so much. I keep expecting him to get better, even though I know he won't...that he can't."

Natalie put her arm around her friend. "We had it so good here for so long. Then everything that could possibly go wrong went wrong. I'm not sure what we did to deserve that." She scooted in the sand to position herself so she could pull Madison's hands away and look her in the eyes. "Listen to me. It was a horrible accident. You can't keep living in the past. There's so much to look forward to. It's been ten years, Madison."

How could she explain to Natalie how impossible that was? Every time she looked at Carl, she felt it again. It never should have ended the way it did. She'd run through so many scenarios since that day, and she was convinced she was the cause of everything that went tragically wrong. She was the catalyst. Even Becca knew that. Natalie didn't.

"It was an accident. No matter how badly you wish it hadn't

happened or that you had done something differently, it still happened." She started to say more, paused, then added, "We *all* had a lot to deal with then and we were just a bunch of kids. But you are holding onto it, and you need to let go. It took me this long to figure it out, too."

Madison hiccupped, wiped her eyes with the palm of her hand and stared at the lake. "Carl deserved better. He was one of the nicest guys on the face of the earth and he deserved better." She quickly added, "And Jared, too."

This time Natalie didn't hold back. "And you deserve better than living like this. You *have* to let go or you'll end up alone. You don't want to be alone. My gosh! We are only human, all of us trying to muddle through life each day. I wouldn't be able to do that without Byron. You don't deserve a lifetime of alone, believe me. If you're avoiding...I don't know...finding someone because of some misplaced loyalty to Carl, well, that's just wrong."

Madison reached over to take Natalie's hand, squeezing it in her own. She wanted to remind her she was certainly not alone. She had the support of her amazing family surrounding her like a security blanket. But she knew that wasn't what Natalie was talking about. "I'm trying. Okay? Every single day, I get up and go through the motions, trying to see the world differently, but it doesn't always work. In fact, some days, it doesn't work at all."

It still felt like a fresh wound, and she feared it would never heal. The accident shook her belief in everything she was because she always believed she was a good person. After, she was no longer convinced of that. Everyone else saw the obvious—she missed Carl. They couldn't see the depths of guilt under which she felt herself drowning every day.

"I never wanted to admit that I...I was jealous of her."

Although Madison was surprised by Natalie's admission, she didn't let on, instead leaning closer, her shoulder touching Natalie's in a show of solidarity.

"She was so...perfect and..."

"Beautiful." Natalie offered.

"Don't forget manipulative."

"Why did she have to change? We had so much fun."

"Remember the talent show?" Madison shook her head. "I still think we should have won."

"We were terrible! Absolutely stink-up-the-auditorium bad. Even my mom thought so. She *accidentally* erased the tape." Natalie laughed at the memory. Gasping for air, she added, "I still say we were doing an okay job until you decided to do what you claimed was a cartwheel."

"I was a little caught up in the moment." Madison's laughter ended abruptly, and she whispered, "Maybe we let her get away with too much. What if we had pulled her aside and told her she was out of control?"

"Wouldn't have helped. She was in her own world by then."

"It was so unfair to Jared." Her fingers had dug into the sand around her, and she released the grip, picking up two clumps of sand and letting it sift through her fingers, back down to the ground next to her. She rubbed her hands together, shaking off the bits of sand sticking to her fingers, and wishing she could shake away the bad memories just as easily.

"And then you had the big blowout with her."

Madison could tell Natalie wanted to know more, but she had never shared the details with anyone and wasn't going to start now.

"I don't even remember anymore what was said, Natalie." That was a lie. She still heard the words in her head as clearly as though she had said them just yesterday. "Whatever it was, I should have just let it go. It was *Becca*. What did I care?" That part was true. What was said should have been of no consequence to her whatsoever, but at the time, she *had* cared. Becca had changed. Their childhood friend had become almost unrecognizable by then, and Madison had a chance, finally, to bring her down a peg or two.

Closing her eyes, she was whisked back in time, as if ten years hadn't passed.

It was clearly her fault.

Her petty need to hurt Becca killed Jared and took away Carl. And now Becca, the only other person on earth who knew the whole story, was coming back to Fairview.

Chapter Nineteen

"I looked in the attic, Grandma, but the letters weren't there. I'm sorry."

A piece of puzzle in her hand, Ruth paused to look at Madison. "I don't know what you're talking about, honey." She gently pushed the piece into the spot she thought it might go, met with resistance, and placed it back in the box next to her, resting her bandaged wrist on the table. "What were the letters about?"

Shuddering at the memory of the cobweb across her face, Madison held in a groan and responded carefully. "At the hospital, you asked me to look for a shoebox with letters in it. You thought it might be in the attic, so I checked." She waved her hand to dismiss the conversation, moving on to what she did find. "I found the box of ice skates, though. We haven't used them in... forever. Do you remember how awful I was? My ankles turned in like this." She demonstrated with her hands.

It felt good to spend time with her grandma. She'd tearfully said goodbye to Natalie that morning before going to work and now was putting off returning to her empty house.

"I don't know about any letters. Who were they from?" Her quizzical look was so child-like and naïve, Madison felt the stab of a familiar pain in her chest. The person before her was no longer the same person she had spent so much time with as she was growing up and she had no idea how to accept that.

Madison shrugged, again trying to draw her grandmother's attention away from something she had no memory of asking for and now wondering if the whole Chuck, Liz, Gordon, and letters thing was completely fictitious. "I don't remember either, grandma, so it couldn't have been important." Madison reached into the box, pulling out a puzzle piece. "Look! I think I found part of the rosebush." But her grandmother was staring off into space.

"He was still working as a caddy when he gave them to me. No, I think he was already in college then." She knit her brows together, her good hand tapping the tabletop and knocking a puzzle piece to the floor. "That was it."

"A caddy? At our course? I didn't know they used caddies at the course." She bent to retrieve the piece. "When was that?" Even as she asked, she knew she couldn't be guaranteed an answer, but sometimes she was pleasantly surprised by the clarity of some of her grandma's responses.

"The boys loved to caddy. That's why Chuck and Gordon came here during the summer." She giggled, sounding like a far younger version of the woman next to Madison. "Well, for the tips and for the pretty girls." She carefully inspected another puzzle piece before discarding it, rapidly losing interest in the puzzle Madison suggested they start. "It's a good thing I never gave Liz one of my cake recipes. Even more boys would have fallen in love with her." She smiled at the memory, putting a hand up to her lips.

Madison wanted to hold on to the moment, the light in her grandma's eyes brighter than it had been in days. "Liz had a lot of boyfriends, grandma?" She thought again about the beautiful picture in the yearbook and couldn't reconcile any of this—the picture and the information from her grandma—with the woman who ran the Cottages and seemed to live a very lonely existence.

"Oh my. That she did, honey. Such a pretty thing." She sat

back, surveying her living area. "You should take the box. I know you wanted the letters."

Madison was confused again. "I didn't find a box, grandma."

"I want tea. Do you want tea?"

"I'll get that for us." Her head spinning, Madison put water in the microwave to heat up as she put tea bags in mugs. Caddies. Liz. Letters. All of this was even more difficult than putting together the 500-piece puzzle on the table.

She had set out to find Chuck, but so far, she hadn't made any progress toward that end. With Natalie returning to Iowa, she would have more time. Of course, there was still a good chance all of it was fiction. It was difficult to tell these days.

"You can get the box now."

"Where's the box?" She asked, setting her grandma's cup of English tea next to her at the table. "Do you have it here?" She was pretty sure this would be another wild goose chase and there would be no box.

"I put it on my night stand."

Madison walked into her grandmother's bedroom, shocked to see there was a box where she had been directed to look. About the size of a large shoebox, it was shabby and worn. She picked it up, carrying it back out to the living room. Her grandma lifted the cover and reached inside, pulling out the familiar small hinged box that once had its home on the pantry shelf. She knew what was inside that box—all grandma's recipes, carefully written in her precise cursive hand. Madison swallowed the lump in her throat as she opened the cover, wondering how long the ink would live on, having already faded to a grayish pantone on the first notecard.

Her grandmother reached into the shoebox again, taking out a fistful of items. "Here you go." She handed the stack to Madison.

The first, an article, was familiar to Madison, because it was the same one framed and hanging on the diner wall. "You should keep this, grandma. I could have it framed for you."

"You keep it. Patrick has one so this one is for you."

Next came two envelopes. Madison gaped at them, bent corners and a few crinkles, but there they were—two sealed envelopes. She held one up, reading the outside. Elizabeth. The letters were real. She picked up the second one, which was the same as the other. "Grandma, if these were for Liz, why…" She hesitated, not sure how to ask the question without making her feel as though she had done something wrong. "Why didn't you give them to her?"

"She was gone. He wanted me to give them to her, but she was already gone."

"Gone? Where did she go?" Madison thought about the yearbook she'd searched unsuccessfully for Liz's picture. "Did she move away when she was still in high school?"

For a second, Madison thought her grandmother was precisely remembering things that happened almost five decades ago. But she lost faith with the next words. "Her mother sent her away." That couldn't be right. Her grandmother had to be confused. "I told you about that. It was her secret. Don't tell anyone else." She picked up the letters and handed them to Madison. "You should give these back to Chuck. Liz won't want them."

She thought about the notes she had on the town's founding family. Agnes and Lawrence Eriksson were the parents of Elizabeth. Her wheels turning, Madison considered the words uttered by her grandmother, wishing she could rely on Ruth's memory being more fact than fiction. Liz didn't want to share any details about her life, and she wasn't sure what tidbits from her grandma were true, but she was certain about one thing. The Liz she'd interviewed for the paper hadn't always been the way she is now.

Her grandmother was looking through the booklet in her hand. "I don't know why I saved this."

Madison leaned closer, trying to figure out what the document might be. As her grandmother closed it, setting it back on her lap, Madison was able to read the title: *Around the Course.*

"This is interesting." She took it, paging through the golf course newsletter. "I've never seen this before." Inside, she saw stories about the successes of local golfers, details about summer league scores, upcoming events, and on the final page, a section called "The Caddy Corner." The edition welcomed a newcomer to the group and included his picture and a brief bio. "Do you have more of these, grandma?"

"I don't think so. But you take it. And don't forget to give Liz her letters. Now that she's back, she might want them. It was so good to see her."

Madison assumed her grandmother was once again confusing Natalie for Liz but chose not to correct her. "I'll do that, grandma."

Madison spread everything out on her kitchen table. On her notepad, she listed a series of questions to guide her search. Foremost among them was finding out who Chuck and Gordon were, and then she would be better positioned to understand their connection to her grandma and Liz.

She turned the newsletter over, tapping it with her pen, and wondering what it could do for her. This edition was dated June 1968. She recognized a couple names of the golfers in it—Ben Johnson, the retired bank president, and Marv McIlson, the foundry owner. He died just a few weeks ago. It was fascinating to her, these glimpses of a time long past that were still so connected to the present.

"The Caddy Corner" segment gave her pause. What were the chances? Turning to a fresh sheet, she jotted some notes on her pad and then considered the two sealed letters for Liz. They likely held the information she needed to help her grandma, but it wasn't her place to open them. She pulled the notepad before her and wrote again. Two items were now on her to-do list: Check the library archives for copies of *Around the Course*. Stop by the

Cottages to see Liz. Madison felt good about the first but was unsure how to feel about the second. She scratched a line through it. She couldn't possibly ask Liz about any of this. Her grandma's memory couldn't be trusted to be accurate and she had caused people in this town enough pain already.

Whatever secret Grandma Ruth kept for her good friend could be problematic for Elizabeth Erikson and Madison had an unsettling feeling that digging too deeply would make whatever that situation was even worse.

―――

Not surprisingly, Natalie voiced similar concerns about trusting her grandma's memory later that evening when Madison called her from the diner where she was enjoying a late bite before going home to review the items once again.

"We already covered the obvious reasons she didn't attend school in Fairview her senior year—she had an affair with a married man, she eloped and then had an annulment, she ran away to California to be a flower child. I have another one to add to the list."

Madison leaned forward, lowering her voice even further, despite the fact the restaurant was almost empty. The two elderly men at the counter were clearly hard of hearing as their shouted conversation rang through the room.

"Do tell."

Natalie hesitated for just a second and then blurted, "What if she went away to have an abortion?"

"What?" Madison almost shouted the word, causing the two men to jerk their heads around and look at her. They weren't as hard of hearing as she had assumed. She quickly composed herself, giving them an apologetic smile.

"Why would you think that?"

There was a brief pause on the other end of the line and Madison could picture her friend shifting herself on the sofa to pull her legs under her in the go-to position Madison remembered from so long ago.

"Such a delicate matter could mean a lot of things. I mean, it was the late sixties and early seventies and they were tumultuous times, with guys getting called up to serve, the whole free love movement and everything." She paused. "If she ended up pregnant and unwed, it's not like she had a lot of options. I doubt she could get an abortion around here. Maybe she went away to have one."

"Oh my gosh, Nat. You might be right." Madison shook her head in astonishment, wishing her friend was sitting across from her yet instead of hours away. "You might be right. Liz might have had a fling and didn't want to be strapped with a baby. Maybe this Chuck guy was the baby's father."

"Well, it could be a lot of things. It's just one more theory."

"There's a story here. I know it."

Natalie's tone changed. "I thought you were just curious. You aren't going to write a story about her personal life, are you?"

"No, I...I didn't mean a story for the paper..." Madison's face turned red. "It was just an expression. I want to figure out what's bothering my grandma." Once again, she wished she could just talk to Liz.

"I don't think that's a good idea to get too involved. It might be best to let it go, Madison. It could end up starting rumors or opening a can worms that could be hurtful to someone." Natalie's statement was firm, leaving no room for argument and Madison was reminded of Jenny Whitebird's reaction to her curious probing a while back. While the town was certainly full of gossips, not everyone participated. And she, of all people, knew the consequences.

Madison crumpled her napkin, tossing it onto her plate. "I wouldn't do anything to hurt someone." Even as she uttered the words, she knew how untrue that was. She softened her tone. "My grandma was caught up in it and I was curious. Nothing more."

Natalie sighed. "I'm sorry. I didn't mean to sound like I was scolding you. Just be careful. I don't believe for a minute you'd try to hurt someone, but your grandma kept the secret for a reason. Maybe it's best to let it be."

Madison said goodbye and prepared to go home, wishing she'd never brought it up.

She thought about the pictures of Liz in the yearbook, and once again wondered what could change someone so much. With a start, she realized she had one answer. A best friend's betrayal. She certainly knew something about that.

Chapter Twenty

This, Madison decided, would be considered an impasse.

If she continued delving into the matter, she might uncover something unpleasant, unsavory, or downright scandalous. But if she stopped searching, her grandmother would never get an answer to the questions she had about Chuck and Liz.

Then she had to ask herself: Was she really doing this for her grandma's benefit or some other selfish reason? What would she be accomplishing? She didn't have that answer, but in some ways, she'd been searching for something for the past ten years. She just didn't know what it was.

Mrs. Blossom eyed her suspiciously, her forehead wrinkles more pronounced than ever.

Somewhat annoyed that the old woman seemed to think everyone needed her permission to learn what they could from the musty storage room in the *public library*, Madison started to roll her eyes and then thought better of it. She was being unreasonable. Someone cared about preserving the old documents and books—the gathered memories of times past. She gave Mrs. Blossom a sincere smile as she thanked her. "And I will follow every rule," she assured her.

As usual, a shiver of excitement coursed through her body as she entered the room, alive with the voices and actions of the past, and she couldn't resist the urge to run her hands along the bindings of some of the books shelved in the room before getting down to business.

From her bag, she pulled the copy of the newsletter her grandmother had saved, smoothing it out on the tabletop. She wasn't sure where to start looking for other issues of *Around the Course*, but she was determined to find them if they existed.

Her excitement soon turned to frustration. Despite her thorough search, she was coming up empty handed, but she also had barely put a dent in the large stockpile of materials in the room. She decided to seek help, finding Mrs. Blossom dusting a shelf near the back of the library.

"Do you recognize this?"

The woman took the document from Madison's hands, paging through it quickly and then scowling, her eyes darting from Madison to the paper in her hands. "Did you take this from the room?"

"No. Absolutely not. My grandma gave me this and I was hoping to find more editions." She was about to give up, but asked, "Do you recognize it?"

She nodded, but her look suggested she needed to keep a close eye on Madison in case she was fibbing about the origin of the document. "The golf course. They had these out on the counter for golfers to take. Started as a monthly thing but then they printed them weekly for a while. We never archived any of them here."

"Oh," Madison replied, disappointment palpable in her face and voice, but then another thought struck her. "Do you know where they were printed?"

"I do," she nodded, turning the newsletter over in her hands before looking at Madison. "That won't help you either. Brittons Printing. Everyone went there. Wedding invitations, church programs, you name it. Burned to the ground in seventy-four."

"Oh," Madison repeated, reaching for the newsletter as Mrs. Blossom turned back to her dusting. "But you could always check at the golf course."

Madison returned to the archive room to pack up, not sure how to feel about the suggestion. A trip to the golf course. A blush crept up her face as she remembered strong arms around her, protective, warm... Just as suddenly, the warmth disappeared as she remembered the business card on the diner's counter. Magenta Enterprises.

Her laptop held three bookmarked sites and it had taken a lot of time and all her research skills to find that little bit of information. The company was buried under parent companies and subsidiaries, but when she did manage to find them, she was sickened by what it could mean for the golf course. Magenta Enterprises seemed to be more about tearing down to rebuild instead of maintaining or improving existing property. If what she saw was true, it was quite possible the course would be developed into high-end condos or vacation property and the golf course would cease to exist. That was the business model for Magenta Enterprises.

She could go to the golf course. There was much to be gained from a visit. Pictures, she told herself. She needed more photographs of the course to create a Hometown Pride layout. Changes might be coming to the course, so it was important to record its current state, preserving another piece of Fairview history. If she happened to run into the manager, she could perhaps get answers to other questions she had.

The late afternoon sun caught her in the eye, so she drew her arm up, trying to ward off the glare.

"Madison Keller. I'm almost afraid to ask what new occupation brings you here today. Do you deliver the mail now, too? I'm expecting a package." Sean Fitzpatrick, handsome in a green golf shirt that made his eyes shimmer in the bright sunlight, was grinning at her, enjoying his joke.

"If it's okay, I'd like to get a few more shots around the course today. I'll stay out of the way of golfers, of course." She blushed, remembering how well she had avoided golfers on her last visit.

"No problem at all. Take any cart." He turned away, still smiling, leaving Madison to watch his broad back as his arms moved in front of him in an imaginary golf swing.

Part of her wanted to run after him, spin him around, and demand answers. But then she would have to look into those eyes again... She shook her head. Getting to the bottom of his involvement with Magenta was her singular interest in Sean Fitzpatrick. Her face warmed with the memory of his strong arms.

Completely exasperated with herself, she climbed into a cart. Because it was busy, she wound her way around the course to get the shots she wanted. The sun sparkled on the lake, and she closed her eyes, the dazzling kaleidoscope of color still dancing behind her lids. It was a perfect summer day.

Back at the clubhouse, she looked around for Sean, determined to speak with him, but finding only a kid behind the desk who shrugged his shoulders when she asked if he might know where she could find the manager.

"Try the putting range. I think he was working with someone out there." He gestured toward the door, and she thanked him before hurrying in that direction, fearful of losing her nerve before she had a chance to say what needed to be said.

Madison steeled herself as she approached, his back to her. This time, she wouldn't let herself get distracted.

"Sean?"

He turned at the sound of her voice, and she noted once again the way his eyes lit up and danced as the sun hit them. "Did you get what you needed?"

She closed the distance between them, ready to start firing with both barrels, but again she hesitated, instead, reaching into her bag for the newsletter, deciding it might be prudent to get an answer about that before diving into the messy part of the conversation she intended to have. "I did, but there's something else I was hoping you could help me with." She held the document out to him. "These used to be printed weekly with golf course news. Have you ever seen any around here, you know, maybe...I don't know...stored someplace?"

Madison watched the veins in his freckled forearm as he took the newsletter and paged through it. "Interesting. Nope. I can't help you with that. Sorry."

She took the document back, ready to ask about Magenta Enterprises. Before she could formulate the thought into words, a golf cart pulled up beside Sean.

"Hey, Larry!" Sean turned his attention to him. "I thought you got lost. Ready for your lesson?" He gave Madison a wave. With a scowl, Madison turned on her heel, not sure if she was upset or relieved that she wouldn't have the opportunity to confront him. She returned to the pro shop, pausing at the counter to carefully store her camera in its bag. Her phone rang, so she did a quick check of the screen. Ben was calling her.

"Madison, hey, sorry to bother you. Do you have some time to stop by when you finish whatever project you're working on today? We need to talk."

Her heart leapt to her throat. She knew Ben well enough to know that tone of voice. Whatever it was he needed to talk about with her was not going to be good news.

Chapter Twenty-One

It was impossible to hide her confusion. She had expected some changes when Gavin took over, but she never thought he would go this far.

"I'm sorry Madison." Ben looked everywhere but at her. Since tears were stinging her eyes, she was grateful that he wasn't watching.

Stunned, Madison took the dummy from his hand, staring at the layout of what should have been her Hometown Pride section for Sunday. Ad copy. The entire page was covered in ad copy.

"It has always been part of the Sunday layout. Is he moving it to a different day?" It was her first look at Sunday's layout, and her stomach dropped as she saw what was supposed to be her photo and caption spread. "This...I don't..." She was a mixed bundle of emotions that was unsure which one to hone in on. Confused, sad, angry, and now, her face burning, embarrassed, she tried to get some explanation. "Ben, what's going on? He cut half of my last story and now..." She couldn't finish. It was too much. Breathing heavily, she excused herself, stepping into the hallway to gather her thoughts and her composure. After Ben's phone call the previous afternoon, they had decided to meet early this morning to go over the information he needed to share.

Why would Gavin do this to her?

Her efforts at self-control failed. Tears rolled down her cheeks as she considered her next steps. Then panic set in. Perhaps she didn't even have a job anymore. She jumped when Ben touched her arm. She hadn't heard him follow her into the hallway.

"I know this is upsetting." His discomfort was obvious, and Madison felt an urge to comfort *him*.

"It's fine." It wasn't fine, but she didn't know what else to say.

"Take a minute. Let me know when you're ready to talk."

She nodded, making her way in the direction of the restroom, and then, needing even more space between herself and everything the newspaper office represented, she left, walking out the front door and away a couple blocks so she could stare out at the lake. Unfortunately, the comfort she usually found there eluded her.

Feeling sick to her stomach, Madison somehow found the courage to re-enter the building, eyes straight ahead, making a beeline to her cubicle. There was much she wanted to get off her chest, which meant she would have to confront Gavin. Hoping nobody would notice her, she made her way to the bathroom, practicing in front of the mirror, but ending in a puddle of tears before she finished the rehearsed speech. She started over again.

It had been for nothing. His office was dark. Gavin never seemed to be around when she wanted to confront him. Was he doing that on purpose? She realized that was a stupid thought. She was completely irrelevant to the man.

Ben was in the break room.

"Madison...I wanted to tell you before you saw it..." He set his cup down, shoving his hands deep in his pockets, like a contrite child waiting to be scolded.

"I just don't get it, Ben."

"Maybe we should discuss this in my office." He was right.

Their conversation didn't need to take place in front of her colleagues.

He picked up his cup and she followed behind despondently, the fight already leaving her. She should have known that everything was going too well lately. That always meant a shoe was about to drop. What had she been thinking?

"Have a seat," he said, gesturing toward the comfortable old loveseat he kept in the office, and closing the door behind her. "I honestly thought I'd have a chance to catch you before you left yesterday, but some things blew up around here and I just lost track of my to-do list."

She sat stiffly, afraid to move a muscle, feeling very much like a block in a complicated game of human Jenga. Everything seemed in a fragile state, ready to topple around her. Ben pulled a tissue from a box on his windowsill and handed it to her. She took it, crumpling it in her hand as she drew in a deep breath, struggling to find the right words.

"You knew about it before I left to take photos yesterday?" It came out accusatory, even though she had no right to be mad at Ben.

"I wish I had more clout around here, Madison. Now that we are corporately owned, a lot is out of my control." He sat on the edge of his desk, as upset about delivering the news as Madison was in receiving it. "Someone else has the final say on *everything*, but I *did* go to bat for you."

Madison nodded in understanding, thankful her voice was stronger than she felt. "I didn't mean to imply this was your fault." She looked down at the almost shredded tissue in her hand and reached over to toss it in the trash. "Do you think eliminating Hometown Pride is a temporary thing? I mean, will I get to do some special editions now and then or something like that?" She couldn't bear the thought of Hometown Pride disappearing forever.

He stood, stepping behind his desk to pick up a folder. "I'm afraid there's more. I know you were expecting to get one last sesquicentennial feature, but that isn't happening."

Disbelief added to the disappointment, doubling the heaviness already settled on Madison's heart. "He...he's taking away a story?"

"I wouldn't call it 'taking away.' I showed him the story list and he did the assignments. He chose not to give you one. I'm sorry, Madison."

She was back to doing captions and short news stories. Glancing at the assignment sheet he handed her, she felt small and insignificant, as though she were right back to being an intern instead of an honest-to-goodness reporter. She didn't dare speak. Nodding, she stood, mouthed a silent thank you to Ben and quickly left the office, making it to the bathroom before the tsunami of tears washed over her. When she returned to her desk, red-eyed, she kept her head down and worked on the tasks she still had as a member of the newspaper staff.

Madison paced in a familiar pattern between the kitchen, living room and hallways of her beloved house, not because she couldn't sit still, but because the well-worn wooden floors squeaked in places and groaned in others, and to Madison, it was the most comforting sound in the world. She imagined the voices of her grandparents in the house, talking to her, letting her know everything would be just fine.

She needed that kind of reassurance more than ever this evening.

The pacing helped. Her heart rate slowed and the cloud hanging over her was dissipating. Every problem had a solution just waiting to be found, her dad liked to say. She just had to find a solution. It might mean figuring out how to get in good graces with her boss.

Plopping down onto a kitchen chair, she noticed the two

envelopes propped against her fruit bowl. The urge to open them was more overwhelming than ever. Who would ever know? Liz clearly had no idea the letters existed; her grandmother would never remember they existed. It would be so easy to open them...

She stood, separating herself from the temptation, and eased open the patio slider. The night air was still warm. Somewhere in the distance she could hear voices, and the faint smell of smoke reaching her nose told her a bonfire was burning someplace in the neighborhood. Loneliness enveloped her, the only feeling left after her stomach-lurching ride on the emotional rollercoaster today. She wished she could tell her grandma about her day. It wasn't that her parents weren't good sounding boards, but her grandma was always her go-to when it came to sharing what was happening in her life.

The sad truth was that her grandmother would no longer be able to offer her the comfort she needed.

As kids, Madison, Natalie, and Becca went through skinned knees, lost teeth, and chicken pox together. As they got older, and their parents gave them more freedom to roam from their own backyards and hang out with one another, there was a tacit agreement they would do just that. If it was sunny, they were on the beach; if it was rainy, they would go to the park shelter. Growing up was easy in Fairview. Then things started to change in middle school.

Becca, the first of their group to blossom, was the envy of the other girls in their class as she developed breasts the summer before eighth grade and learned the fine art of flirting. The wide-eyed, hormonally charged boys didn't know what to make of her, but they watched her every move, little puppy dogs, panting nearby as they waited to be noticed. They eagerly offered to help her with sunscreen. When she spread a towel on the sand, they jostled each other to get the spot next to her. She had a way of making them all feel as though they had a chance at being her favorite. One boy would swim close enough to her, so it was his arm she'd grab onto when the water games started, squealing with delight, and pretending to need saving. The lucky boy would gladly oblige. Another trick the bravest of the boys used was to maneuver next to her and shout out for a game of chicken fighting. Careful planning meant it was his back she'd clamber onto as they all paired up.

Madison and Natalie looked down at their own flat chests and couldn't help but be a little envious of their friend. She promised them, though, it was a terrible burden and they should be happy they hadn't yet developed. They pretended to agree with her.

Madison wasn't a great beauty, but from the day she first met Carl, he made her feel like one. Their conversations were short at first, because she was working. But she remembered every word, replaying them later as she thought about him.

"Do you golf?"

"Does badly count?"

"What do you do for fun when you're not golfing?"

"I take pictures."

When he invited her to join him at the course at sunset to take pictures on the 12th green, a whole new world opened for her. She'd lived in Fairview her entire life and had no idea the most spectacular view of a June sunset could be found if you sat on the knoll overlooking Laurel Lake. She sat next to him as he carefully framed pictures, explaining the lighting and timing. Saving for a car was replaced with saving for the same camera Carl used. She was hooked.

As summer turned to fall and it was time for him to go south, Carl took her hand, squeezing it tightly, promising he would return. She wasn't sure if she believed him or not. Plenty of people came in the summer for a weekend, a week, a month... promising to return every year...and then never showing up again. But Carl showed up. The Thorsens wanted him to return in March, giving him the job of assistant course manager.

Madison wasn't sure which of them was more excited. They spent every moment together that he wasn't working.

She had watched Becca drift away from their group, hurt that she no longer wanted to be part of the forever friends. Hadn't she done the same thing—spending every possible moment she could with Carl?

She deserted Natalie in the same way Becca deserted them. Who was she to judge Becca?

She didn't realize then how natural it was for all of them to grow in different ways—and in different directions.

Karma.

She was finally being punished for her own sins.

Chapter Twenty-Two

Ben's email was brief and left her filled with anxiety. It had only been two days since her meeting with him, and she was submitting the assigned work, the topics dull and uninspiring compared to the feature stories she'd recently done. Making every effort to 'keep a stiff upper lip,' as her grandmother used to tell her, she was doing what she was assigned, despite Gavin's decision to demote her. And yet, she couldn't shake the feeling she was being called to the principal's office.

"When you look good, you feel good," she muttered to herself over and over as she dressed and styled her hair. The mantra served her in the months after the accident, when Madison had trouble simply putting one foot in front of the other, let alone doing what was necessary to make herself presentable for public scrutiny.

After the accident, Madison was unable to function in any way that resembled normalcy. Going away to college was out of the question. That plan was put on hold, and she spent the year living at home, working at the diner, and helping at the flower shop. Most of all, she spent time at her grandma's house, letting stories of the past lull her into a state of mind where everything was better. Her grandmother's house became her sanctuary. Her grandmother's comforting words became her shield. A part of her wished she had lived a generation or two earlier—in a much simpler time. She didn't even attempt to share that sentiment with anyone else. They were already treating her like a fragile glass object. Those words might have caused them to add bubble wrap as added insurance.

There was no way she could describe what she was going through. Carl loved her and in return, she almost killed him. For a long time, she wanted to die.

Immediately following the accident, she had been in a holding pattern, waiting for Carl to get better, to wake up from the coma and smile at her, blue eyes dancing. She was desperate to hear his laugh and tell her, again, he was head over heels in love with her. She craved the feeling of his arms giving her one of his amazing bear hugs or his hand reaching over to take hers, squeezing it for no reason at all. Then, once it became clear he wouldn't "get better," she spiraled even further. She was in love with Carl.

She was in love with the Carl she knew before the accident.

Weeks turned to months and he was healing in some ways, but waking from the coma didn't mean Carl was his old self, and that's when Madison gave in to guilt. All of it had been her fault. She couldn't blame anyone but herself. What would walking away from him now say about her?

With the support of her family, she eventually became something that resembled her old self. She commuted to Brookfield to study part-time at the college there, no longer interested in moving away from home to go to the state university.

Getting swept back into the pain of the past while dealing with the current issues of her grandmother's health was bad enough, but if she was also about to lose her job, she wasn't sure she could handle it. She was tempted to call her mom and tell her to take a day off to spend with her. Or sit next to her grandma and laugh about funny things that had happened during Ruth's years working in the restaurant. She had plenty of people around to catch her as she fell, but it was time to stand on her own two feet.

She fought the urge to put her pajamas back on and crawl under the covers and instead finished getting ready, making it to the office in plenty of time to meet Ben at the appointed time.

She knew immediately he didn't have good news.

"Gavin made his final decision. He wants the space for advertisers." He leaned in close, lowering his voice. "His decision was definitive this time. Hometown Pride is done, effective immediately. Personally, I find it completely sleazy to be more concerned about the bottom line than what our readers want, but he's the boss, Madison. I wish there was something I could do."

Madison nodded. Her hope of the section going on a temporary hiatus was dashed. She could tolerate a lot but losing Hometown Pride completely cut her to the core. The weekly spot gave her free rein to capture all the things she loved most about Fairview and the lake, and their readers loved it, too. Emails poured in each week with ideas and suggestions, and she did her best to accommodate as many as possible.

Gavin Maves had no idea what he was doing. How could that space, just one time each week, make that much in advertising revenue. Surely the number of readers who loved seeing pictures of themselves, their homes, businesses, activities, or whatever was captured by her practiced eye, far outweighed the small cost of ads that would fill it.

"Does he have something against me, Ben? Did I offend him in some way?"

"Don't take it personally. I'm sure this is a Galloway decision, not a Gavin decision. They are looking at it through a business lens."

"I'm glad you have faith in him." She lifted her head, determined not to melt into a pile of mush once again. "I don't trust him. He doesn't care about Fairview, the people here, or the newspaper. I'm not sure what he cares about, but it isn't any of us."

Ben looked sick. "It isn't personal, Madison. To him—and to the company—it's just business."

"Is he here?"

"No, we did a telephone meeting."

"Why is he afraid to show his face here and do the dirty work himself>"

Rubbing his beard nervously, Ben took a deep breath. "I don't know what else to tell you, Madison." He put his hands up as though helping her to pump imaginary brakes. "You are a valued member of this staff. I happen to think this is a storm worth weathering. Someone will replace him as Editor soon. Hang in there."

She stood to leave, asking, "Who else is on the chopping block?"

"You are not on the chopping block, Madison. You still have assignments...."

Any last words he might have added were cut short when she snorted, unable to curb her frustration despite Ben's best attempts to calm her. "He took away what matters the most." Madison was at the door, but turned and added, "And if he can do it to me, he can do it to everyone else around here. You might want to be prepared for that."

At her desk, she took a moment to breathe deeply before pulling her laptop out and opening it. She would avoid eye contact with her coworkers just in case they'd heard about her demotion. The last thing she wanted was to see pity in the eyes of her colleagues.

The little bit of space her pictures and captions took up once a week couldn't possibly make that much of a difference in the bottom line, she wanted to argue. But there wasn't anyone to argue with yet. She knew that stewing and simmering in the injustice of it all was causing her to spin out of control and that was not helping at all. She felt antsy, needing to *do* something.

Gavin was still an enigma. And right now, she saw him as public enemy number one. He might think he was attractive, but all she saw was an ugly heart.

An email appeared from the front desk intern, and she read through it quickly, wondering what unexciting news story someone had conjured for her now, but grateful to have something to draw her attention away from all the negativity. According to the message, she was to call Sean Fitzpatrick at the golf course. It took a second for the message to sink in. Why would Sean be trying to reach her?

He answered on the third ring. "I see you got my message. I have a little surprise for you. Believe it or not, I found more copies of that newsletter you asked me about. I got curious after you left and went on a massive clean-up of the back storage area. I'm not sure if I want to thank you for the motivation or curse you out for the extra work." He laughed, the sound surprisingly pleasant after the morning she'd had. "They are here for you anytime you want to stop by."

"Actually, I have time right now to swing by." She didn't wait for a response. Phone still to her ear, she pushed back from her desk and stuffed her laptop in its carry case. Sitting around waiting for more bad news was stupid after all. She had someplace better to be now, and a mystery still left to solve. Despite her terrible morning, she couldn't stop the smile playing across her lips. Everything else might be crumbling around her, but she could possibly find some answers for her grandma. The thought buoyed her out the door.

The musty smelling box was falling apart on one end, the glue so old it had simply disintegrated. Madison didn't care. Taking the box from the counter, she hugged it to her chest to keep it from collapsing completely. The desire to dig through it was so strong she wasn't sure if she could wait until she got it home to start looking.

Sean laughed at her enthusiasm. "Wow. I thought that smile was because you were happy to see me."

Flustered, Madison set the box back down on the counter. For a moment, caught up in the excitement of his discovery, she had almost forgotten her plan to confront him. She was ready. "Sorry. I've been anxious to get my hands on these." She kept one hand protectively on the box, as though afraid he might take them away once she said what she needed to say. "There is something I have been meaning to ask you, though. What's your connection to Magenta Enterprises?" Her heart raced, but she pressed on, determined to finally have an answer. "Do you work for them?"

His smile disappeared, replaced by a look of surprise. "Oh," was his only response.

Chapter Twenty-Three

The dilapidated box rode shotgun as she drove the short distance back to the office, no longer sure what to make of Sean Fitzpatrick and more confused than ever about what, if any, his role might be with a company that would likely build luxury condos where the golf course now stood.

"I can explain, but I can't talk about it right now." He had looked around the pro shop, as though expecting someone to jump out and say 'gotcha.' And now she found herself planning to meet him for coffee at the diner at 3:00. Perhaps it was her confused state speaking when she agreed to meet him, but now the curiosity was ramping up to new levels.

"Hey," Trista greeted her in what Madison gratefully determined was a perfectly normal way. Maybe nobody else knew about the changes made to her assignments. Relief flooded through her as she picked up her photo assignment sheet and reviewed it.

Relief turned to dismay, however, when she received an incoming email several minutes later. An official Galloway memo, it outlined some "relevant changes" the company would institute, effective immediately. The first was in regard to the amount of lead time required to submit requests for personal days. The second sent Madison's stomach dropping to the floor. There it was. Right there in front of her—in front of every staff member—was the notice that Hometown Pride was discontinued.

Staring at the screen, Madison tried to fathom why Gavin Maves would feel a need to put that information out to the entire staff without having spoken to her personally. For a moment she thought she was going to be sick, but a few deep breaths took that feeling away. She thought about getting up from her desk and marching down the hall to his office suite, but there was no point. Gavin wouldn't show his face today. That was his M.O.

She had to get away from her desk, get out and take pictures, anything other than sitting here. The box of newsletters sitting on the front seat of her Jeep was a siren song, luring her toward it. If she could compartmentalize work as a separate entity she no longer cared as much about, maybe she could ride this out, as Ben suggested—whatever *this* was. Helping her grandma would make her feel more centered. Once she had an explanation from Sean this afternoon, she could spend the evening working through the newsletters. She had no idea what she was really looking for, but even that sounded better than being at the office, under the scrutiny of sympathetic eyes.

———

Shortly before three she went inside to get a cup of coffee to go, taking it out to the picnic table where Sean would be certain to see her. She didn't have to wait long. He waved as he approached and gestured that he would be right back as he went inside. The tinkle of the bell lifted her spirits. Some things truly did not change.

"Thanks for indulging me," he said. "I really like your brother's coffee. At first, I was disappointed that he didn't have an espresso machine, but this is good." He took the lid from the cup, drank some of the steaming beverage and sighed, setting it on the table before him. "Good stuff."

"He's pretty stubborn about some things. An espresso

machine happens to be one of them. He thinks it's too 'new-fangled' for an old-fashioned diner." Part of her hated this small talk because she wanted to dislike Sean and conversations like this made that difficult. She also wanted to get to the matter at hand.

Sean fidgeted, tapping the plastic lid he'd removed from his cup, then sat up straight, looking directly at her. "What's your interest in Magenta?"

Surprised by his question, assuming she would be the one to make inquiries, she opened her mouth, closed it, and then blurted, "I saw you talking to that jerk who almost killed me with a golf ball. I know you're connected somehow and I saw the business card sitting on the counter that day I waited on you." Her voice hardened as she narrowed her eyes at him. "If you're in cahoots to buy the course and turn it into a luxury resort or something, you'll have a fight on your hands. The town council will *never* approve it."

She was infuriated to see he was trying to hide a smile. Nothing about this was a laughing matter and she found her fury rising.

"Let me make one thing perfectly clear. I don't work for Magenta." He took another long drink of coffee, his eyes still on her over the rim of his cup. "I just need to know this conversation is 'off the record,' as they say."

"What are you talking about?"

"I know I tease you about having a lot of jobs, Madison, but I'm not stupid. You work for the newspaper. If you're looking for a scoop of some kind, I don't plan to be the one to provide that for you."

The response infuriated her, leaving her sputtering. "A scoop? This has nothing... How dare you insinuate..." She stopped as a large group made its way down the sidewalk toward the ice cream window.

Sean stood, picking up his almost-empty cup and downing it in a gulp. "I'm getting a refill. Do you want anything?"

Madison stared at him, not even bothering to reply. This was turning into an even stranger conversation than she could have anticipated.

It took a while for the ice cream orders to be filled, but eventually the group moved on, heading back toward the beach. Sean returned, but this time he left the lid on the coffee cup and remained standing.

"Look, I didn't mean to offend you..."

She didn't let him finish and found herself standing also. "You accused me of being some kind of...of...I don't even know. You know nothing about me, Mr. Fitzpatrick, so before you go throwing insults at me, maybe you could take the time to learn more about this town and what makes it special."

He held his hands up in surrender. "I said I was sorry."

Even though she still didn't have any real answer to her Magenta question, she needed this meeting to end. Her day had been bad enough without insults being flung at her. She turned to leave, but he reached out to touch her arm. She paused.

"I really am sorry. I don't work for Magenta. If I could tell you more, I would, Madison, but..." His internal struggle was evident, and she almost felt bad for him... Almost.

"Whatever. You do your job and I'll do mine."

The worst thing about that, she realized as she walked away, was that she didn't even know what her job was anymore.

Chapter Twenty-Four

The sesquicentennial was a mere handful of days away. Banners were strung across Water Street, and residents and visitors alike were getting into the spirit of the city-wide celebration.

Madison was watching the morning news out of Brookfield as she sipped her coffee, preparing to leave for work. Fairview's very own Mayor Stevens was being interviewed by a perky blonde reporter with heavy black eye liner and false eyelashes. The mayor was doing his best to help her along as she struggled to read questions from her cell phone, but there was just enough wind to blow her hair across her face and strands caught in her ridiculously long lashes.

The whole scene made Madison smile. "Fasten your hair back next time," she told the reporter, as if she could hear or would ever take advice from someone else. She remembered how nervous she was to conduct interviews in her early days at the paper. The more important the individual, the more anxiety she felt. This poor girl probably hadn't interviewed anyone as important as a mayor in her brief career with the station.

The smile disappeared suddenly, and her stomach lurched as a familiar face appeared as an inset on the screen. The reporter looked into the camera, excitedly sharing the news that the local girl who had found success as an actress would be the Fairview Sesquicentennial parade marshal. Becca's headshot showed off her brilliant smile and high cheekbones. Nausea overcame Madison as she dove for the remote to switch off the television. Becca would be in town. She had accepted that fact, but she didn't need it rubbed in her nose.

With one last glance back at the newsletters piled on the table, she forced herself out the door and into her Jeep, where she turned music on louder than usual to drown out the thoughts bouncing around in her brain.

Arriving at the office a few moments later, she congratulated herself for her resolve to show up at work with confidence and a good attitude, which was great because she had an especially busy picture-taking week with all the extra activities around town. The paper would have to expand to double its size if Gavin intended to use every photo she was assigned to take. Knowing him, though, he might decide to replace them all with ads.

Her positive attitude took a nosedive. An assignment note was sitting in the middle of her desk, likely dropped there by some intern who had no idea the havoc it would wreak in Madison Keller's life.

Assignment: Friday, 10:30 a.m., photo session with Becca Ristow, Amphitheater/City Park.

She glanced around the room. Was someone playing a cruel joke on her? She knew that wasn't possible because nobody on the staff knew of her history with Becca. The nausea returned with a vengeance and she no longer had any choice. The floodgates were opened and Becca thoughts roared into her brain.

After the accident, her parents kept her close, watching over her. She lost both a classmate and her boyfriend. It was a difficult time for her, and her inability to function frightened them. Going away to school was out of the question, and at first, they couldn't even get her to take a couple classes in nearby Brookfield. They gave her time to heal without rushing her.

Nina took her to the flower shop, watching over her, spending time with her, waiting for her to open up and help them understand what was going on in her heart and head so they could figure out why she was left so debilitated by the events. Madison hated her own neediness, but didn't know how to break free of the pain, and she couldn't bring herself to share with her family her role in the events leading to the accident.

Even now, ten years later, she sometimes needed her mother's voice, a salve that eased her anxiety. With unsteady hands, Madison picked up her phone and punched in her mother's number, needing the magic provided by her mother's voice as they chatted about trivial things. Before long, she felt herself relaxing, her breathing returning to normal. Madison didn't mention Becca or the photo session she was assigned.

"I'm glad you called. Will you be able to check on your grandma tonight? Your dad has a late appointment this evening or he would be able to. I know I can stop by tomorrow."

They managed to have someone check in with her every day, especially since the need for a change to the memory wing was becoming urgent. Josie Ford's son was moving her out to California so he could monitor her health better, which meant a room would soon be available, but in the meantime, they were doing their best to assist the staff by having extra sets of eyes on Ruth.

Something was wrong. Madison could sense it as soon as she stepped onto the floor, still several doors away from her grandma's apartment. Other residents had stepped into the hallway, looking around with various levels of concern and curiosity, and when she realized, with a jolt, from which room the sounds emanated, she forced her legs to continue moving forward.

A cleaning cart was partially blocking the door, and a nursing assistant was standing just inside as her grandmother's voice, almost unrecognizable, rose shrilly, telling the frightened young woman to give something back to her. To Madison's horror, profane language poured from her grandmother's mouth, clearly describing what she thought of the young woman's intrusion. Madison had never heard her grandmother use such language. Even as she took the final step into the room, the cleaning lady, speaking into a walkie-talkie, was summoning assistance for the frightened nurse.

Shouldering the two women aside, Madison walked into the small apartment, shocked at the sight of her grandmother. Ruth's white hair was wild around her head—a dandelion gone to seed. Madison had a fleeting thought that if she blew on it, the white tufts of hair would drift away, leaving the fluffy mass at her feet, like the memories her grandmother was losing every single day.

"Grandma, it's me, Madison. It's going to be okay." She wasn't sure if she should touch her or simply talk to her. She'd never seen anything like this before.

"I've called the Director. He'll be here soon."

"It might be better if you leave me alone with her," Madison said, never taking her eyes from her grandmother.

The nursing assistant, clearly shaken, told the housekeeper to go ahead and finish her work in another room, and then, turning back to Madison, said, "I'm afraid I'm required to stay until a senior staff member arrives. It's a rule."

Madison watched her grandmother's eyes, relieved to see the panic slowly disappear, replaced by confusion. "I'm right here, grandma. Would you like to sit down with me?" Madison desperately needed to see the confusion change to recognition, but so far that had not happened. She was ready to plead with her grandma, to beg her to return to herself, to fight her way back through the fog of her disease.

Her dad's voice startled her. "Madison and I came to visit you, mom. Would you like to sit down?"

It was impossible to measure the relief Madison felt at not having to tackle this one on her own. Her family had once again come to the rescue.

"Greg moved her into the memory care unit infirmary to keep an eye on her. It's like a hospital ward inside that unit. He can only keep her there for up to 48 hours since she isn't 'sick.'" He used air quotes then dropped his hands to scrub them against his face, leaving one hand to tug on his beard. Madison wondered if he even knew he did this when he was deep in thought.

The entire family was gathered in the living room at Brent and Nina's, Piper sound asleep in her grandma's arms. Madison wished she could find the same kind of peace as her niece. It would be nice to just drift away and forget this day had ever happened.

Mya brought a tray of tea mugs into the room, setting it on the coffee table and then placing one in reaching distance for Nina.

"I didn't know Grandma even knew those words." It still shocked her that she'd heard the profane-laced language coming from Ruth's mouth.

"Greg said that's quite common. Thank goodness my last patient cancelled and I decided to drop by." Brent took a mug, sipping its contents slowly, watching Madison over the rim. "You did a great job, Maddy. I'm proud of you."

"She thought the nurse took her letters. I think she's talking about the letters she gave me." Tears filled her eyes, the emotions of the day finally hitting her full force.

Mya moved from where she was seated next to Patrick to sit with Madison on the sofa, her arms reaching around to hold her. "Shhhh. It's okay," she said, the tone one she might use on her toddler daughter. The comforting words and actions served to make Madison cry harder.

"Thank goodness she was next on the waiting list. I hated that we might be waiting for a resident to be moved to hospice care, or worse..." He didn't need to finish the thought. They knew exactly what he meant. "Josie will be with her son in California and my mom will have that room—and the special care she needs."

They looked like a family of bobble heads, all nodding in unison at his words. By the end of the week Josie Ford would be traveling across the country with her son to live in a home much like the one she was leaving, but she wouldn't have a clue she was in a different room, let alone a different state.

"So, deep cleaning, a full maintenance check, and then we can get her situated." Nina was finishing for him. "Greg promised to get it all done as quickly as possible, but the soonest would likely be Monday."

Brent wiped his own eyes with the back of his hand. "We knew this was coming. She was our rock. I can't..." He paused once again. "I know we've been fortunate to have so many years with her. I hate this stupid disease." His voice caught on the last two words, and the rest simply bobbed in agreement. Stupid disease. Nod, nod, nod.

They sat in silence for a few minutes, listening to Piper's heavy breathing, the unlucky one who would never know her amazing great grandmother, while also the lucky one, oblivious to the pain of watching the light disappear from Ruth Keller.

Sorting the newsletters was a good distraction—both from the episode with her grandma and the upcoming photo session with Becca. Lifting the pile of newsletters from the box, Madison set them on the kitchen table and seated herself in front of them. Part of her wanted to grab randomly and read each one cover to cover, but another part of her said she should zero in on certain dates if she wanted to solve this mystery before the turn of the next century. She knew herself well enough to know that once she started reading the documents, she would be lost in them, crawling into the skin of the people she was reading about in the newsletters and living vicariously through them.

Two hours later, she stretched, looking with satisfaction at the ordered piles before her. It had taken a ridiculous amount of time, but now that it was done, she was confident it had been the right way to start.

The newsletters were carefully divided by years. She had almost a complete set of newsletters for April through October of 1967 to 1972, some of them in better shape than others. She poured herself a fresh glass of iced tea and pulled the April 1967 edition toward her. It was, according to the cover, the inaugural edition of *Around the Course*.

A picture of a cold but happy foursome, smiling and holding putters in the air, made her miss Carl so much, she felt the physical ache of his absence. Pushing herself from the table, she paced, desperately in need of the comforting noises of the house to soothe her tensions. Just as she started to relax, her cellphone vibrated and she was tempted to ignore it.

A glance told her she didn't recognize the number so she was about to let it go to voicemail, choosing to pick it up at the last second. A familiar voice was on the line.

"Please don't hang up, Madison."

She hesitated, caught completely off-guard hearing Sean Fitzpatrick's voice and cursing herself for not sticking with her first instinct.

"Hello? Madison?"

Clearing her throat, she responded, "I'm here." There was no invitation for him to continue, but he did nonetheless.

"I owe you an apology...and an explanation." She could hear voices in the background. "Just a second. I need to step outside." The telltale tinkle of a bell told her exactly what door he was stepping through. "There, that's better."

"How did you get my number?" She knew the answer already. Patrick wouldn't have given it a second thought if he believed they were friends—or that she was working on an article about the course. She would have to speak to him about that.

"Your brother. Don't be mad at him. I was pretty persistent. I *really* want to explain."

She was silent for a few ticks, then said, "I'm listening."

He cleared his throat. "Like I already mentioned, a friend told me about the job here. I can't tell you more than that about my friend right now, but I can tell you that person only has the best of intentions for the golf course." His words were coming out faster and faster so by the end, they were all squashed together. "Ihopeyouwilltrustmeonthat."

After a moment's thought, Madison asked, "How will I know?"

"Know?"

"How will I know you're telling the truth...that you're trustworthy."

Sean groaned, "I want to tell you, but I really can't."

She was stuck. Something inside her was saying to believe him, although she didn't know why. When she didn't respond, he continued.

"This works both ways. I have to know I can trust you, too."

This took her by surprise. "Me?" She let out an exasperated noise, adding, "You have no reason not to trust me."

He laughed. "You expect me to trust you, a reporter, but you won't trust me."

"But I'm not writing a story about any of this." She didn't add that she no longer wrote much of anything for the paper at this point.

"Again, you expect me to trust you." There was an expectant silence.

"I get it." And she did. He hadn't done anything to show he was on the wrong side of this, so she decided to take a quantum leap of faith. "I will trust you." She lowered her voice to what she hoped was a threatening tone. "But if you do anything to betray me...to hurt the course...I'll..." Her threat meant nothing, because she couldn't come up with a single thing she could do to get back at him. For some reason, she felt tears prickling behind her eyes.

"I get it. You won't be sorry." His tone changed, all friendly banter now. "Did you have fun with those newsletters?"

She looked down at the piles on her table, wanting to tell him the entire backstory, but that wouldn't be right. Maybe someday... Even that thought surprised her. "I'm muddling through them right now." It was time to end this conversation, so she added, "Maybe I'll tell you the whole story someday." There. She was actually leaving a door open. For what, she didn't know, but it was definitely open.

His laughter sounded nice. "Well, someday, I would like to hear that whole story. I'll let you go. Take care."

She stared at her phone, not quite sure what had just happened.

The next two days were so packed with photo assignments and the subsequent caption writing that Madison didn't have time to think, let alone make progress on the newsletters. She looked longingly at them as she made her way out the door each morning, wishing she could dive into them.

On Wednesday evening, despite exhaustion creeping slowly through her entire being, Madison situated herself in front of the piles, excited to finally have a moment. If she could figure out who Gordon and Chuck were, she would have much more confidence in handing the two letters over to Liz. For some reason, it didn't feel right to do it until she knew more. Jenny Whitebird had already put her in her place once about asking too many questions, so she wanted to tread with discretion.

Madison nearly jumped out of her skin when her phone vibrated loudly near her elbow—an incoming call, and this time she recognized the number. Her heart skipped a beat and she stood, suddenly not sure what to do. "Stop it!" She spoke the words aloud, startling her into action.

"Hello," she said, trying desperately to keep her voice steady but still unable to sit back down. Pacing her favorite pathway in her home, she listened for the reassuring noises from her old wood floors and for calm to find her.

Sean's voice, familiar and unfamiliar at the same time, filled her ear, leaving her a bit lightheaded. "Hey Madison, are you still interested in telling me that long story?" He didn't wait for an answer. "Because if you are, I thought maybe we could meet at the Dockside for an adult beverage."

"An adult beverage? Interesting. And what is the adult beverage of your choice?" She found the banter to be calming, and she made her way back to her chair.

"You're kidding, right?" He guffawed. "Come on, Madison. You're supposed to be a great reporter. I'd think you should know what an Irishman drinks."

"I think I've got this. Irish whiskey?"

"Good guess, but I'm a Guinness guy."

"Not my choice, I must say. I need something with more grapes in it."

"We can discuss this matter over the phone, or you could simply meet me at the Dockside in an hour?"

She looked down at the table, anxious to dig into her research, and she really didn't feel like getting dressed up to leave the house. "I'm kind of in the middle of something here. The newsletters, you know..."

He didn't give her a chance to say no, diving in again. "I promise I won't keep you out late."

About to say no, she caught herself, wondering if one more day of not looking at them would make that much difference. Of course, her grandma's memory was slipping rapidly, so time was of the essence, but the thought of being alone wasn't exactly appealing either. "Okay," she finally said after the lengthy internal struggle, managing to add like a total buffoon, "It's a date."

His voice took on a different note, part teasing and part something she couldn't label. "Yes, it's a date," he repeated, disconnecting.

Shock, exhilaration, and terror took turns buffeting her insides, but she pushed herself from the table to get ready for her date that wasn't really a date. Definitely not a date.

His knee was close to hers. If she moved even the slightest bit, she would bump against it. She couldn't think about anything else for the first several minutes they sat in the booth at the Dockside Grill, Sean drinking his dark beer and Madison sipping a white wine.

After an awkward greeting and small talk about the beautiful weather, they settled in for a more substantial conversation about what led up to Madison's interest in the newsletters. "I never knew about this caddy club before now. It's amazing how much history escapes us. And lucky for me, it might hold the information I need."

Sean leaned forward, elbows on the table, hands folded under his chin. "I love a good mystery. Tell me what your next step is, Sherlock."

Madison didn't need anything further to set her at ease, and she matched his pose, squinting her eyes as she spoke. "You know I'm perfectly capable of figuring this out on my own. Are you assuming I *need* a Watson on the case?"

Conversation continued easily then, and Madison was surprised at how genuinely comfortable she felt as she explained her grandmother's condition and the confusing comments that may or may not be real memories, and even sharing some information about Liz. "I learned a couple interesting things. Elizabeth Erikson never graduated from Fairview High School." She paused, realizing what she'd just said. "That's not necessarily true," she said, deep in thought. "Just because I didn't find her picture in the yearbook doesn't mean she didn't graduate. I'm not sure why I just thought of that."

"That was very Sherlock Holmes of you. Nice use of your

deductive skills." He nodded approvingly. "But now you have to ask yourself, does it matter? I mean, does your grandma's memory of whatever it is that's bothering her have any connection to whether Mrs. Erikson graduated or not?"

"She's not an 'M-r-s.' Liz never married."

"Aha! Another clue."

"How do you figure?"

"I have no idea. I was just getting into the spirit of things."

Madison sighed. "You think this is stupid, don't you?" She took a sip of her wine and set the glass back down, her fingers tapping idly on the glass. "If I can figure out who Chuck and Gordon are, maybe that will help. I'm not sure."

"If there's anything I can do to help, let me know. I would do anything for my grandda, so I get it."

"You're close?"

"We are. When my gran died, I stayed in Ireland with him for a few months, making sure he was going to be okay. It took a bit for him to look and act like his old self, but he's a strong old bugger."

Her eyes brimmed with tears, caught up in thoughts of her own grandmother and how quickly the light in her eyes was dimming. "I miss the grandma I knew, but she'll never be back."

Sean took the tears in stride, reaching across the table to pat her hand. "Aren't we a couple of sad-sacks?" He shook his head in feigned amusement of the scene. "Instead of another round of drinks, perhaps we should order a box of tissues?"

"You're right. Let's change the subject." She used her fingers to wipe away the dampness under her eyes and forced a smile, appreciating his ability to keep her from falling into a funk.

"Tell me about growing up in Fairview."

That was all she needed as an opening to talk about how much she loved everything about growing up on Laurel Lake. She told him about Natalie, mostly, sprinkling in a little about Becca here and there. "If it wasn't for…" A look of surprise crossed her face, and she stopped talking, reaching for her glass.

Sean waited for her to complete the sentence. When she still hesitated, he said, "Well, it sounds like an amazing place to grow up. And I don't blame you a bit for choosing to stay right here. It's a nice little town."

She lifted her eyes, and in the depths of his green orbs she saw his sincerity and knew she could trust him, but still she hesitated, unable to bring herself to talk about the other side—those things that left her with unhappy memories. How would she even start? And what would he think about her? She couldn't do it. "I think that's enough about me for now. Tell me about your family."

It was his turn to oblige, telling her about his life in Philadelphia. "Like you, I had a great childhood, growing up in this amazing Irish-American community, very supportive, lots of loud gatherings, and just a wee bit of drinking now and then." He winked at her as he finished the sentence with a heavy Irish brogue and raised his glass. "My dad wanted me to get a degree in business so I could work with him. My grandda told me to ignore my dad and do whatever it is that makes me happy. You never want to disappoint the people who love you more than anything in the world. Thank goodness my mom helped me find a little compromise in all of it."

She asked the question quietly. "So, are you doing what makes you happy?"

Sean didn't hesitate to answer. "I am. Like I told you, I took this as a temporary gig because I was between jobs, and now I'm *really* glad I did, even if a certain reporter is trying her hardest to distract me." He laughed, and she once again enjoyed the way his eyes lit up. "Aren't you happy, Madison?"

It was such an odd conversation to be having with someone who, for all practical purposes, was a stranger, but she was drawn to him, a magnetic pull that was stronger than her desire to keep everything inside, which was normal for her. She stared out the window, a faraway look in her eyes. "I always liked writing news stories. You know, a strong beginning, detailed middle, and a wrap-it-all-up-with-a-pretty-little-bow ending. That is so *not* what my life is like. I'm kind of stuck in the middle, with a lot of detail I never expected, and I don't see much hope of moving to that pretty little bow any time soon." She sighed, knowing she was making the conversation far deeper than the evening called for.

"You're not just a writer, though. I've seen some of your pictures. You have a great eye for photography."

Her face reddened at his kind words, but her throat was tight. Carl taught her how to take pictures. But she wasn't going to tell Sean that. "My boss doesn't seem to appreciate my photographs. He took away my Hometown Pride section." She was surprised she could share this so openly—and without tears. "I've been demoted. My new boss hates me for some reason. I don't know. Do you ever feel like you don't belong in your skin? Nothing feels right. I don't know if it's me or if it's everything happening around me." She leaned forward, trying to make her point. "I hate how much everything is changing around here, and I can't do anything to stop it. My best friend is moving a million miles away. I got a promotion I wasn't sure I deserved, and then it was taken away from me just as I was feeling confident, you know, like I *did* deserve it. And then there's my grandma..." She broke off, biting her lip to stop it from quivering. "Ever since Carl, I haven't been on steady ground. I feel like I don't know who I am, and I'll never know because everything keeps slipping away just when I feel like I'm gaining some traction."

"Who's Carl?"

Her jaw dropped and then closed as suddenly. She had been so caught up in trying to make her point, she hadn't even realized Carl's name had fallen so easily from her mouth. And now it was out there, leaving her exposed to the elements and not sure where to find shelter.

He didn't push her. Something about Sean made her feel safe and she wondered if she would ever feel comfortable enough to tell him what happened ten years ago to change the trajectory of her life.

Chapter Twenty-Five

SHE COULD NAME THAT TUNE. JOHN PHILIP SOUSA. *Stars and Stripes Forever*? Yes, that was definitely it. At first, she thought the music was in her dream, but then she realized the high school marching band was practicing for Saturday's parade. The music stopped momentarily and then started again. Madison groaned and rolled over. It was only 7:20. What possessed those kids to get up so early in the summer?

The lilting march sounds faded away, and she pushed off the covers, remembering that she was expected to take photos of the rehearsal, as well as about a million other activities going on in preparation for the big weekend. It was oh-so tempting to roll over and close her eyes, though.

As promised, Sean had not kept her out late, but she had trouble falling asleep once she climbed under the cool sheets. She liked him. He was a nice guy. But she wasn't in any position to have a relationship with anyone—and he was only here temporarily. That was all the more reason to keep whatever was happening between them as simple as possible. They were friends. Period. Full stop.

She hurried through her shower and breakfast, getting to the rehearsal in time to take plenty of pictures of tired, sweaty high school kids with their instruments. Then she moved on to the rest of her assignments, racing back to the office to get the captions done by her 4:00 deadline. She was exhausted, but a shot of adrenaline coursed through her when she saw an incoming call from a now familiar number.

"Have you found anything in those newsletters yet?" Sean's voice was filled with laughter, bright blue skies and promises of things to come. She completely forgot about being tired.

"Sadly, I have only had time to sort them." Without thinking, she asked, "Want to help me?"

The invitation surprised her more than it surprised him, because he agreed immediately, as if there was nothing out of the ordinary going on here. This was completely out of character for her, and even as she heard herself sharing the address it didn't feel real. Sean was coming over. She looked around, wondering what she had just done.

There was little time to consider that, because within 20 minutes, he was at the door, his arms laden with a bottle of white wine and a small bouquet of brightly colored carnations.

"Oh," she stammered, "for me?" The words slipped out unbidden, and she wanted to kick herself for sounding stupid. Of course they were for her. He wasn't really the type to randomly carry flowers around wherever he went. She mentally rolled her eyes at herself as she took the flowers, smelling the sweet fragrance before leading him inside.

"This is nice."

He was admiring her home as she pulled a vase from under the sink, filled it with water, and placed the pretty arrangement in it. She could tell they were from Sprigs, and she wondered what her mother would think had she known the handsome young man with the red hair curling up at the ends and a smattering of freckles barely visible across his nose was buying the flowers for her daughter. Sometimes Nina asked her customers questions: "Is this for a special occasion?" "Does your special somebody like roses or carnations?" Her face grew warm as she wondered what was asked and answered at the flower shop counter this evening, probably just moments before Nina was closing up shop for the night.

The deluge of emotions left her flustered and unsteady, and she concentrated hard on keeping her hands from shaking as she pulled out two wine glasses and a corkscrew, passing the latter to Sean. "I'll let you do the honors. Thank you for...everything." Her gesture encompassed the flowers and wine. "It's a perfect night to sit outside, if you'd like." She waved a hand toward the piles. "We can have a glass of wine and then look at these later?"

"Sounds great."

Madison took the glass he had poured her and led the way through the slider. The patio was still warm in the early evening, heat radiating from the pavers below their feet as a gentle breeze rustled the leaves overhead. As they sank into the cushioned patio furniture, she let out a soft sigh.

"I needed this," she said appreciatively.

"Wine?"

"Yes. Well, that and...some company." Her face warmed, surprised she would admit something like that. Then, rolling her shoulders back and rotating her head, she tried releasing some of the week's compounding tensions. "I have had a rough couple of days."

"Want to talk about it?"

She looked at the handsome man sitting on her patio, this man who brought her flowers and wine, who was willing to listen to her stories, and she wondered if she was making a huge mistake she would soon regret or if she could really trust him as someone to talk to.

Because more than anything, she really wanted someone to talk to right now.

Shadows stretched across the patio as they sat next to one

another, knees almost touching, just like on their first "date-not-date" at Dockside.

Madison hadn't shared with her family just how much she still held onto when it came to Carl and the accident—and she couldn't imagine after this much time had passed bringing *anyone* into her inner sanctum of truth. Yet here she was, after a full decade of keeping it to herself, thinking about sharing with Sean Fitzpatrick things she had never even revealed to her own family members. She stopped herself from saying what almost spilled out, because talking about it meant re-living every moment all over again with every word she spoke, a little piece of her torn away from the present and tossed into a past that was trying to swallow her whole.

"Have you been to the Shallows?"

"I don't think so. What is that?"

Madison shifted in her seat, picked up her glass, set it back down, and then shifted again. "It's a submerged sandy area over on the south shore. If you go by water, you'll recognize it right away. Boats anchor next to each other so you can literally climb from one to another. You can swim, play volleyball, or just hang out on the sandbars. It's kind of cool. You should check it out. Even if you don't have a boat, it's a public beach that has one big party, all summer long."

He gave her a funny look, wondering why she would bring up this place. "I'll have to go there sometime. Sounds like fun."

"A group of us planned a big 'last-get-together-before-college' party at the Shallows." She played with the stem of her glass, not looking at him.

She remembered how beautiful Becca looked in a white bikini with a little gold anchor dangling from the bra. Jared kept reaching over to touch it, and Becca would playfully slap his hand away. The action annoyed Madison. Becca could use her acting talent to convince everyone what a great girlfriend she was to Jared, but Madison knew the truth. She wished Natalie had been there. They could have talked about it, and then Madison wouldn't have reacted the way she did...

"We had a good time and a lot of my classmates were there so it was one more time to be together before everyone left for school or the military... It was supposed to be special."

Natalie was long gone by then, so Madison was happy to have Carl with her that day. She had begged him to come as soon as he got off work.

As she lounged on the sandbars, watching Carl play volleyball, she heard Lydia Barnes' voice carrying toward her, deep in conversation with Becca and some other girls from school. "*I don't blame Natalie for leaving town. We all know why her dad killed himself.*"

Madison wanted to stop listening, but she couldn't. She was waiting for Becca to defend Natalie's dad. She *needed* to hear Becca come to his defense. What she heard her say turned her blood cold. "*Everyone knows he was doing perverted things with boys at the church camp. I'd kill myself too.*"

There was no reason to believe any of it, but it didn't stop the others from accepting Becca's announcement as gospel truth, adding their own sick rumors to the mix. Madison sat frozen in place, anger a living, breathing monster unfolding within her. She knew she had to stand up to them, defend Natalie, make Becca apologize for the horrible things she said, but she couldn't do it. Facing the group of girls terrified her, knowing how quickly they would turn on her next.

That was when an idea to get even with Becca was born.

With a start, she pulled herself back to the present, to the patio, to Sean. She had been sucked down a deep hole, the memories dark and heavy around her. Blinking rapidly, she looked around her backyard, surprised that she had made it back from her journey where time had stood still.

"I assume something happened that day?" Sean had been quiet, waiting patiently for her to tell her story, and now he reached over, covering her hand with his own, his voice out of sync with the stillness that had cocooned her. "You don't have to talk about it if you don't want to."

She looked down at his hand, feeling it, and yet so numb, she wasn't sure she would ever feel anything again. There was no way she could tell him the truth, any more than she could tell her family.

"There was a car accident. Some guys driving back..." She was trying to piece the story together without the most important details.

She could see him struggling to understand why that day was so impactful, but there was no way she would let him see what she really was inside.

"I feel like...well, at the time, I felt like I could have done something to stop it from happening." She looked into his eyes and then quickly away, ashamed that she was leaving out the essential pieces of the story—the parts that would make him run away from her as quickly as possible. "I behaved badly and I'm ashamed of myself. Things could have turned out differently that day, but..." She blew out a breath, her bangs lifting from the breeze she created.

"You're probably being too hard on yourself. I'm sure your family has told you that already. You sound like a close-knit clan to me."

She smiled sadly at his word choice. Yes, they were a close-knit clan, and maybe that was the reason she could never share how horrible she was. She desperately wanted to remain a member in good standing of her clan.

"I do have the most amazing family on the face of the earth." She looked away, knowing there was so much she wanted to say at the same time she knew she never would. In the west, the sun would be setting, a molten fireball sinking down into the lake, if they could see it through the line of trees that bordered the back yard.

"Then that makes you the luckiest person on the face of the earth."

She looked at him, wishing she could look at it with the same simplicity. There were all kinds of ways she could have handled that day differently, but she chose to go as low as humanly possible. "Everyone in Fairview was devastated by this horrible accident, and it came right on the tail of my best friend's dad committing suicide." She closed her eyes. "It was all just a lot for a bunch of teenagers to process." No matter how badly she may have wanted to share the whole story with Sean, it was too hard to admit the truth, and even harder to say it out loud. "And now someone who used to be a really good friend is coming back to Fairview and it's all these bad memories piling one on top of another. And seeing her will make me feel even worse." She said the last part so quietly, Sean leaned forward to hear her.

"I've met a lot of people—some good and some bad. You are definitely one of the good ones." He gave her arm a squeeze, picked up her wine glass which she had set down while talking, and handed it to her. "Let's toast."

"What are we toasting to?"

"How about we toast to something simple...putting the past behind us and focusing on the future?"

She clinked her glass against his and they drank. It was a lovely toast, and she hoped she could do just that, but deep down she knew it would never be that simple. Madison looked around at the darkening evening, her earlier exhaustion made worse by talk of her personal past. It was time to delve into someone else's past. That would be a lot easier. She needed to get out of her head—find a distraction from...from too much to even enumerate. "Let's tackle those newsletters."

Inside, he poured more wine as she turned a light on over the table and pulled a notebook from the drawer. She needed to find some of the excitement she had felt earlier about searching the newsletters. She moved the wine glass aside, interrupted by Sean's question.

"Okay, Sherlock. What am I looking for?"

Madison gave him a funny look. "I have no idea, but that's the fun of this kind of project." She glanced at her notes. "We're looking for any reference to guys named Gordon and Charles. Grandma said they were caddies at the club. That's all I know about them."

Sean raised his glass, and she followed suit, tapping it against his. "Here's to finding what we need to find."

"Cheers."

They were quiet for a moment as they each took a newsletter, familiarizing themselves with the layout and then skimming the short articles in search of the two names. That proved useless as they realized there were references to both names in multiple issues. "I guess they were popular names then, and it looks like these are just golfers—not caddies."

"I found several Chucks in the yearbook, but there was only one Gordon, and I'm pretty sure he wasn't the one."

"And you're assuming they were in their late teens or early twenties?"

"That's my best guess." Another thought struck her. "During that time a lot of 'outsiders' came to Fairview to work service jobs. That was really common in resort communities—like Wisconsin Dells, Door County and even here on Laurel Lake. I wasted time searching the yearbooks, but there's a good chance they weren't even residents." She sat back, frustrated that the notion added another layer of difficulty to the process. "I'm hungry. Are you hungry?"

Madison didn't wait for an answer as she pushed away from the table and reached into the fridge and cupboards. Before long she was slicing cheese, and pulling salami from a package, arranging it with some grapes and berries on a tray. They nibbled as they continued making headway with the piles before them.

Sean let out a soft whistle. She stopped, a piece of cheese suspended in midair.

"I think I found them."

The cheese dropped to the table as she moved around to stand behind his chair and look down at the paper in his hand.

A group of smiling young men, about a dozen, were kneeling next to bags of clubs. At the top of the page, she saw the words NEW SEASON, NEW CADDIES. The name of each caddie was included below the picture.

She couldn't see the small print without leaning closer, and she felt his warm cheek very close to her own, his hands holding the document so she could see. "Which ones?"

"Here." He indicated the two at the far right of the photo. "This one is Gordon Cummings and the other is Chuck Lasley." Sean handed her the newsletter and she took a closer look.

"Wow. They existed." She was surprised by the relief flooding through her, knowing her grandma had remembered something correctly. The two young men had certainly been caddies, and Grandma Ruth very likely served them at the diner. The relief was short lived. She set the paper back down and sank into the chair next to Sean. "But I have no idea what to do with the information now. I was so excited about tracking down the names, but what good was that when my grandma can't tell me why they're important or mean something to her...or to Liz. This was stupid."

Sean looked at her, incredulous. "Are you kidding me? That was great sleuthing, Sherlock. I'm impressed."

She smiled despite herself. It felt great to have someone on her side.

"You're right. I know their names. It's a starting point. Once the sesquicentennial events are done, I'll start searching for him."

He continued to stare into her eyes, and Madison felt a funny sensation in her stomach as she wondered if he was thinking about kissing her. But a split second later she jumped up from the chair and started gathering the remaining newsletters, leaving only the one she needed set aside.

"I'll let you take these back to the golf course where they belong, but I'll keep this one if that's okay."

He simply nodded, downing the last drop of his wine. If he did want to kiss her, she would shut that business down immediately. There was no room for a romance in her life—summer or otherwise. They were shrouded in awkward silence. Madison stretched, signaling the end of their evening together.

A short time later, as she waved goodbye to him at her front door, she wondered why she couldn't allow herself a little bit of joy. Carl was never going to get better. Why was she so unwilling to let her own heart heal?

Chapter Twenty-Six

Madison was up well before an alarm roused her, her whole body on high alert as she prepared to face Becca. She dressed carefully, styling her hair, and carefully doing her makeup, asking herself why it mattered but unable to stop herself. She would never pretend to be the beauty Becca was, but she could put in a little effort. And that's what she did. Her anxiety built, making it difficult to down anything other than coffee before she packed her camera in the Jeep and drove to the park.

It was another spectacular summer morning, and crowds were already out enjoying the lakeshore. She counted exactly two fluffy white clouds in the otherwise blue sky. The weekend forecast was a tad iffy, but hopefully rain would hold off long enough for every sesquicentennial event to be a go. Madison would focus on enjoying the festivities—once she made it through the photo assignment. Her stomach did flip-flops and made a funny gurgling sound as her nerves were in full-throttle high-alert mode.

There were few people on earth Madison didn't want to see. She corrected herself. There was only one person on earth she didn't want to see ever again, and that person was Becca Ristow. Madison gave herself a pep talk before getting out of the Jeep. *Breathe*, she told herself. *Just breathe.*

Becca was late, of course. Madison tapped her foot impatiently, checking her watch every couple of minutes, and then pulling out her phone to make sure there were no last-minute cancellation messages. She still had several locations to hit for other picture assignments as well as more work at the office.

An SUV arrived, parking near her Jeep and from it, three people emerged, but not one of them was Becca. One carried a large box from which he unpacked camera equipment. She looked down at her own Nikon DSLR, and had an unsettling feeling she had brought a child's toy to an adult's game.

A young man with colorful tattoos covering both arms was setting up a portable table and chair he pulled from the back of the SUV. Stepping out of the front seat was a heavy-set woman, a floral caftan flowing around her legs with each movement. She lifted a large black rolling case from the back and started setting out make-up, carefully placing brushes, bottles and sundry other items Madison would never be able to identify on the portable table. The assignment was to take pictures of Becca for tomorrow morning's front-page story about the one-and-only Becca Ristow, shining star and parade Grand Marshal. Madison remained nearby, feeling more awkward by the moment. The three were intent on their jobs, giving her no more notice than they would a nearby tree.

A silver BMW slipped into a parking space and then she appeared, showing off a leg as she gracefully unfolded herself from the sporty car and then walked confidently across the parking lot in a stunning white dress and strappy sandals. Bile rose in Madison's throat as she watched Becca move toward the crew that had arrived before her, giving the photographer two air kisses, one on each cheek, as only fake Hollywood types can do so well. Spray tan, veneers, and Botox, Madison thought. Smoke and mirrors.

And then Becca seemed to notice Madison for the first time. Remembering her professional role, Madison closed the distance between them, and for the first time in ten years, looked into Becca's eyes—tiny orbs of meanness that seemed to grow smaller the longer she stood before her. Her look changed quickly, and she was once again as beautiful as ever. It didn't matter how quickly the transition occurred, because Madison had seen Becca's true feelings.

Madison forced a smile, but never had a chance to offer a proper greeting, even though she wasn't sure what it was going to be.

"This is so sweet. The local paper wants pictures?" She pretended to wring her hands and look dismayed, her voice holding a timbre unfamiliar to Madison, as though everything about her had to change, be different, be part of her act. "I'm afraid that was never cleared with my publicist." She gestured toward the crew finishing their set-up. "I don't think that would be fair to the *professionals* who have been hired for the job."

The sick feeling in the pit of her stomach had grown. Something was completely out of whack here—and she was beginning to feel like the butt of someone's sick joke.

Becca was back to smiling sweetly at her, a look of pity crossing her face. "I hope you understand how careful I need to be about what pictures get out into the world." She gestured prettily with an arm jangling with silver bracelets, the sun catching them and sending jeweled sparkles around her, a Disney princess wannabee. "The wrong pictures could start...oh, I don't know... rumors and controversy. And then my public will never know what's real and what's not. You have no idea how messy it can be."

The words were knives, slicing, cutting, deeply hurting Madison. She had apologized ten years ago. She didn't bother apologizing again. It would fall on deaf ears now just as it had done then. "You are absolutely right. I'll let you get to work." She turned her back on the starlet, focusing on the sun shimmering on the lake, diamonds sparkling more beautifully than anything Becca wore on her neck, ears, or fingers. Her *professional* photographer would get some brilliant shots today.

Becca was about to walk back to the crew when she paused, looking directly at Madison. "Do you ever visit Carl?"

Madison felt the color drain from her face. "I visit Carl."

Becca looked her up and down one more time, seeming to mock everything about her, especially when compared to her own stunning looks. "And I assume you visit the cemetery every day, too."

Madison turned to walk toward her Jeep, feeling like a teenager all over again and completely ashamed of her inability to say what she wanted to say to Becca. As she buckled her seatbelt, she closed her eyes momentarily, taking a couple deep calming breaths. When she looked back at Becca, the friendly façade was completely gone. Becca hated her. And she had every reason to.

She watched for another moment as Becca lifted her phone to her ear, talking animatedly to someone before patting her hair in place and returning to the small group waiting to take care of her, to attend to her every need like the star she was.

In the distance, Madison saw the familiar sights of families enjoying the Chamber of Commerce-perfect day at the lake, eerily out of sync with the dark encounter she'd had with Becca. And once again, she felt alone in a world that didn't feel right to her, but instead of wishing for Carl's hand reaching to comfort her, it was, unexpectedly, Sean's hand she craved.

She was running late for every assignment thereafter, and when she finally submitted the last photos and captions, and finished writing a short news blurb about upcoming road repairs, she was ready for the weekend. She stopped at the desk of the layout editor, Mike, making sure he was aware she would not have any photos of Becca Ristow for submission. He paged through his notes, looking at her quizzically.

"I don't have anything here indicating you were assigned photos for that story, Madison. I'm sorry. I'm confused. We were sent over a whole batch a couple hours ago from her agent or publicist or something…"

"Oh." Her face reddened as she thought back on the photo assignment left on her desk. "I guess someone got wires crossed because I thought I was given the assignment..." Her voice trailed off. Someone had set her up. "Forget I was ever here, Mike."

He didn't need to be told twice, his focus back to the work he had to complete for the next morning's issue. Becca had managed to get back at her.

———

She found herself checking her phone yet again. Sean hadn't touched base at all today. It was a little surprising, given how much they had seen of each other in the past few days. She scolded herself for caring, but then wondered if it would be weird for her to text him.

"Everything okay?"

Her mom's voice broke through her reverie, pulling her back to the task at hand—wrapping knick-knacks that would go into storage. Nobody felt up to deciding their fate right now, so until they could figure out a final destination for them, it was best to carefully wrap and store each one, and then at some future date when...when what? Nobody wanted to answer that, either. Her grandma's new space would allow for very few personal items. Her rocking chair was number one on the list. Little space remained after that.

Madison was staring at a beautiful piece, a couple looking into each other's eyes as he dipped her in a frozen-in-time dance move, their love captured in their porcelain eyes and mouths. She wasn't sure who she most saw depicted in the piece—her grandparents? Her parents? The dream of what she thought she and Carl would have? Something possessed her to ask, "Can I take this one home with me?"

Nina looked over her shoulder. "It is gorgeous, isn't it? If I remember correctly, that was the last birthday present Poppy gave her before he died." She looked away, not wanting a fresh set of tears to fall. "Yes, you take it. It deserves a good home."

They finished wrapping, placing the items in two large plastic containers that Patrick would help carry out in the coming days. Everything about the pending move was weighing heavily on all of them.

"That's probably enough for now. We have a big day tomorrow. Let's go say goodbye to Grandma Ruth."

Brent was visiting with his mother in the solarium. Getting her out of the infirmary and into her own room would be good, but it certainly was not something they were looking forward to because the room symbolized another significant change for Ruth and a clear indication of how quickly she was going downhill.

Ruth was wearing a yellow housedress, sitting in a chair near the window, Brent next to her. She looked better today, and Madison was cheered by the sight. She leaned over to hug her grandma. "Hey, you aren't bandaged anymore."

Ruth held her arm up, smiling. "The nurse took it off." She looked around, as if in search of someone. "It was right after Liz and Gordon left."

The three of them exchanged glances over her head, an unspoken agreement to gloss over the comment. But before they could intercede with a distraction, she continued.

"It was so good to see them together again. I couldn't find the letters to give her. Do you know where they are?"

Madison didn't know what to say, frantically looking to her parents for help. They were at a loss as well. "I think...I guess..."

Brent took his mother's hand. "Mom, would you like to go to the parade tomorrow?"

Nina and Madison gave him a surprised look. He shrugged and they understood completely. He needed something to distract her from believing she had visited with a person who died circa 1970.

Madison finally gave in, punching the number of the pro shop into her cell phone, hoping it would be Sean picking up the line. The voice of a young man on the other end caused her eyes to roll. She had yet to meet a single worker at the course with any energy.

Her conversation was brief, and she disconnected with great confusion and consternation. Why had she let herself think she meant something to him? The words rang in her head.

"He doesn't work here anymore. Do you want to talk to Mr. Thorsen?"

Chapter Twenty-Seven

THE MARCHING BAND WAS WARMING UP IN THE FIRE department parking lot, while across the street, on the grassy lawn of the Lutheran church, the local twirling school's brightest little stars were spinning and tossing, readily flashing red-lipsticked smiles whether they caught or dropped their batons.

Frenzied activity showed up in every parking lot designated for parade line-up, and Madison was there to capture it all for the newspaper. She was trying hard to catch the celebratory mood of everyone around her.

The air was becoming heavier, the humidity increasing. It would continue to get hotter throughout the day and she already felt like she was being sautéed in a frying pan.

After the parade, there would be a ceremony at the pavilion. Concessions, games, and a huge flea market were all set up at City Park, awaiting the hordes of people who had come to celebrate Fairview's Sesquicentennial.

Madison wove her way through the parade lineup, photographing anything that caught her fancy. The *Through the Decades* theme was evident everywhere she turned. Float entries were required to capture historical events from the last 150 years, and they didn't disappoint. She paused to take photos of the high school science club's entry, Moon Walk, depicting a larger-than-life astronaut seemingly floating above what was meant to be the moon's surface.

The Waterfront Business Association entry depicting the Roaring Twenties was next in line. Her mom, costumed in a flashy gold flapper dress, its fringes dancing and swinging with her every move, waved from atop the float where she was being harnessed into place. She looked beautiful as she posed for Madison's pictures. Madison waved to Shelly who was about to be seated in a giant barber chair.

Her grandmother would have loved this, she thought, continuing her walk along the line-up of floats. She had borne witness to many of these eras and events. After blurting out the idea the previous night, Brent had quickly back-pedaled, agreeing instead to visit her so she could see their costumes. There was no chance Grandma Ruth would be able to handle the chaos—or the heat—of a day like this. Lost in thought about the many decades of progress Ruth had the good fortune to witness, Madison almost missed it.

Drawing in her breath sharply, heart racing, she stepped behind a tractor attached to the Chamber of Commerce float depicting the post-911 national pride, and lifted her camera, aiming and snapping as she cautiously stayed in the shadows of the float.

Had she really just seen that?

With shaking hands, she looked back at the pictures in the camera's viewfinder, overcome by nausea. Her eyes had not been playing tricks on her, and she had the evidence perfectly captured. Madison no longer knew what was real—but she was getting some sense of who was fake.

In frame after frame, a strange story unfolded.

It was the car that caught her eye. She would recognize that Mustang anywhere. Madison watched Gavin unfold himself from the driver's seat and walk around the car, reaching a hand in to assist his passenger. The woman wore a stunning strapless sequence-covered dress that reflected everything around it like a million tiny mirrors. Her dark hair momentarily blocked her face as she gracefully emerged from the car, but Madison recognized her immediately. The man pushed a strand of hair back from the woman's face with one hand and then leaned forward to kiss her lips.

Madison stared in astonishment as Gavin led Becca to the nearby convertible with the PARADE MARSHAL sign on its side.

This could not possibly be right. She flashed back through the photos once again, making sure her eyes were not playing tricks on her. They weren't. She had captured an intimate moment between Gavin Maves and Becca Ristow, and Madison suddenly understood at least some of what had been happening to her in the past weeks.

Having seen enough, she turned to make a quick exit before either one saw her and walked directly into her dad's chest.

"I have been looking all over for you, kiddo. I was hoping you could get a picture of me with your gorgeous mother after the parade." Seeing her stricken face, he took her arm, drawing her away from the people milling about the daycare center's float. "Are you okay?"

Pale and shaken, Madison nodded, reaching into the bag draped across her shoulder to pull out a water bottle. "I think this heat is getting to me. Make sure you drink plenty of water, too. You must be hot in that get-up."

He looked like a very handsome gangster in his double-breasted pinstripe suit, the red carnation pinned to his lapel perfectly matching the ribbon adorning his jauntily cocked trilby hat. He and Nina would make a stunning pair in a photo.

"I am, believe me." His concern remained. "Maybe you should come sit on our float for a little while, until you get yourself hydrated." Madison wanted to cry. She was so fortunate to have so much love around her. Members of her family were always nearby, ready to catch her as she was falling. But they couldn't help her with this one.

"I'm fine dad. See? Plenty of water." She showed him the almost empty bottle and gave him a smile she hoped conveyed what he needed so he wouldn't ask any more questions.

"Your color is coming back. You looked like you saw a ghost."

Ghost, no. Monster, yes.

"I have to get to the grandstand soon but I promise to get pictures of you and mom after the parade. You're right. She looks gorgeous."

"Maybe we were born too soon," he said, brushing imaginary lint from his shoulder. "We look pretty gangsta."

Groaning, she gave him a little shove in the direction of his float. She needed a few minutes to herself.

She sank down on a bench on the side of the church, finishing her water, and processing what she had just discovered. Her phone was tucked inside her bag, silent and message-less, reminding her how alone she was. Madison felt that loneliness like a winter chill, even as the heat penetrated her skin and the humidity left her feeling like she was drowning.

What if Becca decided to reveal what really happened that day? Already feeling fragile, Madison feared she would shatter into a million pieces.

Forcing herself to focus on the work she needed to do, Madison made her way to her Jeep so she could get to the parade's grandstand. Traffic crawled, and she was grateful for a reserved parking spot in the back lot of the flower shop, one clearly marked Employees Only. A brisk walk later, she was at the grandstand, ready to photograph the parade as it passed by. The mayor, decked out in old-fashioned garb, a top hat, and a white sash across his chest that boldly proclaimed MAYOR, waved to the crowd from his seat.

She took pictures of every float, the marching band, the kids, the horseback riding club, and even the silly clowns on their tiny tricycles with supersized soaker squirt guns sending the crowds backpedaling as they sprayed a powerful stream of water. As the long-awaited convertible arrived, the mayor announcing over the loudspeaker the approach of Becca Ristow, Madison put the camera back to her face, thankful to have it as a shield between herself and Becca.

Tit for tat. Madison had betrayed Becca and turnabout was fair play. It was a clever ploy, Madison decided. She didn't know how they'd met or how long it had taken to concoct their plan, but they'd succeeded. She could figure out parts of it. Becca had a role in a Broadway Across America show doing a six-month run in Chicago. Gavin Maves, when he wasn't terrorizing the staff of the paper, lived in Chicago. Bravo to them, she thought. Becca's best performance to date. Had she not seen it with her own eyes—captured it with her own camera—she, too, would have had a hard time believing that Becca Ristow and Gavin Maves not only knew each other, but knew each other intimately.

So many things made far more sense now as she thought back on encounters with Gavin and his decision to cut her story, cut her job, cut her to the core. It had nothing to do with her ability to do her job.

The parade ended and Madison wove her way through the crowds once again, this time in search of Poppy's booth, set in the sea of vendors. He could use her help right about now, and it would be her sanctuary while she sorted through the emotional tidal wave drowning her.

Patrick and Tino, dressed as old-fashioned soda jerks with red and white striped vests over their starched white short-sleeved shirts, had sweat beading on their foreheads as they scooped ice cream from large tubs set in portable freezers. The canopy provided little relief from the sweltering heat.

A line was already a dozen people deep for the popular old-fashioned hand-scooped ice cream root beer floats. A couple of the high school kids would help out later, but one had just marched with the band in the parade and the other had been part of the science club float so they needed time to change and get back to the park.

"Where do you want me?"

"Take over the counter," Patrick answered without looking up. He was pulling an empty ice cream tub out of the way as Tino replaced it with a fresh one.

Madison set her camera equipment under the table and dove right in with money collecting and passing out the sweet treats. Some kids had visited the face painting booth, turning them into animals, clowns, and imaginary beasts. A little boy, tiger stripes already smearing across his hot cheeks, took the cup from Madison, attempted to put the straw in his mouth, and somehow managed to dump the whole thing at his feet. He wailed inconsolably until Patrick handed him a replacement. His tears and sweat streaked down his face, the artwork melting into messy splotches.

Now and then she scanned the crowds, half expecting...or maybe just wishfully thinking that Sean might have returned, although she had no reason to believe he would.

"Who you looking for? Mr. Right?"

"Yeah. Nope." Her face felt hotter than it had moments before, despite the fact her brother was only teasing her. "I told dad I would take pictures of them—and I should get one of you and Tino, too." She hoped that was convincing. "This rush can slow down any time now," she added, wiping her brow.

"Don't say that!" Patrick pretended to look stricken by the comment. "I have a family to support. Do you know how many root beer floats it takes to pay for braces, and dance lessons, and...?" He threw his arms up, demonstrating the hopelessness of his situation, then readjusted the red and white striped hat on top of his head.

"Okay, okay, drama queen, I get it."

They continued working side-by-side until Christa showed up to start her shift.

"Thanks sis. Get out of here and do your thing. Mya is

bringing Piper in a bit so we can do some carnival games with her."

"Good. I'll watch for them, too." She gathered her camera bag from under the table, looping it over her shoulder and making them pose for pictures. "I sure hope you'll be wearing that lovely ensemble to the dance tonight," she laughed, and then darted away before he could reply. Soon she was swallowed up by the families milling about the concessions and art fair booths, the smell of cotton candy and hot dogs filling the air.

Even as she stopped to photograph kids and families enjoying the festivities, she had her eyes peeled for Becca, certain she could not handle another encounter with her. It was highly unlikely she would be wandering around in the heat and humidity. Of course, knowing Becca, she would still look perfectly calm, cool, and collected despite the rising temps.

Just as she finished taking pictures of three little girls, triplets licking their rapidly melting cones in perfect unison, Madison stopped in her tracks. Coming toward her, grinning from ear to ear, was Natalie, dragging Byron by the hand.

"Surprise!"

Madison clumsily wrapped both Nat and Byron in a close hug. "What…? How…? What are you doing here?"

Byron looked at Nat, draping an arm over her shoulder. "She wanted me to see this place before we go." He shrugged. "Whatever this little mama wants, she gets. It's not everyone who'll jet off to a foreign country for her husband."

Madison looked at Natalie, pleased to see she did indeed look happy. She also knew that joy could be short-lived *if* she ran into Becca, *and* if the wrong things were said… She wondered if it would be possible to keep them away from one another. She had to try.

"Mya and Piper are around here someplace. We should go look for them." She put her arm through Natalie's, taking a few steps away from the pavilion.

"The ceremony is starting soon. Maybe we'll get a chance to say hello to Becca."

Madison nodded, bracing herself for the confrontation that was as inevitable as the storm front that was building.

Twinkling white lights outlined the amphitheater, illuminating the faces of the band members in a magical, shimmering effect. A breeze lifted from the lake, whispering across the crowds, and rustling leaves and branches.

The lead singer stepped to the microphone, caressing it as he whisper-spoke into it. "For all you love birds out there tonight, it's time to slow the pace. So, find your special someone and hold each other tight. You will never want to let go." He slid easily into the slow, romantic number as laughing couples found a spot on the dance floor, and a hush settled over them as the night's magic drew them under its spell.

Twilight had fully settled over the park.

Madison stood off to the side, watching the couples on the dance floor. Her parents moved slowly to the music, her mother's cheek resting comfortably on her dad's chest. Mya was smiling at Patrick, her arms around his neck as he sang the words to the song. Natalie and Byron swayed in time to the music. Madison stood alone. She yearned for arms wrapped around her now, swaying slowly to the music of the night and the band.

There had been no messages from Sean. He left without saying goodbye. She had completely imagined any feelings that might have existed between them.

Shaking away the thought, she tried to focus on some of the positives of the day. Number one on her list was that Natalie never had the chance to say hello to Becca. She accepted her key to the city and then left the stage—and Fairview.

The song ended and Patrick and Mya wandered over, arms

looped around one another's waists. A flash of light in the distance caught their eyes.

"Heat lightning?"

Patrick shook his head in answer to his wife. "I don't think so. We're supposed to have some pop-up thunderstorms tonight. Thank goodness we had perfect weather today."

Madison looked at the sky as another streak followed the first. An unexpected shiver ran through her, and she had the strange sensation that something more than a thunderstorm was on its way.

Chapter Twenty-Eight

THE REAL SLAP IN THE FACE, SHE REALIZED ON SUNDAY morning as she picked up her soggy newspaper from the top step and carried it back inside, was that this would be the first Sunday she would open the paper and not see her special section. Hometown Pride was done. Over.

She moved quietly through the house so as not to wake up her houseguests. Byron and Natalie had to hit the road this morning so they could drop more containers off at Great-Aunt Linda's house and then get back to Iowa to continue packing. They were scheduled to leave August first.

Keeping Becca and Natalie apart had been essential the previous day and, when all was said and done, easy. Rumor had it Becca left immediately after the ceremony to tape some television show, which was fine by Madison. More than fine. That was the perfect scenario. Finally given some breathing room, Madison ran home for a quick shower after the long day at the parade and park. She slipped into a sundress, and was able to enjoy the sesquicentennial dance without fear of a run-in with Becca, who had no reason to stick around her podunk childhood home, thank goodness.

She stirred some cream into her coffee, sitting down to unfold the paper, its smells of dampness and ink an odor not altogether unpleasant. Smiling to herself over what she could only describe as a small victory, that the three of them had been in the same town at the same time and hadn't had any kind of run-in, Madison was ready to put all of that behind her and focus on something positive. And she had just the thing. Last night at the dance, a diner regular asked where he could purchase copies of the photographs he had seen on the diner wall. *Her* photographs. He wanted to buy copies *her* Laurel Lake prints. She would talk to Patrick about making some of her favorites available for purchase at the diner.

Every good thought evaporated. She was wrong bout the slap in the face. This was even worse. There were no ads taking up what had been her section of the Sunday paper. There was, instead, a full-page feature on Becca Ristow. And if that wasn't bad enough, the pictures she saw there turned her stomach.

The first was of Becca in the white dress at the pavilion. Another had her in a black dress, a somber look on her face as she stood, eyes hidden behind dark sunglasses, next to a grave at the Fairview Cemetery. In the next, she was in a blue romper, hair pulled back in a ponytail as she was cheek-to-cheek with Carl, whose expression was the same he always wore, completely unaware of the smiling beauty next to him as she leaned over the side of his wheelchair.

Madison was afraid to even look at the captions, let alone read the article.

Natalie padded in rubbing her eyes, and Madison considered throwing the paper in the trash before she could see it, but she was too late. Natalie was already looking over her shoulder.

"Wow. She was busy. That was nice that she visited Carl."

Her mouth agape, Madison stared at Natalie, then quickly closed her mouth, afraid of the words that might spill from her. Madison stood, busying herself in the kitchen, pulling orange juice from the fridge and bagels from the cabinet.

"Look at this! The article says the local news will be running a pre-taped program called *The Rising Star* twice today." She checked her watch. "I'm going to wake up Byron so he can watch it with us. It starts soon. Very cool."

Taking deep breaths, Madison continued with breakfast preparation, terrified about what the interview might contain. She glanced again at the photos, worried that Becca might have more up her sleeve.

She didn't have to wait long for an answer because in no time at all, Natalie was seated in front of the television, orange juice and bagel on the coffee table before her, Byron pouring himself a second cup of coffee, as the musical notes of the show's opening abruptly signaled the start of the show.

"Welcome to our program, The Rising Star. I am Camile Mills, and we here at WFLV, your source for local weather, news, and sports, are thrilled to bring you this special interview with Becca Ristow." The show's hostess looked into the camera, her glossed lips enunciating each word she read from the teleprompter hidden from view. False eye lashes batted like insect wings as she made the necessary opening comments. *"We are grateful to our sponsors for helping bring this special program to you, our viewers."* Her image was moved to the far left of the screen as sponsor names appeared on the right. They disappeared, and Camile turned her face, directed toward a different camera, a new angle this time as she continued reading, introducing Becca and basking in her glory.

"She looks gorgeous." Natalie sounded a bit star-struck looking at their old friend in a green off-one-shoulder dress and pink Jimmy Choo mules, legs crossed, looking sweet, demure, and very beautiful, making poor Camile look almost frumpy in comparison.

Byron plopped himself next to his wife, leaning toward the screen. "She wears too much makeup but she has nice hair."

Madison stood behind the couch, unable to join in the praise of the woman before them. To her, it was all once more just smoke and mirrors, and she couldn't shake the ocean tides of anxiety swelling within her.

"She was always way ahead of the rest of us with her fashion and make-up, wasn't she, Mads?"

"I guess so." Madison did her best to muster an appropriate response.

"I wonder where they taped this. What a pretty set."

"Hmmm, I dunno," Madison offered. It was difficult to feel anything close to the enthusiasm Natalie had for the show.

After twenty minutes of watching Becca answer the reporter's questions about current roles and achievements, Madison felt her heart rate slow and she let out the breath she didn't realize she had been holding. Maybe there was no reason to feel so on edge over Becca's television appearance.

At the commercial break, Byron stood and stretched. "That's enough for me ladies. I'm taking a shower before we go. What time do you want to head out, little mama?"

"I want to watch the rest of this," Natalie told him. "I'll be ready to go as soon as it's done." Byron kissed her cheek and left, the sound of the water running in the shower and his deep baritone voice created a background to the soft drink commercial airing. And then the show returned.

"*Welcome back. I'm Camile Mills and we are back to continue our glimpse into the life and work of rising star Becca Ristow.*" Camile leaned forward, "*I think your fans would agree with me when I say, your portrayals are always charged with emotion. It seems to come from the heart, Becca. How are you able to give such emotional performances? Where do you find that motivation?*"

Becca looked into the camera and then lowered her chin slightly, a better angle for the camera to catch the single tear rolling down her cheek.

"*Camile, I'm sure you've heard that old saying that you can't sing the blues if you've never had them. I have definitely had them. I loved growing up in Fairview, but it wasn't always easy. I had a hard time trusting people because I was betrayed so often.*" She looked up at the nodding hostess whose eyelashes were fluttering so hard they were in real danger of flying off her eyelids. Her body was leaning into Becca, encouraging her to continue, to fight through her pain, to give her audience what they wanted.

"I think the worst part was the jealousy. There was a lot of that. I was betrayed so many times, you would think I would have learned, but I kept giving kindness even when it was responded to with meanness."

Confusion wrinkling her brow, Natalie turned to Madison. "What is she talking about?"

Unease coursed through Madison. What *was* she talking about?

Byron returned, wet hair plastered to his skull, pouring himself a third cup of coffee.

"It's not easy to talk about this." Becca took the tissue from Camile's extended hand and dabbed it below her eyes before taking a small square of paper from the table next to her. A photograph. Staring down at it for a bit, she let a small smile cross her face before allowing anguish to sweep her features once again. *"For a long time, I had my best friends to get me through everything, but like everyone else, they let me down, too."*

She dramatically touched the photo before handing it to Camile who looked at it and then held it so the camera could zoom in on it.

"Hey, that's you!"

Natalie looked back at her husband and then returned her eyes to the screen. "What is she doing?"

Madison went cold, unable to respond. The photograph was one she knew well. Natalie's mom took the picture of the three girls while they sat on the old dock, feet dangling in the water, the sun warm overhead. Nancy had the day off work and wanted to treat them to ice cream. They had been giggling wildly about something that 10-year-old girls find amusing when Natalie's mom said, "Look over here girls." She had a copy made for each girl. Madison kept her framed copy tucked away in a drawer. It hurt too much to see the pure joy on their faces.

"Soon after I graduated from high school, we had a terrible accident that claimed the life of a classmate. He was very special to me." She paused, practiced looks of anguish, pain, sorrow playing across her beautiful face. "I believed he was my soulmate. His death was devastating." Her voice caught, and Madison could sense Byron and Natalie leaning forward, as though drawn by some invisible strings, hanging on her every word. "I close my eyes and I can see every detail of that day like it was yesterday and not ten years ago. Ten years ago." She shook her head in disbelief, tipped her face back and blinked rapidly to ward off more tears so she could power through the story.

"We were a bunch of kids out having fun, but it took just one person, and this is hard for me to talk about because she was truly my closest friend for as long as I can remember..." A camera zoomed in for a close-up as she looked down again at the picture, shaking her head in disbelief that she could have been victimized by someone she cared about. "Lies were carelessly thrown around about another dear friend's dad we lost to suicide. Some very crass, horrific comments were made that day." Natalie gasped, her face turning red. "I tried to be the voice of reason."

Camile paused, letting the emotions build, filling the space with suspense. "What happened next, Becca?"

"There was nothing I could do to stop this...this bully. Jared Bales died that day. He drove away, upset by the horrible things being said. He drove away and was in a terrible car crash. He died. The passenger, Jared's friend...our friend...was helping me calm everyone down before Jared got in that car, but..." Natalie was letting tears fall unabated down her cheeks, putting on the performance of a lifetime. "Jared died. The boy I loved died. My friend Carl was left with permanent brain damage."

Becca looked at Camile, sighed, and then continued in her practiced cadence. "These are the life events I dig into for my emotional scenes. I never have to dig too deeply because the pain is so *close to the surface every day of my life. But I learned something important about forgiveness since then. If all of Fairview could forgive my friend Madison for her actions that day, then I needed to find it within myself to forgive also."*

The camera zoomed in on Camile, her eyes glistening with unshed tears. *"That is a beautiful message of compassion from Fairview's one and only, Becca Ristow. After a word from our sponsors, we will find out what Becca's next project will be. Don't go away."*

Madison picked up the remote control, shutting off the television. Silence roared around them.

Natalie was still staring at the screen, trying to piece together what she had heard. She turned a stricken face to Madison. "You need to tell me what really happened that day."

Caught between a rock and a hard place, Madison weighed her options carefully. How could she explain to Natalie that what she had just witnessed was a carefully crafted, well-rehearsed means of getting even with *her*? Natalie was collateral damage. And now it would force Madison to tell Natalie the one truth she always wanted hidden from her dear friend—that the gossips of Fairview spread unspeakable lies about her father, and she, her best friend, had not stepped up in her defense.

She couldn't divulge everything. The truth would chase Natalie even further away than her father's suicide had already done. Natalie would never come back again if she knew.

"I told you what happened that day. Becca just made all of that up for this interview."

"I don't know why you can't be honest with me." She waited a moment to see if Madison would change her mind, and when she didn't, she stood. "We need to pack, Byron." She left the room. Byron, with an apologetic look at Madison, followed his wife into the bedroom. Thunder boomed in the distance as the previous night's storms continued rumbling through. Madison remained rooted in place, quicksand ready to swallow her no matter which way she stepped.

Chapter Twenty-Nine

MONDAY DAWNED GRAY AND RAINY, JUST LIKE THE DAY before. Madison cursed her luck that Saturday hadn't seen this weather. If the day would have been a washout, everything canceled—no parade, no dance, no sesquicentennial celebration at all—then she wouldn't have to be feeling this way.

Groaning, she rolled over to check the time. 6:12. She had last checked it at 4:30. Before that, 3:00. She might as well get up. Sleep had been an impossibility with the world as angry at her as the skies seemed to be right now.

As though in agreement, a gust of wind sent a slashing of rain against her bedroom window, scolding her, berating her, reminding her she was a terrible person. It was time for coffee. Lots of rich, dark, let-me-forget-the-rest-of-the-world-exists-for-a-moment coffee.

Seated at the table, head in her hands, she let the rich aroma of the beverage seep into her being before taking a sip. Before her, the newsletter her grandmother had first handed her was propped against the fruit bowl. She knew why her grandma saved it. On page three there was a picture of a man holding a golf ball. Tad Richards. His first hole-in-one. The shot had been witnessed by

"Poppy" Keller. That simple mention of his name drove her grandmother to keep the document.

Madison had some keepsakes herself. What she had not kept was a secret.

Becca's secret, to be specific.

She set her coffee cup down on the table and returned her head to her hands. A single tear dropped, splotching onto the woodgrain of the table, forming a shallow pool. She was mesmerized by the growing spots, separated at first, but filling in to form one puddle. It wouldn't take long for that pool to slosh onto the floor, saturate the room, and then fill the entire house. She could slip under the salty deluge and drift away forever.

The thought of going into the office today was unbearable. She could not possibly face her colleagues after... She couldn't. She called in sick. And she already knew she would do the same thing tomorrow and maybe even the next day. Quitting was possibly her only option. Leaving Fairview might follow that.

She sat up, that last thought hammering in her brain. Leaving Fairview. That's what Natalie and her mom did after the suicide. It's what Becca did after the funeral. Leaving was not an option for her, and she knew it. That meant facing the situation head on was all she had left. Closing her eyes, she thought back to the day that started it all—the day she was supposed to become the keeper of the secret.

Becca came to them for help. When she found herself in trouble, it wasn't her drama friends she could count on.

The three of them were on Natalie's bed with its pink bedspread, legs crossed Indian style, knees just touching. Blowing her already red nose, Becca groaned, "I don't know what to do."

"Are you *sure* you're pregnant?"

Becca nodded at Natalie, a fresh wave of tears starting. "My parents will kill me. They've spent a fortune on acting classes and drama camps...Oh, God, this sucks."

That was her greatest concern? Outwardly, Madison showed support, but inside, she was disappointed. It was bad enough that

Jared, her long-time crush, started dating Becca during their junior year, but to find out he would be so careless sickened her. This would be devastating for him, too. "What did Jared say?"

Becca lowered her head and sniffled loudly. "I can't tell him."

Natalie and Madison exchanged a look.

"You really should, Becca. He should know what he...what you..." Natalie's face flushed with the words. "He should help make a plan."

"I can't," Becca repeated. "It's not his."

Madison had to fight the urge to grab Becca by the shoulders and shake her. Jared was handsome, kind, smart. How could Becca want something other than those qualities? How could she betray him like that? "Whose is it?"

"Steve. I met him at a party and..." She looked with pleading eyes at her friends. "It was a party at a frat house in Brookfield. I was stupid."

"Does he know? This Steve guy?"

Becca shook her head, fresh sobs accentuating her next words. "I don't even know his last name."

Madison had difficulty hiding her disgust. It was clear Becca was desperate for help, and in a strange way it did feel good that she turned to the two people she knew she could trust, but Jared certainly deserved better than this.

Natalie took Becca's hand. "Tell us what you need."

They developed a plan. Becca's secret was safe with them, and they sealed it, the three of them putting their pinkies together as though they were seven-year-olds instead of seventeen-year-olds.

It all worked out. They pooled their resources, made an appointment, and feigned a trip to a museum in Brookfield. Once the pregnancy was a thing of the past, Becca drifted away again.. Becca no longer needed them for their support, money, alibi, or other help, so she returned to her other "friends." Nat and Madison didn't have much time to wallow in how used they felt, because just a few weeks later, Nat's dad killed himself and neither gave Becca's desperate pleas for help another thought.

Becca had used them, whether she and Natalie chose to discuss it or not, and Madison could have let it go, but when she overheard Becca, she had seen red. After everything Natalie had done for Becca, how dare she?

But Becca had reason to punish Madison, and so she had done just that.

Opening her eyes, Madison saw that nothing had changed. The rain still came down from the gray sky. The coffee was getting cold in the cup before her. And she was the one who betrayed her friend, got Jared killed, and left Carl a mere shell of a human being.

She could not have hated herself more than she did in this moment.

A shower did little to wash away the guilt or the ache in her chest. She wasn't entirely surprised to find her mom in the kitchen shortly after. Turning off her phone the previous day was not going to deter her family from showing up—whether she was ready for them or not.

"I brought bagels. Would you like coffee or tea?"

Madison wanted to throw herself into her mother's arms and sob, but she was well past the age when she could let her mom take away all her problems.

"Your dad called the station Sunday morning. He threatened to sue if they ran the program again. They were certainly out of line for putting that nonsense on the air."

Madison nodded, her breath coming in gulps as she held back sobs. Nina pulled Madison to her, wrapping her loving, protective arms around her. "Mom..."

"We can't make what was said go away, but it is definitely time you told me what really happened."

Ten years after it happened, Madison finally came clean, telling her mother every last detail—even the most painful of them.

And for the first time in a decade, Madison felt like she wouldn't have to carry the weight of the world all by herself. Someone else would finally understand the loathing she felt for herself—the events of that day an albatross around her neck, heavy, smelly, and impossible to shed.

———

Their coffee was all but forgotten as Madison neared the end of the story. "I wanted to hurt her, mom, like she hurt everyone around her." The plan to get even with Becca proved she was childish and vindictive, but Madison was determined to tell her mother everything—exposing even the worst parts of herself. "It worked. I just told one person what I knew and then I sat back and watched. I could have stopped it at any time, but I didn't."

The sights and sounds of the summer day at the Shallows surrounded her. She continued watching the volleyball game on the beach. A car full of underclassmen showed up, the six girls joining in the fun and festivities. It gave Madison the perfect opportunity. Pulling one of the girls aside, she whispered to her, "*Can you believe what Becca Ristow did? Some frat boy in Brookfield got her pregnant and then she had an abortion.*" Her plan worked. She didn't have to wait long that day, simply letting the natural tendencies of teenage girls take over, as she observed how the story flew from group to group, taking on a life of its own. Until eventually, conveniently, inevitably, it arrived in earshot of Jared. "*Did you hear? It was some college guy. He got Becca pregnant and she had an abortion. Jared doesn't know so don't tell him.*"

Jared had stormed away from the group, his anger palpable, and Madison saw her opportunity. She slipped away after Jared to console, commiserate, and share in his disgust and betrayal. For the first time, she felt as though Jared *saw* her. Finally.

And in those moments of comforting Jared, she didn't give Carl another thought.

After a bit, Jared drew her into a hug, and her heart raced. When she stood, brushing sand from her shorts, she saw Becca standing nearby, watching them. Madison could tell by the look on her face she had put it all together. Perhaps Madison wore a tell-tale smirk and perhaps she was unable to hide her pleasure. It was difficult to remember, but she was pretty sure she whispered *Gotcha* to herself. *That* would teach Becca a lesson, bring her down off her high horse. She had been asking for it for years.

Then everything unraveled quickly.

Becca and Jared were nearby arguing, their voices carrying. Carl sat down next to her, gesturing in the direction of the two. *"What's going on there?"*

"I'm not sure," she'd answered, shrugging her shoulders. *"Lovers' quarrel, I guess."* Carl, older by a year or two than everyone else in the group, probably felt some sense of responsibility. As Jared stormed over, gathered his things, and started toward the parking lot, Carl rose from next to Madison and followed Jared a short distance away, caught up in a serious conversation.

Not sure what they talked about, Madison watched as Jared started toward the parking lot and Carl returned to her side. *"I can't get him to stay, so I'll ride back with him and make sure he's okay."* Carl had taken her hand. *"I'll see you later."*

Carl hadn't seen her later. A few miles out of Fairview, Jared's car crossed the center line, veered back to avoid an oncoming car, and crashed into a tree. He died at the scene. Carl's traumatic brain injury left him comatose for months, and then disabled for life. Madison was unable to free herself of the guilt and shame.

Her mother held her as she cried.

Chapter Thirty

It was not at all surprising to Madison that her family kept her close, circling their wagons around her and making sure she was getting through this in one piece—just as they had done ten years prior.

This time was different, because she was older, wiser, and finally talking about the events of that day in a way she never had before. And this time she was honest with herself...and in the retelling of what happened.

Her mother's words did not sink in immediately, but simmered, bubbling away in Madison's being until she could take a step back and hear what Nina was telling her. She replayed the conversation in her head.

"No matter what you choose to share now, Madison, nothing has changed. The accident was just that. An accident."

"I'm so ashamed of how I acted. I should have been a better friend. I should have stepped up and defended Natalie. Instead, I became the very thing I despised about Becca—manipulative—so I made everything worse."

"At the time, you also thought you were helping Nat. It's a lot easier to look back from here—ten years later—and think about every 'would have, could have, should have.'"

Madison covered her face with her hands, the shame still a fresh wound. "I have no idea who I am anymore. I thought I loved Carl, and I pretended we would have this whole future here. Then when I was with Jared, I was wishing I had told him how much I liked him for all those years. I betrayed *everyone*...even myself."

"You were a child, Madison. You had a lifetime of learning and growing in front of you. Nobody expects an 18-year-old to have all the answers. You didn't drive the car that day. You didn't tell the boys to get in that car. They made decisions for themselves that were outside your control. As for telling Becca's secret, you have to figure out how to forgive yourself. It was a learning and growing experience—not a life sentence."

She looked at her mother and then away. "I don't know who I am or who I am supposed to be. Everything I have ever done is because of someone else. Why did I join the swim team? Because Patrick was on the team when he was in high school. Why did I join the newspaper staff? Because Jared was on it. Why did I take up photography? Because Carl liked taking pictures. Maybe if I had figured out who I was I wouldn't have hurt everyone else."

Nina studied her daughter carefully. "You are a little piece of everyone who has ever influenced you. We all are, Madison. You were in the process of discovering who and what you wanted to be but the accident side-tracked you. You've done a darn good job despite that. You have a home, a career, a family that loves you beyond words, and the most incredible bond anyone could ever have with a grandmother. Focus on all those good things." She took Madison's hand in hers. "You hated that Natalie wouldn't visit you here, so you went to her. She didn't realize just how much she needed to keep that connection, but you gave her that. And now she's been here twice in one summer. A piece of Fairview will always be in her and you reminded her of that. You gave her that, just like everyone gives you a little bit of themselves in different ways." They sat in silence for several minutes.

"I don't know what to do from here."

"You'll take some time to think about it. If you don't want to work for the paper, then you find a different job. You have your whole life ahead of you. It's time to forgive yourself and move forward." She stood then. "And we expect you to come to dinner tonight."

Madison started to protest, but Nina held up her hand to stop her. "And keep visiting your grandma. She's settled in her new room and will need lots of memory triggers."

Patrick assured her almost nobody watched the interview. Mya insisted that anyone who did watch probably believed it was an episode of one of Becca's soap operas. Her dad simply hugged her and told her he loved her.

She appreciated their kindness, but she still had to make things right with Natalie so she steeled herself to pick up the phone later that evening.

Natalie's voice on the line was enough to make her cry, but she had to say what was on her mind. "Natalie, I was wondering if you could use an extra set of hands to pack. I'd like to help. And maybe we can find some time to talk about what happened."

"I would love that."

Madison used her saved vacation time to step away from the newspaper. It was time well spent. She and Natalie packed and taped boxes, preparing them for the long journey to Iceland. They cleaned the apartment from top to bottom. They had the difficult conversations that Madison should have had with her a decade earlier.

"I let you down in so many ways. After your dad died, I didn't know what to say to you. I spent time with Carl instead of you. You deserved a better friend. Then, I should have shut down the conversation at the Shallows right away and none of this would have happened. I let Becca and her crew say things that were untrue and I didn't confront them. Instead, I was petty and vindictive. It had absolutely nothing to do with you, Nat, and everything to do with me being too chicken to do the right thing—to look Becca in the eye and tell her to stop."

"You were never responsible for me or for defending what my dad did." She laughed humorlessly. "There was no defending his decision to take his life. And as for letting the cat out of the bag about Becca's abortion, I wouldn't be surprised if most of Fairview already knew."

"I guess that's possible. People do talk..."

She looked up from the box she had just taped, making eye contact with Madison. "Are you ever going to tell me what they said?"

Madison shook her head. "There's no reason for you to know. I'm going to keep that a secret. And this time, it's staying in the vault." She reached out and locked pinkies with her friend, confident that they were, indeed, forever friends, no matter how many miles separated them.

Madison was away from the office for a matter of days, but a lot had happened. Adele was at home with a new baby girl. Ben had been named Editor-in-Chief. (That had probably been the plan all along. Gavin and Becca needed their moment to humiliate her in as many ways as possible first). Galloway sent a message to the staff introducing their new regional manager. No more Gavin, thank goodness. And there among the other messages was one from Liz Erikson asking Madison to call her.

Curiosity drove her to punch the number even before she finished looking through her other emails.

"Miss Keller, I understand you have some letters for me. Your grandma mentioned when I visited her several days back that she gave them to you."

Shock and disbelief prevented Madison from responding coherently. "The letters? You visited? You knew about them? I do. Uhm..." She shook her head, trying to clear it of whatever cobwebs were preventing her from responding like a normal human being. "Would you like me to drop them off at your office?"

"If it isn't any trouble, that would be wonderful. How about tomorrow morning. Ten o'clock?"

"I'll see you then."

Her grandmother had accurately remembered a visit from Liz. That was something, at least. Of course, she had also claimed that Gordon was with her, so she hadn't been entirely correct. Madison decided to count it as a small victory for her grandma regardless.

The lake looked entirely different than it had a couple months earlier when she'd arrived at the Cottages to interview Liz Erikson. There was no wind on the glasslike surface, and families were enjoying the beach. Business was clearly good for Liz this summer.

With a sinking feeling in her stomach she tried to push away, she wondered if Liz had seen the television interview. Even if she hadn't seen it, small town gossip had likely reached her ears. Madison hoped Liz didn't ask her about it.

Feeling scrutinized by members of the community was a horrible feeling, and she now had a real taste of what it must have been like for both Natalie and Becca—believing everyone was talking about them behind their backs.

She parked in front of the converted barn and walked to the reservations desk. A young man directed her to the back where Liz was waiting for her in her office. Madison was surprised to see she wasn't alone. Jenny Whitebird was sitting at the table, coffee cup in front of her.

"Good morning." Liz motioned her in and Jenny smiled warmly.

"Good morning. I uh..." She started pulling the letters from her bag, then thought better of it. Perhaps it was a private matter Liz wouldn't want handled in front of Jenny.

"Have a seat, Miss Keller. Would you like coffee?"

"Please call me Madison." She sat next to Jenny. "No thank you," she responded as Liz pushed an empty cup closer to her.

Liz Erikson smiled. "Thank you for coming by, Madison. I've been looking forward to chatting with you. Jenny and I were just talking about the letters. Do you have them?"

Madison looked from one woman to the other before pulling the two envelopes out of her bag.

Liz let one drop to the table before her, inspecting the writing on the outside of the one in her hand, and then holding it up for Jenny to see. "That's his writing all right." Jenny rolled her eyes, nodding.

"So, you know who they're from?" She asked the question without thinking and then flushed with embarrassment, hoping Liz wouldn't tell her to mind her own business. Jenny had basically done that once already earlier this summer.

The women laughed. "Oh, yes," Liz answered with a shake of her head. "We know. He gave us plenty to laugh about all those years ago."

Madison looked from one to the other. "Did you go to school in Fairview, Jenny?"

"I most certainly did. We were best friends." She waved her hand back-and-forth between Liz and herself.

Again, Madison was guilty of sticking her foot in her mouth. "I don't remember seeing you in the yearbook." If possible, her face, already warm from her previous comment, was now burning up.

Jenny smiled, glancing at Liz. "Well, I did look just a tad different then." One finger reached up to run the length of the scar.

"Oh…I didn't…I'm sorry…" Mortified, Madison looked at the door, then back again to the two women. "I am so sorry. I'll let you get back to your coffee."

Jenny rose, finishing the last of the contents of her cup and walking to the counter behind her to set it down. "I have a class to teach so I need to get going. It was nice seeing you, Madison." She patted Liz's shoulder as she walked by. Stopping in front of Madison she said, "The next time you look in the yearbook, look for Jenny Smits. After the...accident...I took my mom's maiden name. Made me feel closer to her Ojibwa roots."

Madison stared after her, wondering how she had missed her. She must have looked significantly different.

"Are you sure you wouldn't like some coffee? I expect him to be here any second..." Before she could finish, the door opened again, and a tall, dark-haired man she guessed to be about Patrick's age walked in. Since she had never seen him before, she assumed he was renting one of the cottages.

"I was running a little late. Sorry grandma."

Chapter Thirty-One

MADISON STARED AT ONE AND THEN THE OTHER, mouth agape.

Liz smiled, reaching out her hand. The young man stepped to her side, taking her hand. "Danny, I want you to meet the young lady I was telling you about. This is Madison Keller."

"The photographer. Pleased to meet you." His warm smile lit up his face. "I'm Danny O'Connor."

Confusion and disbelief left Madison unable to immediately respond. She held out her hand to shake his, leaving it extended a couple beats longer than she intended, her eyes darting back to Liz. Grandma. Grandma? Nothing was making sense to her.

"I brought the designs." Madison watched him hand a file folder to Liz, who smiled broadly.

"Perfect timing."

For the second time since arriving, Madison felt as though she were intruding and should take her leave. Just as she was about to excuse herself, Liz pushed the folder in front of her, tapping the cover in her enthusiasm.

"I wanted to show you these so you know what you would be committing to." Seeing Madison's confusion, Liz laughed, surprising Madison with the joy she heard in the sound. She never associated Liz Erikson with joy and laughter, but they were in abundance today. "Now that the sale is final, we want to move forward with this." She nodded toward the folder.

Sale? She couldn't have been more confused had she walked into a room where everyone was speaking a foreign language. Danny sensed this, and patted Liz's arm. "You might want to take this a little slower."

"You sold the Cottages?"

"Good lord, child. No! We bought the golf course."

Madison looked from one to the other, then opened the folder. Before her were sketches of beautiful buildings, different in shape and silhouette, but all with modern, sharp lines. Still struggling to figure out what they were talking about, she blurted, "You're building these houses on the golf course?" The last word caught in her throat. How could Liz Erikson, of all people, want to destroy one of Fairview's greatest attributes?"

"Why would I do that? No, I'm taking down the cottages and bringing this tired old place into the twenty-first century." Again, the smile, so unfamiliar to Madison, showed up.

Danny took a stab at it. "We bought the golf course. We didn't want to jump into any changes here until the sale was finalized. If another buyer had come in, we don't know what might have happened to the property but it wouldn't have been good for us."

Us? Madison's head was still spinning, but a clearer picture was slowly beginning to form. "You bought the golf course and now you are building..." She picked up the folder, turning the pages. Each "cottage" was depicted with bright, open spaces, clean lines, a minimalist design. Most importantly, they fit perfectly into the landscape. "They're beautiful."

"Modern Scandinavian design. This," she spread her hands out, looking around the barn, "will be a spa."

It was a lot to take in—especially the image of Liz Erikson being excited about a spa. Then something struck her. "Wait. What did you mean? What would I be committing to?"

"All those clean, white spaces need to be filled. We want to commission you for that task. I saw your prints at the diner. They are perfect. Every single one of these," he said, tapping the folder, "will have your Laurel Lake prints, if you're interested."

"Tell her the rest." She didn't wait for him, though. "There's so much more than that. We need someone to help us build a website, promote our packages...oh, the packages. Tell her."

He laughed. "We are doing a good job of confusing this poor woman." He turned back to Madison. "Our plan is to build golf packages, spa packages..."

"And some winter spa and snowshoeing packages."

Their enthusiasm was contagious and Madison smiled. "You want me to work for you?"

Liz nodded. "You bet that's what we want. Your Hometown Pride section, your feature on the Cottages...I think you are the perfect person for this job. If you want it, of course. And it won't be right this minute so you have time to think about it and prepare for it."

Madison shook her head again, still trying to make sense of it all. "I thought Magenta Enterprises was going to buy it. I thought they would build condos on the property."

"That would have definitely meant the end of my business." Liz looked at Danny, a glint in her eye. "That was a concern for us, but we knew what we were dealing with and had to let everything play out. We had someone on the inside keeping a close watch on things for us, staying on top of what Thorsen was doing. I brought in a surveyor to shake things up, get him thinking about the fact that his course was built a few feet onto my property." She laughed. "Yep, we were staying on top of things on the inside. Not that we were doing anything illegal or anything, but it was a tad unorthodox."

Pieces of the puzzle continued falling into place.

"A friend contacted me..."

"...growing up in this great Irish-American community."

Danny O'Connor. She looked over at him, noticing there was

nothing Irish looking about him despite the Irish moniker. The thoughts niggling in the back of her mind were starting to form into coherent ideas. "Danny, did you by any chance grow up in Philadelphia?"

He looked to Liz before answering. When she nodded, he said, "I still live there."

"I think I'd like to tell you a story, Madison." Liz poured them all a cup of coffee and then looked pointedly at Madison. "And *this*, Miss Keller, is completely off the record."

For the next hour, Madison learned about a Liz she never knew…and she was forced to rethink her notion that people in small towns knew everything about one another.

Chapter Thirty-Two

"It is absolutely crazy."

She was breathlessly filling Natalie in on what she had learned that day, unpacking it one layer at a time. There were many layers.

Although it had been hours since she left her, Liz's voice still rang clearly in her head. Part confession, part explanation, taken as a whole, her story was heartbreaking and heartwarming at the same time.

"Gordon lived with his elderly grandparents in Brookfield but came here in the summers to earn money to help them out. He was working with the grounds crew at the course and saw how much money the caddies were making. Oh, my goodness, that boy was driven. He worked his tail off to learn everything he could about golf and being a caddie. And he did it.

"Chuck, on the other hand, was used to having everything handed to him. He was a cocky son-of-a-gun. When I rebuffed his advances, he turned his frustration on Gordon. You see, they went to high school together, but didn't run in the same crowds. Anyway, Chuck spread all kinds of stories about what a low-life Gordon was. And then when some money went missing at the club, it was convenient to blame it on Gordon.

"I loved Gordon. I knew he never stole anything." She took

Danny's hand in hers once again. "Your grandfather was the most honest and decent person I knew. He was devastated by the accusations but held his head high and kept working the grounds crew even when they didn't want him back as a caddy. I convinced my dad to give him some part-time work to make up for the money he lost when he stopped caddying.

"But then his number came up. I hated saying goodbye." She blushed then. "I guess we took our farewell a little farther than appropriate. I didn't even know I was pregnant until after he left for Vietnam. I was going to write him a letter and tell him everything, and then I learned he had died. He was over there only three weeks. I wanted to die, too.

"Then my mom discovered my... my condition. She couldn't tell my dad. It would have killed him, especially after he trusted that boy enough to hire him on. So, she sent me to Philadelphia, pretending I would be a live-in caretaker for her Aunt Martha." She laughed ironically at this. "That was all a lie. Martha was a headstrong, cantankerous old bird who would never allow anyone to take care of her. It didn't matter because I really went to the Women and Children's Center in Philadelphia. Once the baby was born, a beautiful little girl, I had already earned my high school diploma. Night school. Now that was an interesting cast of characters. Anyway, I was feeling like I could handle anything. I figured I would keep my little Anna, get a job in Philly, and happily live out my life.

"I was wrong. I couldn't take care of her and work enough to support us. I couldn't bring her back here and humiliate my parents. I did what was best for my baby girl. I gave her up for adoption when she was two months old."

Madison relayed the entire story, and just as she had done when Liz told it, she shed tears for the woman they had always seen as cold, stoic and even strange. How wrong they had been.

"I couldn't get Liz to say more than a few words when I interviewed her in May. This morning she talked nonstop. Honestly, it was one surprise after another. I can't believe she had a baby. And

I understand, I guess, why they kept it a secret from her dad. Her mom, my grandma, and Jenny were the only ones who knew."

"Can you imagine handing your baby over after two months? I couldn't do it."

"She was lucky that Marybeth and Daniel O'Connor wanted the baby. Liz cleaned their house, so that's how they knew each other. The O'Connors stayed in touch with her over the years so she still had Anna in her life to some extent."

"Is her daughter visiting, too? Did you meet Anna?"

"That part is even worse. She had Danny when she was still in high school—just like her mom. She was able to graduate and was ready to take college courses...and then she was hit by a car and died."

"That's horrible."

"Liz always hoped Danny might want to come to live with her, but his grandparents—Anna's adoptive parents—wanted to keep him there. Remember the game room in the barn? She did that for Danny...always hoping he would one day live here. Liz helped put him through college—and then law school. And now Danny is her business partner and wait until you see how they are redesigning the Cottages."

Natalie laughed. "Take a breath. This is a lot!"

"Tell me about it! And get this! Liz and Danny visited my grandma and she thought it was Gordon. They didn't tell her he was really Gordon's grandson, but I can see why grandma thought that. Liz showed me pictures and they have the exact same dark hair and dark eyes."

"I guess that's one mystery solved."

"And remember those letters my grandma kept for Liz? Here's the best part." She drew in a deep breath before plowing on with more of the story. "She ripped them up into shreds without even opening them. I just sat there with my jaw practically touching the floor. I mean, honestly, my grandmother has had them since 1969, and she ripped them to pieces without reading them."

"Did she say why?"

"What I could make of it is Chuck was a jerk—really full of himself—and because Liz liked Gordon, he was trying to push himself on her—and then his girlfriend came to visit and that really made everything blow up in his face. Not that he ever had a chance with Liz. You should have heard the way she talked about Gordon. She was madly in love with him. Oh my gosh, Natalie! This is like a soap opera."

"I wish I would have been there to hear all of that."

"It was better than any movie I've seen, to be honest."

Madison didn't tell Natalie how guilty she felt, knowing Jenny kept Liz's secret for decades. There were some things she would have to continue to work through.

"It's a shame about her daughter, though."

"Thank goodness she still had her grandson to ease the pain a little. She wanted to live in Philadelphia to be near her daughter even after she gave her up for adoption, but then her mother needed her back here when her dad was sick. She took over the business as soon as she returned. They never did tell him about the baby." She paused, another thought coming to her. "I wonder if maybe he knew, but let them think he didn't."

"We'll never know."

Madison finally ended the call, her head spinning just as much in the retelling of the story as it had during the original hearing of it. She wondered if Danny was planning to move to Fairview and help his grandmother. She hadn't thought to ask that. And what about the things she couldn't ask? What was the accident that left Jenny with a scar?

We'll never know.

The words repeated in her mind. Natalie was right about that. There was much she would never know.

She considered Carl, sitting in a wheelchair staring at a television set. Missing the Carl she knew was an ache she would forever carry, but maybe, just maybe, that summer would have been the end of their story no matter what. It was possible she was only meant to love the 21-year-old-version of him and they both would have moved on to other loves.

Jared's smile flashed through her mind. She had such a crush on him for the longest time. Joining the school paper to be near him may have been a silly reason, but she did manage to turn it into a career path. Long ago she told Carl she liked writing for the paper because it was a chance to observe life and document that we were here. Those hadn't even been her words. She once heard Jared say it and simply used it herself.

She thought about her grandmother, moved into her new room, and getting the focused professional care she so needed. Ruth was confined to a single wing, able to visit the activity room or solarium, but not leave the floor. Most often, she sat in her rocking chair, tapping her hand on the armrest. Maybe she was lost someplace in time with memories that made her happy. Her family wanted to keep reminding her of the here and now, but maybe the *there* and *then* had been so perfect to her, she was satisfied to be forever caught in the past.

We'll never know.

Chapter Thirty-Three

THE CURSOR BLINKED ON THE BLANK WORD document. She was again assigned feature stories, but had yet to feel the excitement she first did. Ben was still working with Galloway to have Hometown Pride restored, but so far, they were adamant that the space was crucial for advertising.

Thoughts of her new job crept in far more frequently with each passing day. The groundbreaking for the first two new cottages was still weeks away, but Liz asked Madison to start with them in November. In the meantime, she was spending every free moment taking pictures of the beautiful scenery in and around Fairview, filling orders for prints, and visiting her grandmother whenever she had a moment.

It was time to finish this story and get outside. The waning days of September were warm by day and cool by night. Madison's plan was to take a bike ride and enjoy the post-Labor Day quiet of Fairview.

Still she stared at the blank screen, for some reason thinking about the letter her grandmother had encouraged her to write to Carl ten years ago. In the pre-dawn hours of a day much like this, she found a notebook in the nightstand and started writing. Had she ever actually sent it to him or had he been able to read it, Carl would have known how sorry she was for her part in everything that happened. She asked for his forgiveness, but she would never know if he was capable of forgiving.

She'd written a second letter. This one told Jared how wrong she had been...to never let him know she really liked him, but more importantly, to apologize for her cruel words about Becca that day. She never meant to hurt him. His death would leave a void in her soul forever.

Maybe she should write a letter-she-would-never-send to Sean. She had stupidly believed something was happening between them, but she was wrong. Stupid, stupid, stupid. But if she *was* to write the letter, she would tell him how disappointed she was in herself for not trusting him enough so she could open up to him. Then again, there was no point in showing him how messed up she was inside. He left; she was nothing to him. And now she would never be able to look into those green eyes again.

She quickly finished writing her story. There was something important she needed to do.

Madison rubbed the wrinkled hand she held. She didn't have to write this letter because she still had time to say what needed to be said.

"Grandma, in case I haven't told you lately, I love you more than anything in the world. You have always been a shining star in my universe. Thank you for everything you've ever done for me." She watched a smile play across her grandmother's face and felt her hand turn to squeeze Madison's.

"Liz and Gordon came to visit me."

"I know, grandma. That must have been wonderful for you."

"It was. It was." She rocked and smiled.

Madison let a single tear run down her cheek as she reminded herself that Grandma Ruth might be perfectly happy living in whatever world she found herself in at this moment. She continued holding her hand even after she drifted off to sleep.

"Oh honey, it's so good to see you. Carl will be thrilled to have company."

Madison stepped through the door Sara held open for her, turning sideways to maneuver past with the bulky package. "I brought Carl a gift." She pulled the brown paper back to reveal a beautifully matted print in a rustic frame. "I can help you hang it if you'd like."

Sara put her hand to her chest, staring at the picture. The lake was calm, reflecting the clouds scattered across a perfectly blue sky. "Madison, this is...this is spectacular."

She should have done this years ago. The photo was taken from his favorite spot—from the knoll on the 12th green. "I thought he might like to look at it."

Sara set the picture aside and drew Madison into a hug. "Thank you." She drew back, looking into Madison's eyes. "Carl is lucky to have you as a friend, and you are welcome to come here to visit him any time you want." She hesitated, then continued. "Don't *ever* feel like you are obligated. You have your life to live, Madison. Get out there and do that...for Carl."

Madison cried most of the drive home. When she was drained of tears, she allowed herself a smile as she remembered the time she spent with Carl on Laurel Lake.

Piper held a twig out. "Look, Auntie."

Squatting next to her, she helped Piper poke holes in the sand, laughing along at the little girl's giggles of delight.

"Do you want her sweater?" Mya was at the gate holding the pink knit garment.

"She's fine." Madison waved her off, continuing down to the dock where the pontoon boat was on its lift. Her dad would be putting it in storage in a couple weeks. She remembered what a great time they'd had touring the lake when Natalie visited. The BPB had served them well for another season.

Piper dropped the stick and tugged Madison's hand.

"Baby in tummy?" Piper pointed to Madison's midsection.

"No honey, mommy has a baby in her tummy." The big announcement had been a wonderful surprise for all of them at dinner. Another baby in the family. Madison hoped Patrick and Mya stayed in Fairview forever. It was the best place in the world to raise a family.

Piper reached down to pick up a leaf that had blown onto the dock. She dropped it over the edge and they watched it float away. It belonged to the lake now. Madison thought about the hours and hours she had spent in Laurel Lake. It had been the constant in her life.

The leaf floated out of sight as Madison thought about the laughter, tears, joy, and pain the lake had witnessed. Maybe it was the keeper of all their memories.

She took Piper by the hand and led her back to the house. Her family was there, celebrating the present and the future. Madison felt herself letting go of the past a little more each day. Lighter and brighter. Shelly's words came to mind. Yes, she was feeling lighter and brighter. And now they had a new baby to look forward to. Her mother was right. She was a little bit of everyone from her past. Piper and the new baby would take pieces of her wherever they journeyed in life. The thought made her smile. There were so many wonderful memories to create.

Chapter Thirty-Four

On a perfect October day, as the leaves were turning brilliant shades of red, yellow, and orange, and the days had just enough chill to warn that winter was on the doorstep, Danny O'Connor called.

"Can you meet me at the golf course? I found a perfect place for some pictures I want taken. If I show you the exact spot, you can get whatever shots you need at your convenience and when you have the right light...or whatever it is you photographers need."

"Of course." She had seen him only once since the day with Liz. "I didn't know you were in town. Are you planning to stay for a while?"

"No, so if you could meet me at about 5:00, I would have just enough time to show you before I have to head out."

Danny was a mover and shaker with a busy schedule. She smiled, thinking about the strong family roots that helped establish that inner drive. He had Erikson and Cummings blood in him—combined, apparently that was a force to be reckoned with.

"I'll see you at the course."

Danny O'Connor was nowhere in sight when she arrived. Only a couple cars were in the lot—and those likely belonged to staff. Very few golfers braved the cooler temps, and soon the course would close for the season.

She stepped from her Jeep and didn't have a chance to close the door before a cart pulled up beside her.

"Miss Keller?"

Expecting Danny, it took a moment to figure out how the worker knew her name. Frankly, she was also surprised someone who worked here knew something about etiquette. It was definitely a step in the right direction, whether it was Liz's influence or not.

"I am."

"Good. I'm Alex. I was asked to give you a ride to the knoll. Climb in."

She smiled. She had been right about where Danny wanted the pictures taken. There was no comparison to this perfect spot. Her spirits were higher than they had been in a long time. The opportunity Danny and Liz were giving her was the shot in the arm she didn't even realize she needed.

A brisk wind picked up, blowing her hair across her cheeks as the cart made its way along the path. She pulled her jacket tighter, watching the sun sink lower in the sky.

Alex pulled up next to an empty cart and she climbed out. "He said he would be just over the rise. Have a nice evening, Miss Keller."

Madison took a few steps and started up the hill, fully prepared for the spectacular view that would open before her as soon as she reached the top. She was not prepared for what she saw. Sean was waiting for her.

She hesitated, looked around for Danny, started to turn around, but was stopped by his words.

"I was afraid you wouldn't take my call so I had to enlist a little help from a friend."

She was afraid to move, afraid to feel the many emotions washing over her.

"Is Danny here?"

"No, he's still in Philly."

"Oh." She looked around, not sure what to do, and then made up her mind. "You left without saying goodbye."

"Because you told me you never wanted to hear from me again." He shook his head. "I tried to stay away, but I couldn't."

Even more confused by this statement, Madison was at a loss for words, racking her brain for some memory of such a conversation. A momentary panic set in. Was she losing her memory, just like her grandmother? "I don't remember saying that," she finally admitted.

"Your email said exactly that."

"Email? I never sent you..." Understanding dawned. "Was it from my work email?"

When he nodded, she knew she was right. Gavin and Becca had left no stone unturned in their attempts to sabotage her life. How had they found out about Sean? Small-town gossips? She rolled her eyes, imagining someone like Armando passing along tidbits of gossip. It probably had not been all that difficult to piece together.

"I didn't send you any message, Sean. It's a long story, but trust me, I didn't."

His quizzical look turned to a smile. "Thank goodness. I do trust you, Madison Keller. I do. That's why I was going to tell you Liz wanted me back in Philly to meet with Danny and my dad. But then I got your email..."

"Your dad?"

"Our financial backer. There's a lot of money going into this project. I guess Liz and Danny didn't talk about that part of our plan with you."

He took a step toward her, reaching for her hand. She was too focused on the word "our" to resist. She looked down at his fingers entwined with hers, still unsure what to say. There were so many dots still waiting to be connected.

"Madison, I liked you from the moment I first saw you. I almost told Danny and Liz that I was out because I thought I would lose my chance with you. I wanted to tell you everything, but I promised them I wouldn't until the sale was final. But then I didn't get the chance because of your email." He squeezed her hand. "Tell me I didn't lose my chance with you."

Every one of their conversations played out in her head within the moments she stood before him. He was working with Liz all along and didn't tell her. He had even helped her solve part of the mystery involving Liz. She wanted to be angry with him, but realized he was doing exactly what Liz asked him to do...keep their arrangement a secret. He was better at such things than she was, apparently. "Are you going back to Philadelphia?"

He shook his head. "How can I manage the Erikson resort properties if I'm back in Philly?" Grinning, he added, "Even my dad is happy now that we are doing business together." He pulled her closer, the gap between them mere inches now. "Madison, this is going to be my home now."

She felt something inside her release. Was she finally letting go?

"I thought my grandma sent me on a wild goose chase." The unopened letters, the golf course newsletters, the memories of Liz, Gordon, and Chuck—it *was* a wild goose chase. "But now I think it was all some grand design because it led me to you." The catalyst, she thought.

He pulled her to him, and she felt the strong arms around her once again. They were a promise of how he would care for her, protect her, and love her. Madison breathed him in. She slowly pulled back to look at him.

"I still don't understand how all of this happened, but you can explain it really slowly to me." She smiled up at him. "Your big Irish clan, right?" Her brow furrowed. "Wait. Danny isn't really Irish."

Laughing, he nodded. "You're right. Some of us are born into it; some are adopted into it." He winked at her. "And some marry into it."

Her heart skipped a beat. She was far from thinking about marriage, but the comment didn't scare her, either. "Let's start by working together, okay?"

"And maybe visit Philly so I can show you my clan?" He raised his eyebrows. "Better yet, I'll take you to Ireland to meet the real deal, my grandda."

"Ireland. Wow. We have a busy schedule ahead." It was her turn, though. "And then a quick trip to Iceland?"

"Sure!"

It was all just silly banter, but somehow, it felt like more than that. Much more. For the first time in ten years, Madison could envision the future.

Together, they walked down to the shoreline, stepping close to the softly lapping water. Three fishing boats bobbed before them, and the sound of laughter drifted on the breeze from a pontoon moving across the horizon.

Madison let the warmth of the evening and the familiar sounds of the lake wrap her in a comforting blanket, just as it always did. And like so many other times, she knew she would forever remember this moment on Laurel Lake.

About the Author

Karen Gibson is a retired professor who now dedicates her time to writing. She spent a couple decades teaching English and Speech Communication to middle and high school students before joining the faculty of the University of Wisconsin Oshkosh as a member of the Educational Leadership and Policy Department.

Karen divides her time between Wisconsin and Arizona (for obvious reasons!) When she isn't writing, she is cheering on the Wisconsin Badgers, Milwaukee Brewers, and the Green Bay Packers. Speaking at library events and appearing at book festivals are also high on her list of fun things to do. She spends as much time as humanly possible with her family and friends.

karengibsonauthor@gmail.com
www.karengibsonauthor.com

 facebook.com/KarenGibsonAuthor
instagram.com/kmgibson_author

Made in the USA
Monee, IL
15 April 2024